Maggie & the Pirate's Son

Maggie & the Pirate's Son

ROSE PRENDEVILLE

First published by Eridani Press.

Cover by Poshie

Names: Prendeville, Rose, author.

Title: Maggie and the Pirate's Son / Rose Prendeville.

Description: First edition. | Nashville, Tennessee : Eridani Press, 2024.

Identifiers: ISBN 978-1-955643-12-2 (trade paperback) | ISBN 978-1-955643-13-9 (ebook) | ISBN 978-1-955643-14-6 (audiobook)

Subjects: LCSH: Highlands (Scotland)—Fiction. | Man-woman relationships—Fiction. | Pirates—Fiction. | Romance fiction. | Historical fiction. | BISAC: FICTION / Romance / Historical / Scottish | GSAFD: Love stories.

Classification: LCC PS3616.R452 | DDC 813/.6—dc23

LC record available upon request.

Prologue

The ancient mud was just thick enough to hold Bastian's laundry peg sailors at attention like the standing stone they surrounded. They were naval marines, of course, the kind who sailed tall wooden ships far out to sea, beyond the beyond, leaving the MacLeods and the Macaulays alone, with Bastian bouncing back and forth between them.

The laundry peg navy had traveled inland to investigate the circle of stones, rowing little boats like the Lewis fishermen used to cast their nets. Now they stood in a line—one, two, three—on guard and awaiting orders. The captain, however, was engaged in a rather rude argument with his first mate over whether or not to retreat.

Stomach growling, Bastian looked up to find the sun beginning to dip behind the massive old stones. The captain had best hurry up and make a decision. Miss Macaulay would already be sore at him for pilfering more laundry pegs to fill out his regiment. If he was late for dinner too, even his dimples might not save him.

With another glance skyward, he scooped up the sailors and stuffed them in his pockets, slapped on his cap, and turned down the hill towards his village.

She was a good sort, Miss Macaulay. He didn't like to vex her. Of the five different homes he'd lived in since his mother's passing, Miss Macaulay baked the best shortbread and gave him the largest portions of fish pie. She said it was so he could grow up big and handsome like his da—the only warm description he'd ever heard of his sire, who was usually mentioned with grim-faced curses—and so in this case, Bastian didn't mind the comparison.

With his dark hair and golden-brown skin, he didn't stand out as much as Ma had, but he didn't match the fair and ginger children who speckled the island like white-fleeced lambs, and he quite liked the notion he might grow up to be thought handsome.

Memories of his ma tugged several different strings within his heart all at once, so Bastian hummed the song she'd taught him before he'd even learned how to read.

The king once built a town so fair,
Red hibiscus lined the square.
Dance a waltz, then dance again.
Down the hill, an empty lane.
Andrew's spire calls out to thee.
Hear the bells, but do not see.

He scrunched his left eye, trying to remember the next part, and then started the nonsense rhyme over again.

As he neared home, he spied a ship way out in the harbor and peered through his fist like a spyglass, tempted to run along the beach until he could make out the colors of its standard. But cooking smells already assaulted him from every stone house along the lane, so he put exploration momentarily aside, determined to eat his fill before going out again.

When he lifted the latch and opened the door, the first thing

Bastian noticed was the fire still banked. No delicious stew simmered on the hob, no bannocks wafted their rich doughy scent to greet him. Miss Macaulay leaned against the cold stove with her arms across her chest while a long-legged man in an expensive dark waistcoat sat at the table in Bastian's own chair, drinking the medicinal whisky.

For a moment, Bastian stood in the doorway, staring at the adults who stared right back at him, very much wishing he'd taken the time to chase down that ship after all. He'd lived with Miss Macaulay for nearly a year, and in all that time, Bastian had never known male suitors to call on her.

His belly rumbled for a different reason this time. It knew without being told that his days of hearty, loving portions had come to an end.

"Come and say hello to your father, Sebastian," Miss Macaulay said in Gaelic, with a tremor in her voice instead of the warm, honeyed tone she used when she called him handsome.

"Tell me the boy can speak English," the man growled.

"Have you forgotten your Gaelic then, Neil?" she spat back in English, with a tone that sounded all wrong coming from her mouth.

Bastian slid his gaze over the stranger and weighed his options, trying not to linger on the man's hard, cold eyes. He was fast for nine and a half, but the man lounged in his chair like a cat feigning laziness, flicking its tail, ready to spring the moment a mouse ventured out of the shadows.

If he ran, Bastian might stow away on that ship out there in the harbor, but if this man was indeed his wayward sire, then the ship most likely belonged to him. Bastian wanted to ignore the man and race into the protective arms of Miss Macaulay, but her arms were still closed, wrapped protectively around herself instead.

Steeling his courage, Bastian stepped to the man's side as he was bidden, this figment of so many imaginings, who had always loomed larger than life, now made flesh before him.

The stranger assessed him for a moment and then said, "Well he's certainly her child. I don't know if he's mine."

"He has your nose and chin."

The man shrugged. "Get your things," he said, and took another sip of whisky.

What things? Bastian wondered. *Fishing things?*

"Cornelius, you can't mean to take him with you," Miss Macaulay pleaded.

The stranger slammed his cup down on the table, but his words were the hushed steel of a cutlass being drawn from its sheath. "You wrote you couldn't keep feeding him."

"But a ship is no place for a child."

"What did you expect me to do? Send coin?"

His laugh was laced with anger, and Miss Macaulay's face crumpled. "You could give up the sea. Come back here, make a life together. You promised me that once."

The stranger snorted, and tears sprang to Miss Macaulay's eyes, which she tried to hide by fussing about with a kettle on the cold stove.

"Go and get your things, Sebastian," she said in a scratchy voice. "I'll wrap some shortbread and bannocks for your journey."

Any excitement was tempered by the squirmy feeling in his empty belly, but Bastian gathered his clean sark and breeches into a satchel, along with one clean handkerchief because it would please his gran. With a heavy heart, he emptied his pockets of the laundry peg sailors, keeping just one for himself. Miss Macaulay wouldn't begrudge him the one, even if his dinner portions had been too large after all.

His mother's wooden locket already hung from his neck, but he checked to make sure both their likenesses were still safe inside. She smiled out at him, and he smiled back, tucking her safely inside his sark.

Just before leaving, he snatched his granda's gold-and-black tartan from the bed and crammed it in so the satchel bulged. He might never grow into the plaid, but he couldn't leave it behind.

Eager to see the ship up close, Bastian followed the silent stranger out of the village and down to the port where awaited as large a two-masted vessel as he'd ever seen. The figurehead was an ugly, scowling youth, its outstretched arm clutching a writhing serpent as blood seemed to drip from the youth's bared teeth, and Bastian could swear its eyes followed him, even as he stepped aboard *Auldfarrand's Revenge*.

Chapter One

1730, EVIE, ORKNEY

It was a brigantine ship, with two tall masts and square-rigged sails, and the fact that Maggie knew so much about a pile of floating timber reaffirmed she'd lived in Orkney far too long. She watched anyway as it deftly maneuvered through Eynhallow Sound instead of docking in one of the large ports where such a ship belonged.

Perhaps the nearest port was already overrun by ships laden down with letters full of bad news like the two in Maggie's apron pocket. Her sister Ellen's note had been brief and kindly meant: an offer to move back to the mainland to live with her and Silas MacKenzie, the big Laird Kintail, at Castle Leod. Much as Maggie missed her quiet, gentle sister, she couldn't stomach the thought of residing there, playing widowed governess to the growing brood of MacKenzie children—beautiful, lively children who would fill Maggie's days instead of children of her own. She couldn't face such a vision of her future, and yet the other letter in her pocket was far worse. She could feel it even as she sat on an old stone wall, watching the ship navigate the sound. It burned hot in her pocket, as though inked with fire, and heavy as though writ on stone.

Her father wrote that Maggie's one year and one day of mourning were coming to an end, and he'd already picked out a new husband for her: one of his former students, Michael MacFadyen. He and Michael would arrive in one week's time to collect her and take her back to Inverness, for, at twenty years of age, she was still young enough to try her hand at marriage again.

If she'd been a boy, there would be no trying again. There would only be marching herself down to the captain of that ship and signing on to his crew.

"Maybe this time he's picked someone better suited," her neighbor, Lorna, replied when Maggie related the sorry news, and she almost laughed in the other woman's face.

"Anyone who knew my cousin Jory would have known she was the least-suited woman on earth for holy orders," she replied. "But that's what he chose for her when the choice was his. Nor would any have thought my sister a fit match for the son of a laird."

"The Lord works in mysterious ways," Lorna chided.

"Aye, Father got lucky with that one. Still, I reckon suitability's the last thing on his mind." If it had been, he would never have matched her with Jeremiah Budge the moment she came of age. Back then, Maggie had only been suited to fairytales and romantic novels, not to becoming the real-life helpmeet of a fully grown man.

The truth was, there'd been no dowry left for Maggie's keeping. Her father had given it all to Silas MacKenzie when he wed Wee Ellen, and while Maggie had felt certain her brother-in-law would have settled a dowry on her himself two years ago, her father had refused to even hear of it. He'd made up his mind she would wed his former student and wouldn't be swayed on the matter.

Jeremiah Budge had owed a debt of unpaid tutoring fees, and so Mr. Mackintosh had written off the debt as the amount of his younger daughter's dowry, claiming he got the better end of the bargain, for wasn't Maggie finally off his hands?

This new man, Michael MacFadyen, was another former student, one who used to ogle Maggie as if he could see right through her stays before she'd even turned eighteen.

Maggie shuddered. She couldn't marry him. She refused.

As a girl, she had always imagined marriage to be some magical adventure filled with laughter and cozy picnics, whispered secrets and bubbling joy. She'd been sorely disappointed the first time. There wouldn't be a second.

"Jeremiah brought you here, that's a bit like an adventure," Lorna had suggested in a pathetic sort of way. Even she knew it was ridiculous.

Maggie didn't laugh in her face because she'd learned some amount of tact in the two years since her wedding, but Orkney had been less of an adventure than a prison sentence—her husband's sudden death a blessed reprieve.

Still, Lorna must have read the incredulity on her face because she refilled Maggie's cup with strong, hot tea and said, "Go on, then. What sort of adventure would you want if you could have one?"

Staring out towards the sound and the smattering of islands across the water, Maggie tried to recall the girl she used to be. "I always thought... all I ever wanted was to wed a devilishly hand-some young man and mother a passel of mischievous, deliriously happy children. But"—she went on quickly, cutting Lorna off before she could suggest Michael MacFadyen might have grown handsome in the years since Maggie had met him—"now, I suppose all I want is to be someplace warm. I've never once felt truly warm here. Even sitting before the fire there's a chill nipping at your back like the creeping fingers of a shadow."

Lorna frowned but didn't defend her home, and Maggie was a little sorry for being quite so blunt.

"And perhaps to swing through the trees like a monkey," she added to make the other woman laugh.

"A monkey!"

"Jory was forever climbing trees when I was small, and I was desperate to join her. Now I suppose I've missed my chance."

Lorna's face said she couldn't fathom such a thing.

"She looked so free. But even when I was little, I was afraid—"

"You? Afraid?" *This* was the notion that finally caused Lorna to laugh. How little they knew each other.

"Not of the tongue lashing I'd receive for mussing my pinafore. I was afraid the lads wouldn't like me if I were as wild as I wanted to be, and oh, but I was desperate for the lads to like me."

"And now?" Lorna asked, amused.

Maggie fingered her short hair. It had grown back almost curly after she'd shorn it when her husband died, a final act of rebellion against his accursed soul. "Now I don't care what the lads think at all, but there aren't any trees to climb," she laughed helplessly.

Lorna's face was open and easy to read. She had always found Maggie a bit silly, and though politeness demanded she try to hide it, some things weren't easily hidden. She'd grown up on Orkney and married a local fisherman she'd known all her life, the same fate as most of the island's young women. He spoke little more than grunts in Maggie's presence, and she wondered how well even Lorna knew him. She cooked his food and mended his clothes, bore his children, and offered no complaints. She took life as it came without any thought to whether or not she particularly enjoyed it. Perhaps she was even fond of her fisherman in the way that familiarity can breed affinity as well as contempt. They seemed companionable at least, both of them too tired or even-tempered to fight.

But Maggie had seen the fire crackling between Finn and Jory, even from across a crowded room. She'd witnessed her sister bloom under the sunshine of Silas MacKenzie's worship.

Now, after one year of marriage and one year in mourning dress, she couldn't help thinking she'd imagined it all. Such love was all right for fairytales, but if it could be found in real life, well, then perhaps *she* was the problem. Maggie wasn't a heroine from fairy stories. She was as stubborn as the sun that refused to set in summer, too wild and self-centered to take care of a husband or children the way they would need.

That night, she lay in bed staring up at the discolored spot where the roof used to leak. After Jeremiah's funeral, the village men had turned out in force to repair the thatch so she could almost pretend her husband had never been there at all, as though they hadn't fought, and she hadn't thrown the bucket full of rainwater at his head, as though he hadn't climbed up on the roof in the middle of a lightning storm just to prove a point.

The lightning strike had accompanied the loudest crack of thunder Maggie'd ever heard. They said the roof would've caught fire if Jeremiah hadn't been struck instead.

Shivering, she burrowed deeper beneath her quilts. She'd meant it when she told Lorna she longed for warmth. How sad that all her youthful dreams had been reduced to something so basic and primal. At least if her father took her back to Inverness, she could enjoy a bit of summer weather before MacFadyen dragged her off to whatever place he had in mind. God help her, if he put her on a ship to America, she would throw herself into the sea. Not because of any particular objection to the New World, but because the choice wasn't hers.

When it came down to it, she supposed she was an ungrateful brat. There was really no getting around it. She despised this low stone house at the end of the earth, miles and miles from everything she'd ever known, loathed the uncle who died leaving the place to Jeremiah, and perhaps hated her father most of all for deciding they must wed. Michael MacFadyen might surprise her by being the kindest man she'd ever met, but she didn't want him, and so she hated him, too.

Disappointed by her father's selection of Jeremiah Budge, Maggie had initially underestimated the former pupil. Lanky and scholarly, she'd thought Jeremiah was a timid sort. He was still a bachelor at thirty-six, and she'd naively expected him to be putty in her young hands. Instead, he was constantly annoyed by her inexperience and found her lacking in every way.

For starters, Maggie's stitching wasn't prettily done. Her cooking, when she didn't burn the soup, was far from savory, her housekeeping abysmal, and her thighs never spread wide enough or often enough for his liking. The only thing he seemed to approve of was her hair.

Pushing herself up in bed, she snatched her sewing shears from the table and trimmed it even shorter, the tiny chestnut curls dropping to the floor like autumn leaves in a place which had no trees. See if her father's new stud pony would take her now!

From her perch atop the tumbledown broch wall that morning, she'd watched sailors spill off their brigantine like sun-browned ants marching about their busy lives. They must be merchant mariners sailing back and forth from somewhere quite warm to be so tan. Mercy, how she envied them—such freedom, such endless adventures. She couldn't begin to fathom the things they must have seen, because she'd read all the wrong kinds of books.

Even now, they were probably swapping stories in the tavern over pints of ale and bowls of mutton stew, laughing and singing, strangers to the notion of setting down roots anywhere as windswept as this.

Hugging her knees to her chest, it struck Maggie again that if she were a boy she could run away and join them.

She laughed grimly.

If she were a boy, she wouldn't be in this situation to begin with. She wouldn't need to run away and join them, because her father wouldn't be so desperate to be rid of a son. No, he'd find a son very useful indeed, apprenticing her out and demanding she hand over all her wages.

If she were a boy, she might have run away to sea long ago just to find a taste of freedom from her father.

Freedom.

She shrugged back down under the blankets, but the thought wouldn't let her go so easily.

Freedom.

She tossed and turned like she was caught in a whirlpool eddy.

It would be an easy thing, she supposed, to creep on board and hide amongst the cargo. By the time they found her it would be far too late to shoo her on her way. They might not be happy about it, but they'd have to keep her then, at least until the next port. She had a little money which might be used to buy passage if they were truly fussed.

Maggie had never been one to pray overmuch. She had long since given it up altogether, but when she'd read her father's letter yesterday, she'd certainly muttered an oath begging for deliverance. It could almost have been construed as prayer-like.

What was the brigantine, then, but an answer to her almost-prayer, appearing from the fog like some kind of beacon? There was no good reason for the ship to drop anchor in the sound instead of the harbor.

Jory had once run away from a future she didn't consent to, forging the one she preferred instead. Maggie could run, but on an island, she'd eventually be spinning in circles.

That ship out there was her chance to escape, to choose whatever path she wanted. She'd be a fool to sit back and let it sail away.

Leaving her bed before she could talk herself out of the decision, Maggie dressed quickly, throwing on her warm Mackintosh earasaid and drawing it up over her chilly head. What else did a lady pack when running away to sea? She filled one pocket with dried beef and another with dried strawberries. She collected her sewing kit and a spare chemise and tucked away the folding frame containing likenesses of Ellen and Jory, drawn by the big MacKenzie's younger cousin, Bram.

A tiny pang of regret bit Maggie for making such a fuss when her father had teased the match. Bram would be about fifteen these days, and she could be idly biding her time in Inverness waiting for him to grow up instead of widowed and facing another inconvenient match with a stranger. But none of that mattered now. Adventure was calling.

After writing a hasty note to Lorna and another to her parents, Maggie crept down to the shore before she could change her mind. The deserted beach called to her like a selkie of old, as the brigantine rocked gently against its moorings.

She glanced around to make sure no one was watching and was startled to find a cream-colored cat with glowing yellow eyes staring back at her from a wooden plank abutting the vessel. Flicking its tail saucily, the cat turned and scampered up the plank and over the side as though welcoming her aboard. She followed on tiptoe, freezing each time a timber creaked.

The cat, which she immediately named Custard, led her across the shadowed deck and down a ladder into the gaping maw below.

Descending the ladder in her skirts and earasaid was quite the challenge, she soon discovered. Twice she nearly slipped. How on earth had the cat managed it without raising a ruckus?

Once her feet finally touched solid boards again, she sagged against the bulkhead in relief. Custard just blinked its golden eyes and turned down a corridor.

Was it called a corridor on a ship? She wasn't sure.

Not eager to be discovered until they were well out to sea, she hurried in the direction the cat had fled before being swallowed by the cavernous abyss. Candle lanterns at the entrance did little to light her way. To call it dark would be like describing the

Orkney wind as chilly or Jeremiah Budge as cruel: factually accurate but far understating the situation. She couldn't make out her own hand in front of her face.

Feeling each step almost one toe at a time, she crept forward, following the rumble of Custard's purr as she shuffled with one hand on the wall for guidance until it gave way to a wider area, just as dark and almost more cramped, packed with crates and barrels of all sorts. A stack of them loomed up out of the darkness and she froze, certain one strong exhale would send them all crashing down.

The cat led her through a maze-like area where her outstretched fingers tangled in netting that hung from the low ceiling—hammocks for the crew, she realized, making them out in the glimmer of twilight from the portholes and scurrying past as quickly as she could. When she stubbed her toe on what felt like heavy iron, she bit her lip hard, and swallowed the cries.

As though Custard sensed her pain, the cat rubbed against her legs, making a figure-eight between them before heading off again, blinking at her over one shoulder like it knew its eyes were just about the only thing she could see. Then it turned a corner and she followed once more, down, down down, coming to a stop when she finally did bump into a stack of crates, causing a chorus of squawks and clucking.

Borrowing some straw from the sleepy chickens, which warbled softly in irritation, she made herself a little nest in the furthest corner she could find, piled high with more crates to shield her from view. Maggie had never heard of feline messengers from the heavens, but perhaps the cat was some spirit's familiar, sent to guide her on her journey. She would never have found such a clever little hiding place on her own, and Custard almost seemed smug the way it curled up on her lap, as though she were precisely where it wanted her to be.

Had she done the right thing? Her knees and shins ached from the many obstacles she'd tripped over, but bruises would mend. They were a small price for warmth, and most of all, adventure. How funny it would be when she presented herself to the captain. Like her father, he would lament the need for someone to take her off his hands. Then she'd offer him her money, and he'd shake his head in annoyed amusement and warn her to stay out from underfoot.

Heart still pounding after skulking through the darkness, Maggie was now so excited that even the gentle rocking of the ship and the warm, purring cat couldn't lull her to sleep for quite some time.

BASH WOKE WITH A START AND STRAINED HIS EARS AGAINST THE night, but all he could hear was the familiar creak of timber and flap of sails, the gentle thump of the surf against the hull, and the snores of the crew who had finally stumbled back from their shore leave. His heartbeat slowed as he adjusted himself in his swaying hammock and pulled the old black-and-gold MacLeod plaid up from where it had slipped to the floor. Summers were blasted cold in the islands, and Orkney was almost far enough north to kiss the pole.

He kept listening, for what he couldn't say. Something was off besides the chill. The entire journey to Scotland had been ill-advised, not only because they couldn't afford it. His stomach grumbled, reminding him that the cod he'd caught and fried for dinner hadn't been enough to fill his belly. Fish never did for long. Had the others fared any better in the village tavern, with barely enough coin for a pint of ale between them, let alone provisions to see them back across the Atlantic?

Probably. If this place was anything like the village of his youth, they likely turned the taps for free just to keep rowdy sailors peaceful. Might feed them, too, crusty bannocks and bowls of hearty stew. His mouth watered, but Bash didn't really mind fending for himself. It was just about the only peace he got—when the crew went ashore, waving and blowing him kisses as he stayed behind, captain's orders. He couldn't even remember what land felt like under his boots.

With the sort of certainty he only ever felt in the marrow of his bones, Bash knew the captain had dropped anchor here for his own personal torment. Orkney was so close he could taste home, but not so close it mattered. It mollified him somewhat, realizing the mad old man needed him and was just a little scared Bash might leave, scared enough he hadn't sailed directly to Lewis. So, he wasn't wholly confident his orders that Bash never leave the ship would be obeyed.

And what would Bash have done if they had gone to Lewis instead? After thirteen years away, there was nothing on the island for him now. There was nothing in Scotland for any of them, except rumors that Willy Walsh had packed it in and taken his sloop back home, a pirate's life no more.

Bash rolled his eyes and put an arm behind his head. Fucking nonsense. If Willy Walsh were going to give up the life, he'd have done it twelve years earlier when the King offered a pardon. Indeed, rumors suggested he'd done just that, and if the old pirate had the captain's lost treasure, Bash would eat the main sail. He was hungry enough.

Before they left Nassau, Bash had plotted a course up the eastern coast of the colonies to harass the English merchants and navy alike, from Florida on up to Boston, where supposedly rampant lawlessness and stirrings of rebellion made easy pickings for pirates. But Mad wouldn't hear of it, and the captain always knew best.

The crew had a year or two left at most before they'd be caught by the navy and hanged, or even just starve to death. Despite not having set foot on land in ten years, Bash still hadn't saved enough coin to strike out on his own. Raiding fishermen around the Caribbean didn't bring a heavy purse, and they hadn't encountered so much as a schooner during the Atlantic crossing. With the ever-present threat of pirate-hungry vessels patrolling the British coast, Bash reckoned the *Revenge* would be lucky to make it back to warmer waters in one piece.

Captain Mad MacLeod was truly earning his nickname with this ridiculous voyage, and everyone knew it. But they followed orders because none of them had any better ideas. Election or no, the captain wouldn't step aside without a mutiny, and mutiny wouldn't put coin in their pockets or food in their bellies. So they all just pretended to believe there was gold at the end of the rainbow. And maybe there was, but the rainbow didn't end in Willy Walsh's cargo hold.

If there had ever been as much loot as Mad let on, which Bash doubted, and the captain had really buried more than he'd spent, which Bash also couldn't believe, then Mad had forgotten where he left it, plain and simple. It was a twenty-two-year-old mystery no one would ever solve.

Whether he'd accepted it or not, Mad knew the gold was lost, but he was canny enough to see his crew growing thin and fractious. They were trapped in a life which was no longer prosperous, and even Bash couldn't chart a course out of it.

Coming to Scotland had been a charade to boost morale, nothing more. Tomorrow, Mad would declare new rumors of Walsh's whereabouts, and he'd instruct Bash to sail them straight back across the ocean to where they'd begun.

With any luck, they'd dodge the navy and even take a merchant ship or two. The pay would either be enough for Bash to slip off and start some new life, or so little the crew would finally mutiny and toss Mad overboard like so much rubbish. Bash wasn't fussy which.

He held his breath at the sound of light footsteps padding

towards him, like someone trying to sneak, and reached for his dagger.

"Mrow?" a cat murmured, springing up to sit on his chest.

Letting out his breath, he held up a hand for the cat to sniff, and then its bristly whiskers brushed against him in greeting, and he scratched behind its ears. It must have snuck aboard, lured by the smell of cooking cod perhaps.

"Go on now, Mouser," he whispered. "If you set sail with us, like as not you'll wind up eaten before we reach t'other side."

The cat's purring stopped, and it jumped down and padded away as if affronted at the very notion of hungry men eating cat and mushroom stew.

If only changing course were so easy for Bash. He'd spent more than half his life on this bloody ship. Pirating was the only occupation he knew. Even if he managed to take his leave with coin in his pocket, what was he going to do? Join the navy? Hire himself onto a merchant fleet? One whiff of his past, and he'd be food for the fishes. And that would be after he was hanged.

No, to reinvent himself he'd need a lot more than the pittance they could earn these days. He would need gold on par with the rumored stash the captain had misplaced all those years ago. And that was why he stayed—why they all stayed, even as they knew this way of life was ending—had ended long ago.

Mad Cornelius MacLeod clung to the illusion that piracy was still viable, and the crew clung to Mad. Any port was better than none when a storm was brewing.

Bash squirmed in his hammock, unable to shake the pall hanging over the night.

Maybe it was just being back in the islands making his nerves so jangled. It had been at least a year since they'd encountered the naval captain with a vendetta against Mad, long enough for a false sense of security to settle like a blanket. If Bash were paranoid like his captain, he'd say they were overdue for a visit from HMS *Pursuit*.

He tried not to be paranoid, as a general rule. Indeed, he tried very hard not to be anything like his sire at all, but he'd feared the specter of the Royal Navy's Captain Constantin and his *Pursuit* for more years than he hadn't. It was second nature to shudder at the thought of Mad MacLeod's old nemesis.

Snap out of it, he told himself. He'd feel better once he was back under equatorial stars. The cat had been a good omen. Still, it wouldn't hurt to check everything was in order. Tomorrow they must depart, for the day after was Friday, an unlucky day to set sail no matter the weather. It had to be tomorrow.

He rolled out of his hammock and shuffled to the ladder, pausing to strain his ears towards the stern of the vessel where nocturnal creatures scurried, no doubt carefully stalked by his industrious feline companion.

Bash curled his lip. He'd always hated rats, and by the sound of it, they'd taken on some very large ones. At least there'd be extra protein when the chicken ran out.

He climbed the ladder and stepped out onto the deck, looking up into a cold, twilit sky. Even the moon shone differently here, or was his imagination overdoing it again?

Dogwood blossoms, moonlight glow...

A line from some faraway song floated into his head like a butterfly that refused to land. Maybe Mad was smarter than he realized—something about being back in Scotland was making Bash maudlin and edgy.

A familiar shadow stepped up to his elbow.

"So few stars," Dutch murmured.

"Aye." It should have felt familiar, but it was only disconcerting after more years spent sailing the equator than playing in the Lewis dirt. "What are we doing here, Dutch?"

The old quartermaster shook his head. "Following orders, son."

Bash smiled. Dutch called everyone son except the captain, and one word had never carried more meaning. Disappointment, ridicule, condescension—all had their place, but most of the time Bash heard pride. Shared history. Even love. Whichever side Dutch came out on in the end, that was where Bash wanted to be, preferably not side by side wearing matching rope necklaces dancing for a crowd at Gallows Point.

"Don't suppose Willy Walsh turned up in the tavern?"

"Just missed him," Dutch replied.

Bash snorted. "Rotten luck."

"We head after him at dawn."

"What'll we do if we catch him?" Bash asked, not quite teasing. It was bound to happen eventually, if the pirate really hadn't hung up his rapier and made peace with the King, and unless his ship, the *Woebegone Whale*, was sitting heavy with gold, the crew really would mutiny at last.

Dutch turned to him, the whites of his eyes bright with anticipation. "Pray we never do."

"Might not be the worst thing," Bash murmured. "But what's Mad's plan? He should be searching for gold, not chasing a figment he knows doesn't have it." It was his own sort of madness, trying to second-guess the captain's strategy, but Bash couldn't help wondering aloud.

"He's spent a dozen years searching," Dutch said with a shrug.

"Still, he must know what'll happen if we catch the *Whale* and there's no gold. D'you suppose he wants it? Death by mutiny? Just to make a tidy end of things?"

It would be insanity, no doubt, to try and force a revolt, but it made some kind of twisted logic. The captain had refused the royal pardon. He would never surrender his ship, not until it was pried from his cold, dead grasp.

"But then why not just let the blue devil catch him?" Bash whispered, wondering, not for the first time, how they'd been so lucky, always slipping past the navy at the last moment as though fate or Providence were on their side.

The quartermaster shook his head. He had no answers. The captain kept his own counsel.

They stared in silence at the heavens a bit longer, until Dutch finally turned to go below deck, patting Bash's shoulder as he went. "Keep your wits about you, son. Weather's coming, and it always gets worse before it gets better."

He'd been saying the same thing for more than a decade, and after so much time, Bash was overdue some fair weather of his own.

Chapter Two

Boats and Maggie had never really been a good match. Two days after her wedding, she and Jeremiah had set sail from Inverness in a tiny boat, making their way up through the North Sea to the Orkney Islands. They were tossed about on choppy waves until Maggie was sick all over herself and vowed never to set foot on another such vessel for the rest of her natural life.

Over the course of two years and everything that followed, she had conveniently forgotten the horrors of boating in her hasty decision to stow away. She forgot right up until her next great adventure hauled anchor and sailed out into the rough open sea. Taking deep, soothing breaths as Jory had once taught her elder sister to do, memories of the Orkney crossing came flooding back, but Maggie consoled herself that the brigantine was much larger than the tiny fishing vessel which had carried her as a newlywed, and as soon as it broke free from the coastal tides, everything would settle down.

She could not have been more wrong.

The first day of sailing felt as turbulent as any she might have imagined, and soon they were beset by storms that made the ship creak and moan as though it were a man being pulled apart on a rack. Even deep within the dark heart of the ship, the cacophonous thunder seemed to echo all around her. She could feel it in her bones as though it vibrated the very ocean floor. Only the lightning was missing, for, hidden as she was, not a flicker could reach her. The disorienting lack of warning somehow made the thunder all the more terrifying.

Maggie heaved constantly into the straw she'd taken as a bed, though her stomach was long-past empty. Retching and snuffling, it was a wonder she'd not been discovered straight away, but the sailors were likely busy doing whatever sailors did in a storm to make sure the brigantine stayed afloat. At least she hoped that was what they were doing, as she relieved herself in a nearby corner, little better than an animal. She had certainly not thought this plan through any better than an animal, and perhaps worse, considering squirrels buried nuts and built nests.

Had she not been so weak and miserable, Maggie might have crawled out of her hiding place to gasp fresh, cool air and announce herself to her new traveling companions, but as it was, she couldn't manage much more than dozing in a puddle of filth and misery.

She had no idea how long it lasted. Days? Weeks? Long enough that she was surprised when she realized the storm was finally over, and after noting her relief, she promptly fell back into a fitful sleep, battered by dreams of another storm and Jeremiah climbing up onto the leaking thatch roof.

Sometime later, she was awakened by a rough stroking of her hand. She blinked in the darkness, jerking her arm away when she realized the wet smacking sound meant some creature was licking her. She shuddered. What sort of diseases could a person contract from being licked by a rodent? Had Jory ever mentioned such a thing? And was it licking her in preparation for biting?

Two golden eyes turned to look at her as though insulted by the question, and she skittered deeper into her corner, cracking her head against timber before she realized it was only the same cat who had led her to this hiding place.

"Custard," she croaked, reaching out to pet it, her throat as dry as sand.

The cat rubbed its whiskers against her hand, licking her thumb once more for good measure.

"How's your adventure going?" Maggie asked, scratching under Custard's chin.

In response, its golden eyes turned away, and in the darkness, she could just make out its shadowy form disappearing.

Were they far enough from Scotland that the captain wouldn't turn around and drop her on the nearest Hebridean beach? She drew her earasaid closer around her arms. How long until they reached someplace warm?

Her stomach growled plaintively and she sucked on a dried strawberry, but it didn't make her mouth water as it should. It was all she could do to chew it up and choke it down. Soon her meager provisions would run out and she'd be forced to show herself. Would these merchant marines begrudge sharing their portions with her? Would they accept what little money she'd brought as compensation?

She refused to give in and call the anxiety which gripped her throat and hammered her chest *regret*. She was having an adventure, and she was going to enjoy it, damn it. Perhaps she should remain hiding—slip out to find something edible and potable in the dead of night, though how she'd know if it was day or night in this cave of perpetual shadow, she was uncertain.

That was a problem for later. At the moment, she felt far too weak to stand, let alone scavenge, and was more inclined to go back to sleep. Then she heard footsteps shuffling towards her, and she froze, not yet ready to be discovered.

When Custard reappeared, popping out from behind a stack of crates with a "Mrow?" Maggie released her breath, perplexed by how one small cat could make so much noise.

A larger figured stepped out to join the cat.

Maggie gasped and shrank back into the hull, knocking her head hard enough to see flashes like a meadow filled with fireflies.

The newcomer wore a loose white shirt with a darker colored waistcoat. He stood a good few inches taller than Maggie, with a thick, muscular neck and arms, and a patch flipped up above his left eye.

"What in God's name have you done?" he whispered, as though she were guilty of more than poor judgment and profuse vomiting, which couldn't possibly account for the full range of stench pervading the cargo hold. There was something distinctly bovine about the smell, and no matter how filthy, Maggie hoped she wasn't capable of smelling like a stable.

"Nothing," she rasped back, her hackles rising.

Not enjoying the way he towered over her, Maggie pushed herself up the wall to standing, though her legs felt weak and wobbly, and her head began to swim.

He glared at her even harder, now she was close to his eye level, and she scowled right back at him because squinting made her feel less like collapsing.

Then a flickering light appeared behind the man, and her eyes watered from the sudden brightness, while the man's face turned absolutely thunderous.

"Well, well, well," a weaselly voice sang, as an equally weaselly little sailor with white skin and wispy white hair limped out from behind another crate holding a candle lantern. "Tsk, tsk, tsk, tsk, tsk," he clucked his tongue. "What do we have here?" he asked in a gleeful tone that made the hairs on Maggie's arm stand.

The first man turned his head only slightly towards the second and sounded almost sad as he answered, "Stowaway."

The older man took out a long pipe and tucked it between his teeth unlit, looking slyly at his younger companion. "Just found her down here, did you, Bashy?" he asked, his words tinged with an accent Maggie didn't recognize.

"Aye, just now, same as you," the young man rumbled. " 'Twas Mouser found her first."

"Sure and you didn't help her aboard?"

"Of course not, Rooijakkers."

The second man spoke around his pipe once more. "Well, come on, then. Best take her up top. Mad'll be none too pleased."

"Aye."

Even as a little child, few things aggravated Maggie more than being spoken about like she wasn't standing right there, and she would have told off both men properly, if she weren't half so fatigued. And perhaps a touch nervous. She hadn't expected her hosts to be overjoyed by her presence, but the way the young man kept glancing between her and his companion, along with the fact she was being taken to someone called Mad, made her insides as much like jelly as her knees.

"You coming, or shall I carry you?" the older man asked her, leering over his shoulder, but the first held out an arm to usher her forward almost like a gentleman—albeit a sullen one. When she brushed past him, he stiffened as though she were covered in nettles, but he followed close behind, scandalously close, as they ascended the ladder. And a good thing, too, for she hadn't found her sea legs yet and she took several missteps, grateful to have his solid form behind her to break a fall. He kept his hands at her hips to steady her, all propriety left behind on the Orkney shore. There was no room for propriety on an adventure, she reminded herself.

Once on deck, she shut her eyes tight against the blinding sunlight and gasped in great lungfuls of the crisp, ocean air, tangy with brine, as she reached for the nearest solid object she could lean against, a mast pole. His left eye now covered by the leather patch, the young man guided her with a firm grip on her upper arm to the far railing where she could lean casually, or vomit over the side, should such a need arise.

The sailor who had climbed up ahead of Maggie roused the

other men, directing their attention towards her until she had quite a crowd gawking. Turning away from the hungry, leering faces, she blinked in awe at the square sails hanging limp and torn after the storm.

"What's all this?" The deep, bassy murmur came from a tall, black man. He stepped close to her, but her young captor just shook his head once and peered sternly down at Maggie.

"Nav?" another sailor asked, coming out of the crowd to scan Maggie with warm, curious eyes. This one was as white and fair as Maggie's sister Ellen, or would have been if he wasn't burned to a crispy, painful-looking red. No wonder their mother always fussed about bonnets.

She'd never seen so many varied faces or heard so many differently accented words in her life. As the men drew closer, she suddenly realized quite how foolishly precarious her situation was, and this time she felt only gratitude when the young man who had discovered her moved between her and the rest of the men.

"Don't say a word," he whispered for her ears only.

The crowd parted as a tall gentleman who could only be the captain strode forward. He wore an impressive tricorne hat of brown leather, a gold earring, and a long, black coat with a row of brass buttons. His mouth curved ever so slightly on the left side as he studied her from top to bottom and Maggie shivered, shrinking back against the railing.

What did you think was going to happen? She could hear her cousin's words, spoken in exasperation each time one of Maggie's impulsive notions had resulted in a cut lip or scraped knee, only this time Jory wasn't there to take care of her. Maggie was very much alone.

BUGGER BUGGER BUGGER. WHEN BASH HAD FIRST DISCOVERED the girl hiding amongst the cargo, he tried to convince himself she was a ghost. He'd heard tales aplenty of apparitions, despite never seeing one himself. Eyeless, mouthless bastards were supposedly condemned to wander the lonely seas after having been murdered. Women, green with algae, were said to scream their misery in the dead of night.

The girl was certainly pale enough, though he'd never heard of ships acquiring new hauntings after decades at sea, nor to his knowledge had there ever been a living woman aboard the *Revenge*. And while she looked a bit unkempt and sickly, there was nothing of the tormented soul in her lovely face. No, for now she was very much alive, more's the pity.

As they had stared at each other for that split second before the bloody Dutchman interrupted them, his mind flew through possible courses of action that wouldn't result in either of them being keelhauled, a way to hide her until he could put her on a bloody boat back to bloody Scotland. Then the damn cook sidled up like he'd known she was there all along and was just waiting for someone else to find her so he wouldn't get the blame.

Now the vultures were circling, and it would be a miracle if Bash could save either of their skins.

"A woman," the captain said, stepping up to examine her, his lips curving into a wolfish smirk. With one long finger he tilted her chin up, forcing her to meet his gaze. "Where did you come from?"

"Inverness," she said in a husky whisper. "By way of Orkney, sir." At least the silly girl recognized the captain's authority.

In the sunlight, it was plain her lips were dry and cracking, her eyes a bit sunken. Had she drunk a drop since coming aboard? She must be dangerously thirsty.

"Inverness by way of Orkney," Mad repeated, stepping back from her a pace. "Welcome aboard *Auldfarrand's Revenge*, madam," he added, gesturing around them.

She blinked back at him. Bash could almost see her mind working as she realized it was no ordinary merchant ship, not with a name like *Revenge*. She licked those poor parched lips, while the captain scrutinized his pirate crew.

"Who brought a woman aboard my ship?" Mad demanded, his voice soft but cold as chert.

The men looked from one to another suspiciously, but none came forward.

"Who?" Mad yelled, and the girl flinched but lifted her chin defiantly.

"No one," she answered, but the captain ignored her.

"Was it you, Langley?" he asked the youngest lad, a lanky, sunburned boy of seventeen. "I'll bet you like them young and pretty."

Young Langley shook his head. "No, sir, Cap."

"Duffy?" Mad barked, and the next youngest, a ginger sailor with gangly limbs and a beaklike nose, snapped to attention, shaking his head. "Roo?" Mad asked the cook. "You're down in the hold more than anyone else. What say you?"

Rooijakkers shifted his weight from foot to foot, no longer so eager to expose the girl now Mad's suspicions rested on him. "Well, now I—"

"Roo?"

"It were Bash with her down below when I spied 'em just now," the damn cook offered, casting a shrug Bash's way.

Mad turned back to Bash with a delighted sneer. "You brought a woman onto my ship?" The surprise in his voice didn't quite mask a note of something like pride.

Bash stared straight ahead and didn't answer. There'd be no winning anyhow. The captain wanted it to be him, and maybe if he drew Mad's wrath he could at least protect the girl.

"The cat," Mad ordered without taking his eyes off Bash. And he didn't mean the mangy mouser which had led Bash right into this godforsaken trap in the first place. So much for good luck.

His bowels twisted, his palms beginning to sweat, but Bash would be damned if he let any of them see it.

"Captain, you know it wasn't him," Dutch argued in his placid, even way. "He's not allowed ashore. Where would he find a girl to smuggle aboard?"

Mad cut his gaze to the quartermaster. "Perhaps he's disobeyed more than one order," he hissed. "Bring me the cat o' nine tails."

Dutch glanced sideways, but when Bash didn't protest or even acknowledge him, he stepped away to retrieve the dreaded sack while Mad continued his grandstanding.

"You see, madam, there are rules on my ship. Forty lashes," he reminded Dutch when the quartermaster removed the blood-stained whip from its bag. Thirty-nine may be customary, but Mad always liked to go that one extra.

Bash removed his waistcoat and shirt, then stepped towards the post, extending his wrists for binding. He reached for a faraway place in his mind, but the imprint of the girl upon his senses made the fog difficult to access. She gasped when she saw the nine-tailed whip, and likely the scars adorning his skin. He willed her to shut up and turn away until the business was over.

Instead she exclaimed, "Wait!"

"You may not have known the rules, madam, but Bash most certainly did," the captain advised her.

"But he didn't bring me aboard," she argued in that surprisingly low, raspy, lilting voice of hers, unable, it seemed, to simply hold her tongue.

"Who did then, miss?" Dutch asked her.

"No one. I brought my own self. So if anyone's to be whipped, I suppose"—her words wavered—"I suppose it should be me."

Christ.

Bash closed his eyes as a rumbling murmur went up from the gathered men, and Dutch stood frozen, unsure what to do.

Bloody foolish girl, playing games with her life and she didn't even know it.

"Seems reasonable," Dutch murmured to the captain.

After decades sailing under Mad, the quartermaster was skilled at whipping so as to inflict the least damage possible. He wouldn't kill her, but it would be a torture right enough, for her and for anyone decent who watched.

"Shall we vote?" Dutch called to the rest, before Mad could order elsewise.

Bash hazarded a glance around at the crew, all of them nodding and shouting their approval. Even the most bloodthirsty, eager as they were to see him thrashed, would rather see the girl stripped bare for whipping and nodded their eager assent.

"Fine," Mad agreed, and the girl nodded, though her face was all scrunched up with worry, and even more pale than before.

Dutch waved her forward, and Bash slipped his shirt back on.

"No." Mad held a palm out towards Dutch, whose eyes widened, but he handed over the cat, unwilling to openly defy the captain.

Bash froze. If Mad meant to do it himself... but then the captain gleefully shoved the whip at Bash. "You found her. You do it."

"'Tis the job of the quartermaster, not the sailing master," Bash protested, but his words were drowned out by the cheering of the horde, and the captain pressed the whip into his hands. There would be no getting out of it. Mad would torment him one way or the other. He knew whipping the girl himself would be worse than having Bash's own back flayed open yet again.

Mad tilted his head and growled, "You or me, boy," forcing Bash to take the whip.

He hated touching the thing. It was all he could do not to drop it on the deck like it was on fire. He glanced at Dutch for guidance, and the quartermaster's eyes darted toward the ladder and the deck below. It might work. Anyway, what was there to lose?

"Fine," Bash said, thinking quickly. "But she's a lady, not some common whore. I'll not do it up here." And before there could be any argument, he grabbed her roughly above the elbow and shoved her towards the hatch, weaving through the men who hooted and hollered and refused to step out of their way, each one salivating for a chance at a poke, as they realized they were being deprived of the best entertainment they were likely to get all year.

Bash stared them down one by one as he forced his way through. With his lips so close they brushed the soft shell of her ear, he whispered, "Don't try to run. Do exactly as I say. You've no idea how much danger you're in. Bloody fool."

He hadn't meant to say the last part out loud, squeezing her arm a little as he murmured it. The girl shot him an angry look, but she scrambled down the ladder and waited for him at the bottom, glancing nervously at the cat o' nine tails still clenched in his fist. Not pausing to flip the patch off his left eye so he could better see her in the dim light, he took her arm once again to guide her away from the leering sailors above.

Not yet accustomed to the sway of the ship, she tripped along the narrow passage to the almost-private alcove where he hung his hammock, and he shoved her inside, releasing her arm to draw the curtain closed.

The two of them certainly filled up the tiny space in an intoxicating sort of way. Even the ceiling seemed suddenly too low, though there was normally space aplenty.

"Don't say a word," he breathed harshly when she opened her mouth, and jerked his head to remind her of their audience. At best, the men would be crowded around the hatch to hear her screams.

She snapped her lips closed and then opened them again and drew a breath.

"Not a word," he whispered once more, close enough to take

in the heady scent of her hair, then he stepped back, putting some distance between them.

How in Christ's name did he end up here? The whipping wouldn't be the end of it. She was a woman, after all. Mad wouldn't keep her aboard. If she wasn't a specter when he'd found her, she'd be one soon enough, haunting him and the *Revenge* until their final days, more efficiently than the navy had ever done. Even if it wasn't by Bash's own hand, the stain of her death would forever taint his soul for having found her and failing to prevent it. What the hell was he going to do?

Chapter Three

Maggie was the sort of child who, upon being scolded for misbehavior, would look her parents dead in the eye and misbehave again. If anything got her dander up faster than being bossed around, she couldn't think what. This once, though, her sense of self-preservation, honed through marriage and a scant amount of maturity, outweighed any childish rancor.

Truthfully, the whole adventure seemed more and more like a very ill-conceived, impulsive mistake. Like every rash response to Jeremiah's goading, whether it was burning his dinner or throwing it in his face, she had a feeling she was going to regret ever running away.

She eyed the whip her captor—Bash?—still held at his side. Did he earn his name by hitting people? The raw white knuckles of his clenched fist might indicate yes.

He heaved a sigh, and she allowed her gaze to travel up his taut, tawny forearm to his broad shoulder, and so what if it was broad? This young man was just another man, and one who'd been ordered to whip her, at that.

Swallowing her nerves, she forced herself to meet his gaze. He worked his square, stubbled jaw like he was chewing his thoughts, the muscle popped beneath a thin scar bisecting his left cheek, right along the ridge of chiseled bone. Maggie licked her lips and leaned back against the bulkhead, forcing herself to meet his gaze.

And his eyes? Mercy. They looked as fierce and turbulent as the storm she couldn't quite believe they'd survived. And yet, there was a glint of something like lust until he caught her looking. Then they softened briefly, and he tossed the nine-tailed whip onto a tiny desk and turned away.

Her relief was short-lived, however, for he picked up a leather strop from a nearby shelf and turned back to face her. She licked her lips again, tasting bitter iron that threatened to make her heave, and she struggled to swallow it down.

Bash stepped closer again, close enough she could smell the scent of citrus and sea, so close there was definitely not room for the Holy Ghost between them.

With a glance towards the curtain he'd drawn at their arrival, he loosed the tie of his linen breeches.

Whatever Maggie might have been expecting, this wasn't on the list. Perhaps it should have been. After Jeremiah, nothing should have surprised her. He'd seemed so timid and inexperienced, even shy, until they were alone as man and wife.

Stumbling backwards, she clunked her head against the wall hard enough to make her eyes sting and gave an involuntary yelp.

Jeremiah had shown her what men were like, but he'd never once touched her before their wedding night. This man, this Bash, and likely all his seafaring companions, offered little pretense at gentility or refinement as Jeremiah had. Mercy, but she was a fool. If she survived this misadventure long enough to share the story with Jory and Ellen, they would never let her live it down. Well, Ellen would, but Jory wouldn't, not that Maggie deserved to.

He let his breeches fall to mid thigh, but his shirt hung down low enough Maggie couldn't see the necessary bits, not that she was looking. Well. Not that she was meaning to look.

Jutting out her chin, she glared at him defiantly, and he glared right back as he raised the strop. She braced to absorb the blow. Where would he strike her? On the hand like a cruel governess? In the face like Jeremiah?

He brought the strop down hard on the bare skin of his upper thigh, and Maggie jumped, gasping her surprise as though it had been her own flesh he'd struck. He stepped even closer to her, and another loud crack made her flinch. She stared straight into his dark brown eyes, which held her own gaze captive, as surely as if she were tied to that post on the deck.

"Scream," he demanded through clenched teeth, and the puff of his breath tickled her cheek right where the scar would be on his own. What had marked him that way? she wondered.

He brought the leather down for a third time on his own bare skin, and Maggie didn't even mean to when she cried, "Stop!"

He nodded with an approving grimace and slapped himself again with even greater force.

"Stop, please," she cried again, her eyes burning but dry.

Another blow, and Maggie moved her lips to form the word please, but no sound escaped.

Another, so hard he grunted when the leather made contact with his thigh, and when she stood in silence, her mouth hanging open, he whispered, "For Christ's sake, cry," and struck himself again.

Seldom one to be stunned into silence, Maggie willed the tears to come, but, though hot and aching, her eyes remained dry. Here he was, taking her beating for her, and she couldn't even cry for him.

Ashamed and confused, Maggie bit her lip and held out her palm. He frowned at her, but she nodded fiercely.

Glowering, he let one strike fall across her palm with far less force than he'd used on himself, but enough to wrench a howl from her throat, and he looked away, breaking eye contact for the first time. She turned away too, staring down at his raw, red skin, even as he slapped himself again, and Maggie began to weep, loudly and openly, as though every ounce of bitterness and grief that she'd trapped inside herself since the day she turned eighteen was finally bursting free.

It was like that one, furious wail had uncorked an ocean and loosed a tempest all her own, face flushed and head pounding, though still her eyes stayed dry. Was she so broken, she could no longer even shed tears? Somehow the thought made her moan louder, as she wrapped her arms protectively around herself.

He was standing so close that even in the dim light she could see he'd broken the skin in places, that he'd done so for her, when none of this was his fault.

Bash tossed the strop aside, breathing heavily, and resecured his breeches before reaching out a hand to cup her cheek, running his thumb across the bone as though wiping away the absent tears.

"Good girl," he whispered, his accent some lovely mix of faint Scots and who knew what else, the lilt of wind and wave. "You need to drink. Your body's all dried out. Now listen carefully. A woman aboard is the worst of bad luck. There's many a man would toss you overboard and not blink an eye. Maybe more of another mind," he added soberly. "And when they got through with you, you'd wish you'd taken your chances in the sea."

He didn't need to elaborate. When he'd dropped his breeches, reality had finally set in. She'd seen the sailors practically salivating as they encircled her on deck.

"But I'm married," she protested weakly, and when she noticed his brow crease for a split second, she felt the need to clarify. "Widowed."

"And you think that's some kind of protection?" he whispered.

Maggie could only shrug.

He turned away from her and rummaged in a cabinet cleverly concealed within the hull.

"Here," he shoved another pair of breeches at her along with a sark that was definitely not clean, but it smelled like him, and she found she didn't hate it. "Best I can do at the moment. What's your name?"

"Maggie Mackintosh." She paused, realizing she'd left off her married name. "Budge."

"Now it's just Budge," he said.

She scrunched up her face in disgust and shook her head. "No. It isn't."

He tilted his own head at her refusal, but gave in. "Magnus then," he said with a nod, and she nodded once back. "And you're a lad of fourteen."

"I'm twenty!"

He grinned a cheeky, dimpled smile that made her stomach flutter. "That's the bit you take issue with? You're fourteen, and I discovered you were disguised as a woman when I lifted your skirts to tan your hide."

He stared openly at her bosom for a moment and frowned— not the reaction she was used to, though they'd diminished a bit as she'd grown thinner the last two years, wasting away on that blasted island. Bash rummaged around the alcove some more and handed her an old cream-colored neck cloth. "Will that be long enough to bind them down?"

Heat flared across her cheeks as she both nodded and shrugged, then he turned his back, waiting for her to disrobe.

"You'll be taken on as part of the crew, a cabin boy, mostly fetch and carry, and mind you behave yourself because next time" —he fingered the brutal whip—"it won't be private and neither of us will survive."

"It's barbaric," she murmured, getting down to the business of undressing in the tight space. "Could you...?" she asked, turning to give him access to her buttons.

He obliged with quick, nimble fingers, chuckling soft puffs of breath on the back of her neck that made her shiver all the way to her toes.

"Barbaric," he repeated. "Aye, darlin'."

Something about the way he said it made Maggie instantly hot between her legs, even as she wanted to *want* to roll her eyes at him.

"Aye. You're among pirates now."

She froze, halfway through wrapping his cravat around her chest. Pirates? Were they not as fictitious as dragons and fairies?

He glanced back at her, and then spun immediately away again, clearing his throat, and she finished pinning the wrap in place. She'd have to come up with something better for the long term. How long would this dreadful voyage last?

"I'll make it clear you're under my protection and not to be touched." He cleared his throat again, trying to dislodge the rasp. "None will dare harm you when I'm around."

"Because you're so big and fearsome?" she teased, knotting the linen trousers tight around her waist.

He drew himself up straight. "I'm the boatswain and sailing master of this ship."

She'd insulted him.

Maggie reached out to touch his arm in apology. Something like lighting sparked from her fingers, and she looked at them in wonder.

CHRIST, THE GIRL HAD FAIRLY BRANDED HIM. HE TURNED TO assess her disguise. She had a sweet round face with luminous eyes as deep and blue as the Atlantic. It would be a damn miracle if they pulled off this ruse, but it was the only thing he could think of in the moment. At least the men were drunk most of the time. They'd see what they expected to. If they could mistake a sea cow for a maiden then surely the power of suggestion could turn even a lovely young woman into an untried boy.

"This is a stroke of luck," he said, reaching out to tug one of her haphazard, short-cropped curls, not at all the locks of a fashionable lady. More electricity jumped between them, and he grinned.

"What?" she asked, touching her neck where the shock must have scorched her.

"St. Elmo's fire," he explained. "Once means bad weather. Two times, and it'll be fine."

"Thank heavens for that," she murmured. "Another week of those storms, and I'd be done for."

"A week?" he laughed. "We've been at sea three days, darlin'."

Her eyes widened in disbelief, and he allowed himself the luxury of cupping her cheek once more under the auspices of pulling down the eyelid with his thumb.

"When did you last drink?"

"Orkney."

No wonder she looked half dead and couldn't cry.

"We'll get you some rum. Drink every drop, understand?"

She nodded.

"And... try and act like your arse has been skelped within an inch of your life?"

She nodded again, with only a slight look of annoyance crossing those eyes, and Christ but this was never going to work. She was too feisty and too beautiful. He was half hard just standing next to her. No one would believe she was a lad for long. He'd have to keep a constant vigilance. Even pretending she was a boy wouldn't keep her safe. There were some among their ranks who'd be just as happy to take a boy as a woman.

"What should I call you? Sailing master, you said?"

"No such ceremony here. Just Bash'll do. Come on, we'd best get back before they think I've... that is..."

She turned her face away to hide a smirk, catching his meaning. She didn't know the half of it.

The sooner they reached Jamaica and he could toss her on a ship back to Scotland, the better.

"This way, Magnus," he said, overly loud, pulling back his curtain and leading her to the galley where he wiped a tankard clean with his shirttail and filled it with spirits.

When he handed it over, she took a tentative sniff and grimaced.

"It was so watered down Roo had to doctor it up with spices and the like. Calls it bumbo, though it barely passes for that."

She took a sip and shook her head in disgust.

"Every drop," he reminded her. She looked up at him like she had stopped herself mid eye roll. "When you finish that, you come back down here and fill it again. You'll get used to the taste. Cheer up. We'll soon run out of rum and you can choke down watery ale instead."

She huffed but drank a little more. A lady's throat moved in an awfully delicate way when she swallowed, didn't it? Her eyelashes were fine, too, like the fraying edges of softest linen or the downy feathers of a newly hatched chick.

He shook his head to clear such thoughts away and handed her a fistful of dried beef and a hardtack biscuit. "Ready?"

For a moment she scrunched her face as though she might cry again, but then she took a deep breath and swallowed it down with a nod, and he led the way back to the hatch. God help them, it was either going to work or it wasn't, and then they would both sink or swim.

Too late, he realized he should've told her what to do if they were thrown overboard, to flip on to her back and float for as long as she could and hope the tide would carry her someplace dry.

It was the plan he'd concocted as a boy, swaying in his

hammock or keeping watch across a blackened sea. He would run calculations in his head: how long it might take to reach inhabited land or a deserted island, how likely to meet another vessel and what sort of ship it might be. It passed the time, and, though grim, he liked the security of having a plan. Sometimes he imagined a friendly dolphin taking pity and allowing him to hold tight to its dorsal fin as it scurried with the current to safety on a remote Jamaican beach.

This time, he ascended the ladder first, which would hopefully support the narrative that Maggie was a chastened boy but would also save him from having every detail of her arse outlined in linen a foot before his face as he climbed.

For both their sakes, he resisted the urge to turn and help her out of the hatch, leaving her to struggle to her feet, sloshing her rum. In the sunlight, her pale face looked red and almost tear-stained, despite being too dried out for actual tears.

The nearest men stopped pretending to work and openly stared at her once more.

"Meet the newest member of the crew, lads," he announced, putting on his boatswain persona and swaggering toward the middle of the deck.

"Say again?" Dutch asked.

Bash pretended not to notice the captain watching them both shrewdly, but he couldn't pretend away the sweat beginning to bead on the back of his neck.

"Quite the thing," he boasted loudly for all to hear. "I take the lady in hand and lift her skirts, and what do I find but a tiny prick and two balls staring back at me. Not a lady at all, but a lad of fourteen. Seems young Langley ain't the babe of the crew anymore."

Samson and Duffy cheered and jostled Langley, who grinned a sheepish gap-toothed smile.

"I wore him out good and proper anyway, on account of the ruse," Bash went on.

The girl did a fair job of looking chastened and focusing on her rum, but Dutch narrowed his eyes and studied the pair of them just as the captain had.

"What's your name, son?" Dutch asked.

She glanced quickly at Bash before answering. "Mag—Magnus, sir," she said, that raspy voice even lower and more sultry than it had been before. Christ.

"D'you have any skills, Magnus?"

Another glance at Bash, which he supposed was helping to sell that he'd thoroughly blistered her. "He says I'm to fetch and carry." Then she nodded towards a ripped sail flapping in the breeze. "I could mend that. Wouldn't look pretty, but it would hold."

Dutch nodded. "I'm quartermaster of this ship. You do as Bash tells you, and we'll be square. You need anything, come and find me."

She nodded solemnly, but Bash didn't allow himself to draw a relieved breath yet. The older man cast another suspicious glance his way. Dutch wouldn't call her out publicly, but he might not be easily convinced.

The captain wasn't either. "Magnus, was it?" he asked.

She nodded.

"I didn't catch that."

"Yes, sir," she said in that same low voice.

"Are you in the habit of trespassing, Magnus?"

She shook her head once. "No, sir."

"And yet. You invaded our privacy. Threatened our property. Infiltrated our home."

"And I whipped him for it," Bash interjected. "He'll not sit comfortably for a week, I assure you, or I'll take him in hand again."

The captain nodded. "I, of all men, understand the lure of the sea, the irrepressible desire, the drive, that once your mind is made up to take action, nothing can stop."

The girl nodded her head as though he had perfectly understood.

"But why did you do it in a dress?"

Bash's stomach dropped. He hadn't thought up that particular part of the fiction.

The girl merely shrugged. "It was the only way I could slip down to the beach. I was supposed to be doing my chores while my sister was allowed off to the market. Only I tore my britches scrabbling with another lad, and my mam would've tanned me good for it. So I pinched my sister's clothes right off the washing line and slipped away down to see your ship." She shrugged again. "And then I decided, why not come aboard?"

The captain threw back his head to laugh, and then tsked his tongue, and Bash finally allowed himself to breathe. "Subterfuge and petty theft—he'll fit in better than you, boy. Perhaps you should whip him again for his mother's sake."

"I'm fairly tempted," Bash agreed, pretending to frown at Maggie's quick, if rambling lie. "And lest anyone gets any ideas," he added, raising his voice for the whole company to hear, "It'll be me alone who whips him. He's mine, understand? My responsibility."

A few guffawed lecherously, while others cast knowing winks and smirks his way. Most of all, the captain seemed pleased. It was enough to turn Bash's stomach, but better to be assumed a pederast than the alternative consequences.

Only Dutch's look of deep disapproval really cut him. He would laugh, though, when Bash explained it all someday. For now, at least, the girl was safe.

"Sometimes my sailing master forgets he's not in charge," the captain said, stepping closer and clapping a hand on Maggie's shoulder with a meaningful glance tossed over her head at Bash. "As it seems you'll be staying awhile, I'm Cornelius MacLeod. You may address me as Captain. Welcome aboard *Auldfarrand's Revenge.*"

"Thank you, sir," she whispered.

"Bring the axe," he called, and then Maggie turned a bit green. Mad was loving it.

"Aye, you must sign the articles over the axe to be official," Bash rushed to explain. "Can you write?"

Maggie nodded and licked her lips, watching nervously as the boarding axe was brought forward and the ship's rules laid over it for signing. Looking to Bash for approval once more, she accepted the quill Samson offered her and only faltered a little over signing her assumed name.

"I'll get you a needle and twine," Dutch told her when it was done, heading off to round up the supplies.

Nodding to herself, Maggie sat down on the deck to wait, but immediately sprang to her feet, rubbing her backside while the nearest men snickered, and Bash's heart rather burst with pride.

Chapter Four

The air was brisk and bright on deck, a mixture of cool from the wind that filled their sails and warmth from the unrelenting sun. It would singe Maggie's face to a cherry-red crisp and make her freckle something awful. A part of her old self still cared a little, wondering briefly if she could treat them with lime juice from the bumbo to make them lighten. But the new, adventurous Magnus laughed at this vain line of thinking. What would a whole face full of freckles matter amongst pirates? If anything, they might improve her disguise.

Pirates... she still wasn't used to the idea, still couldn't quite reconcile what she was learning with all she'd thought she knew. Now she had signed on as crew, agreeing to abide by their code: no stealing from each other, lights out at eight, no women, and no gambling allowed.

She flexed her hand and shifted uncomfortably on the wooden deck. Despite no actual smacks to her bare behind, after three days in the cramped hold, her bottom was sore anyway, and the thin linen trousers favored by sailors offered far less cushion than her skirts and earasaid had done.

The palm she'd offered up so Bash could make her cry still

stung something fierce, her awkward grip on the heavy canvas exacerbating the chafe. Now the fingers of her other hand were beginning to cramp as she struggled to wield a thick sewing needle. She worked it back and forth to form a jagged scar across the sail resembling the one upon Bash's cheek.

It had been the truth when she said her sewing wasn't pretty. Despite years of tortured practice, her stitches always turned out rough and uneven. Her sister could embroider lovely designs in delicate silk. Even Jory, who claimed to eschew all of the feminine arts, could sew lace fine enough to reattach a butterfly wing. Not Maggie. She was impatient and impulsive, and besides that, her hands were simply too large for dainty work.

Her hands had been one of her husband's chief complaints. Or at least one of his first.

She should have realized what was in store the moment Jeremiah tried to slip the wedding band on her finger and found it too small. Such anger had flashed in his eyes. Maggie had been a little embarrassed, but she didn't blame him in the slightest. After all, her father had sprung the whole thing on her, and she supposed Jeremiah hadn't had time to adequately prepare either. But when they visited a smithy to have the band resized, Jeremiah had snidely remarked that he hadn't expected his young bride to possess such mannish hands.

A month later, he stumbled home from the tavern after ripping his shirt doing God knew what, and he threw it at her. "Time to do something useful with those idle meat hooks," he'd grumbled. Her hands shook as she clumsily repaired the damaged garment. Such a small tear, but she'd wanted to please him, so she had labored over it by candlelight for more than an hour to get it just right.

In the morning he'd thrown the shirt into the fire.

Not to be outdone, Maggie had taken her sewing shears to the rest of his tops and cut gaping holes in the lot of them, tossing those bits in the fire as well. It had been war between them ever after.

Marriage means war, Jory liked to quote her mother's favorite saying, and Maggie often wondered if she somehow inherited her particular character flaws from the auntie she'd never met and with whom she shared no blood. Because she supposed it had been a war of her own making. She'd always been that way—starving for someone to look after, impetuous and spiteful when her efforts were spurned. Hadn't she spent half her life being a brat to Ellen and Jory because Ellen needed none but Jory, and Jory needed only herself?

Maggie had also spent most of her life dreaming of a handsome husband—one who couldn't survive without her devotion, as well as the many children they would give each other. The reality of marriage and the truth of her auntie's famous words had proved a crushing disappointment.

And yet... feisty Jory and meek Wee Ellen had somehow each found her perfect match.

Finlay Shaw was Jory's fiercest supporter, teaching her to fight and proud of her independent nature. He also challenged her more than she allowed anyone else in all the world to do, pushing her to see every angle of a problem and solution.

Ellen's Silas MacKenzie had a heart as big as he was, but one that needed both gentle nurturing and a firm push in equal measure. Somehow, they'd both seen the people inside the other's skin, the perfect complement to the ones inside their own.

Both women had flourished in their partnerships with the two gorgeous men, made lighter by having someone to share their burdens, and that was it, wasn't it? Theirs were partnerships.

For the past year, Maggie had tried to analyze what precisely went wrong in her own marriage. When exactly had it become doomed? Why was it the furthest thing from a partnership? Her conclusion, night after dismal night, was that *she* was what had gone wrong. She might wish to take care of those around her, but anyone could see she was incapable, and then she proved them right by hurting them over and over again.

Stabbing the needle through the stiff canvas sail as though it were a lance capable of vanquishing her dreary thoughts, she gouged the sharp steel into her thumb by mistake. Quickly, she sucked the sore finger, willing it not to bleed all over her work. The captain might not like that.

When she'd confessed to Lorna her desire to visit someplace warm, she had envisioned lying on her back in the soft sand, pondering the shapes of passing clouds. She really was a perfect fool, sneaking into a den of thieves in the dead of night. So far, she'd been very lucky, but what would happen if her luck ran out?

Nearby, the bell was rung six or seven times to signify the hour, and then a shadow fell across Maggie's work. She examined her thumb for signs of blood, afraid to look up and see which rotten-toothed pirate was looming there. But then Bash squatted down before her, a bit of dark brown hair peeking from his open collar, thighs filling out his breeches, stretching them obscenely tight, as he studied her work up close. He smelled of tangy sea brine and citrus, and he placed a fresh tankard of spiced rum before her.

"Drink."

When she reached for it, he caught her wrist, not hard, but firm enough to make a shiver run through her belly. This braw young man might be the stuff of her teenage daydreams, but she was there for adventure, not a dalliance. Besides, when had reality ever measured up to childish dreams?

"Did I not tell you to refill your cup?"

"I was busy," she explained, lifting the sail and bracing herself for his stern critique.

"When did you last urinate?" he asked, and her eyes shot open wide at the blunt question. She also couldn't remember, and he knew it. "Drink," he said again, holding her gaze with such seriousness Maggie dared not refuse.

She gulped the foul-tasting stuff, and he nodded approvingly. She could almost hear the whispered, "Good girl," from earlier and it made her tingle. *Settle down.*

"This is very well done," he said, admiring the sail.

"Oh, stuff it," she muttered before she realized his praise was genuine. "It's not even straight," she added.

"You're not embroidering a tablecloth, darlin'. You've lined the edges up perfectly, and these stitches look tight and strong."

He ran his fingers over her mending—long, fine fingers—and for half a moment, Maggie imagined him running those fingers down her torso, around the curve of her breast, and over her ribs. *Settle down.*

"Like scar tissue," he murmured, with something akin to awe in his voice. "Stronger than even before it was torn."

His praise made her glow with warmth from the inside out. Who'd have thought so many years of frustrating needlework would land her employment aboard a pirate ship?

"I did my best," she explained.

"You've done fine work, Magnus. This'll hold up well in the next storm."

"The next one?" Her eyes snapped up to meet his. They were such a deep, dark brown, like the richest earth after a rain.

He grinned at her, a dimple showing its face just beneath the scar on his cheek. "There's always a next one, darlin'."

She frowned, and he shook his head, bemused.

"What did you expect when you ran away to sea?"

She glared up at him because a ferocious temper was her only possible weapon. Bash couldn't be much older than she was, maybe two or three years at most, and yet he was wise to the ways of the world and thought her a foolish, silly little girl. And wasn't she? Didn't everyone think the same, except for the men on this ship who, for the time being, thought her a foolish, silly little boy? No one expected anything from her and never had, because she was flighty and dramatic. A nuisance.

And there *he* was, too handsome and bossy by half, with some kind of authority over men twice his age, the politics of which Maggie didn't yet understand. She'd wager he didn't need much looking after and wouldn't take kindly to anyone's efforts to try. Not that she was looking to try. She'd been down that road before. Foolish she may be, but she seldom made the same mistake twice.

Anyway, he'd found no fault with her stitching, and that was something.

He was still staring down at her with dark, volcanic eyes. It made her sweat more than the full force of the sun shining on her face, and she squirmed under the intensity of his glare.

"Something else?" she finally demanded when he didn't look away.

He nodded at her half-finished tankard, and she rolled her eyes, tempted to slosh it back in his face. Except she still didn't feel certain of the rules here, despite having signed a false name to them, and she had some inkling that such insubordination, at least if observed by others, would find her breeches around her ankles for a session with his strap, for real this time. Or perhaps not. He'd warned her the next time would be public, which would end the ruse for both of them, and besides all that, she really was thirsty—so thirsty she almost didn't notice anymore.

Bash held her gaze, as though he could hear every immature thought tripping through her head, but he waited patiently to see what she would do. So she picked up the tankard and drained it to the last drop. He nodded, satisfied, and for some reason she longed to hear that whispered, *Good girl* again, as he took himself off up the prow.

ALONE ON THE FORECASTLE, BASH PEERED THROUGH HIS spyglass at the endless ocean waves, pretending to be busy so he wouldn't be caught looking at her. They were far off course after the storm, and wasn't that an apt summation of how he felt, from his head clear down to his groin, and she, the gusty wind that made him so.

After a time, Dutch joined him, and they stood in silence, shoulder to shoulder, staring out at the vast wide world. The ocean had always been their domain, his and Dutch's, and Bash was reminded of the first of many thousand hours they had spent in just this way.

He, a boy of nine, had staked out this very spot, wondering whether anyone would care if a strong gust of wind tossed him overboard. When the tall West African had joined him, not uttering a word but simply taking up space alongside him, Bash had known the wind wouldn't dare. Now an unusual tension separated them in a way it never once had done before.

Bash retracted his telescope and said, without turning, "You're not usually one to hold back speaking your mind."

Dutch stayed quiet a minute longer before replying, "Just wondering whether you've lost yours."

"That's more like it." Bash grinned. As long as they could speak plainly, things would be all right.

"Your cabin boy, Bastian?" Dutch spat with disgust.

Or maybe not.

He fought to keep his face impassive. No one could read him like Dutch could.

"You know as well as I do what can happen to a lad who goes unclaimed."

"That's all it is?" Dutch's voice softened.

"Aye, same as I should've done for Langley," was all Bash dared reply lest some tell in his voice give him away.

"Langley wasn't your fault," Dutch argued, his voice tinged

with the same guilt that chafed at Bash's conscience, believing his own words as little as Bash did.

Well anyway, together they'd set things right for Langley once they realized he needed them to. They'd fed him up and taught him to fight. No one bothered Langley anymore, Bash had made certain of it.

Dutch cleared his throat. "None could blame you having needs, son," he said in a conciliatory tone. "Man wasn't meant to be cooped up his whole life as you've been."

"That's all it is, Dutch." Bash studied his feet. "Same as you and me," he added softly. It wasn't a lie. Sure, the girl was beautiful, but he was nothing if not disciplined, and he was determined to keep her safe.

"Good. Still, I'll have a word with Mad when we reach Port Royal. He can't object to your visiting a brothel or two."

Bash snorted. "Too afraid I'll find his missing gold up a whore's—"

Dutch cuffed him, and Bash shut his mouth immediately, not because the quartermaster outranked the sailing master, which he did, but because this quartermaster had a sixth sense Bash trusted with his life.

Sure enough, moments later the captain stepped around the mast to join them.

"Any sign of the *Woebegone Whale*?" he asked, and Bash had to credit the man's commitment to his own farce, but they were far enough off course it almost felt deliberate, and Bash meant to understand why.

He shook his head. "No sign of the *Whale*. This close to England, I'm more concerned about running afoul of the *Pursuit*."

Dutch glanced at him sharply. The navy was a legitimate concern, but mentioning it to the captain was tantamount to poking a bear.

Mad's eyebrow twitched up and he tapped his spyglass two

times against his thigh. Then his lips quirked into a jagged sneer. "Still the same frightened little rabbit, are you boy?"

"It's His Majesty's ocean," Bash replied with a shrug.

Mad bared his teeth and laughed, but it sounded more like a hiss. "Exactly why the blue devil won't be looking for us here. I haven't dodged the bastard this long by playing it safe," he boasted. "I mean to find the bilge-sucker Walsh."

"And Walsh left word he was headed to the colonies, did he?" Bash countered. "I told you before, we're too far off course. We'll come to port in Boston at this rate."

Mad cut his gaze to Dutch who simply shrugged.

"To be clear, I think New York or Boston could be extremely lucrative, but if Walsh is bound for warmer waters, then we've under corrected after the gale." Bash said *we*, but they both knew he meant the captain had failed to follow his navigational advice.

"I've been sailing longer than you've been alive. Perhaps your compass is wrong."

"The compass?"

Mad shrugged. "Many an inexperienced sailor lets his tools get tossed about on a choppy sea. Maybe you've lost true north."

Bash sighed. *'Tis a poor worker blames his tools.* His granda's words echoed in his head like it was yesterday, making sure his grandson learned the lessons his firstborn had not.

"Shall I recharge it, sir?" Bash asked in a clipped tone.

Mad inclined his head ever so slightly, and Bash nodded once before striding away to retrieve the lodestone from his berth.

He stormed past Maggie, who glanced up at him with such a look of startled delight that he rather wished he could take her below with him, hang the captain, the navigation, his promise to Dutch, and everything else. He ignored the urge, ignored her completely along with his sudden erection, and counted to a hundred while focusing instead on cold wet sleeves, and cold, thin gruel, and the sear of the hangman's noose.

Dutch had made himself scarce in the few minutes Bash was

gone because nothing made the captain dig in his heels like having an audience.

"Will you do the honors, sir?" Bash asked, offering up both navigational tools, but Mad gestured for him to continue, as though the very suggestion were beneath him.

Bash showed the captain the current reading, then removed the compass needle and drew it across the lodestone. When he returned it to its casing the reading was exactly the same. They were sailing west-nor'-west even still.

The captain shrugged. "Perhaps your stone is faulty." He'd never admit to an error. Either he would course correct for the Caribbean in secret, or they'd have the opportunity to harass the colonies after all. Bash didn't particularly care either way, so long as there was a port and a ship headed back to the British coast with Maggie aboard.

"Before the earlier excitement," the captain said, glancing at the girl as though reading Bash's mind, then taking out his spyglass to scan the sea, "there were murmurs of a ship."

Whispered rumors had reached Bash's ears too, but he shook his head. "I've seen no sign of the *Whale*."

"Not the *Whale*," Mad said, his eyebrow twitching up again as he stared down his crooked nose at Bash. "A converted galleon. Idle chatter, of course, but is that why you fear the *Pursuit*?" He tapped the spyglass twice more against his thigh.

Bash pursed his lips to suppress a smile at the captain's tell.

In truth, he'd only mentioned the navy to elicit a reaction. Because despite his best efforts not to surrender to paranoia, or maybe because of them, Bash had begun to wonder whether Captain Constantin was any threat at all or a mere figment, his aptly named *Pursuit* a ghost ship of Mad's own conjuring. What better way for the captain to maintain order in lean, uncertain times than by uniting his band of thieves against a common foe?

Bash would rather believe it was a ghost ship. The vessel had pursued Mad across time and space in an effort to retrieve the very same gold he'd lost twenty years ago, and they'd been outrunning the ghost ever since. But even now, he couldn't quite decide what was true.

Bash shrugged. "I've seen no ship."

The captain stared hard, like he didn't quite believe him, as though Bash weren't painfully aware that capture by the Royal Navy would mean death for them all. A pirate was a pirate, regardless of rank, and the navy had a powerful appetite for seeing pirates dangle.

"Alert me at once if you do."

"Aye, Captain."

Mad turned away, hands clasped behind his back, and strode off as though he hadn't a care in the world, but Bash knew better. The old man was cracking into pieces, and his single-minded pursuit of a hoard that only Dutch seemed to believe had ever existed would kill them all if the navy didn't do it first.

When they finally docked at whatever harbor found them, Bash wouldn't only have to book the girl passage back to Scotland. He needed to find a way off the ship for himself as well.

Chapter Five

Flexing her hands to prevent them becoming permanently fixed in a cramped lobster claw, Maggie surveyed her work. She had mended two full sails, and as she'd finished each one, Bash looked it over, gave a satisfied nod, and then ordered it hoisted up the rigging. Now she stood back to admire her handiwork in action.

The ship had been plodding along before, helped occasionally by teams of rowers, but with the wind filling its freshly patched sails, they were flying.

"Well done, Magnus," Bash said, clapping a big warm hand on her shoulder. "Whoever taught you to sew would be proud."

She snorted, rather doubting her mother would appreciate anything about her present situation.

"I mean, except that you're using your skills to aid and abet our sorry lot," Bash amended.

"I only hope they hold."

"Couldn't have done better myself, and I've been stitching up sails since I was nine years old. Come on, you've earned your grub tonight. You can start on the rest tomorrow."

What kind of childhood entailed mending ship sails? Perhaps

his father had been a harbor master or merchant marine? The siren song of easy riches likely lured away many a man's son. Had Bash joined this pirate crew for money? Or was it simply the promise of freedom on the open sea? Freedom had been the draw for Maggie, after all.

She stretched her aching back, rolling her neck side to side and rubbing feeling back into her sore fingers. Exhausting work, but she couldn't help a flush of pride.

Below deck, more candle lanterns had been lit, so Bash didn't flip up his eye patch, though to Maggie the scant light was still dim as the devil's cupboard. A variety of smells assaulted her from every direction as they traversed the belly of the ship. There was the usual undercurrent of bilge, almost masked now by the sweaty musk of sixty or eighty men, and perhaps the combined stench of their farts. On top of all that, someone had been preparing food.

Bash led her to the galley, where he drew two tankards of rum. "What's cooking, Rooijakkers?" he asked the older man who had found them in the hold and forced her above deck. Was that only this morning?

The pirate cook gestured towards an iron stove set atop a stone hearth. Inside burned a wood fire, surrounded by sand. Over the fire, a large pot of something green and sludgy blurped more than bubbled. "Cackle fruits and peas." He grinned at Maggie. "But you'll have to sit down to eat it."

Without meaning to, Maggie rubbed her bottom, which was rather sore from sitting on the hard wooden deck all day. The cook burst out in a guffaw and slapped his thigh. "Poor young'un."

"I'm sure the young'un could do with a cup of fresh milk," Bash suggested, putting an abrupt end to the cook's merriment.

"No milk," he said with a frown.

"Before the cat led me to this one, I could swear I heard the lowing of a cow. But no, said I, we couldn't possibly have bought a cow on Orkney. We could barely afford a barrel or two of watered-down ale."

The cook stared him in the eye and shrugged. "There's cackle fruits and peas," he repeated.

Bash nodded. "Serve it up then, man," he snapped, and the cook slopped some of the green gunge into two rather fine china bowls, placing, not fruit, but a whole brown hen egg atop each.

Maggie swallowed. "Thank you, Rooijakkers," she tried to say, tripping over the unfamiliar name, but the cook laughed and waved her off.

"Bashy's the only one can pronounce it. 'S why they call me Roo."

She nodded, staring glumly at her egg, then up to Bash for guidance. Was she meant to eat it raw? To suck it from the shell like a weasel?

"Relax. It's boiled," he whispered, reaching into a barrel to retrieve a handful of the same dry round biscuits he'd given her that morning. "If you've no stomach for it, at least try some hard tack," he added, handing her one. "Though it's best to eat fresh while you can."

He led her through the galley to a sort of dining room, where the fart smell Maggie now recognized as boiled eggs intensified. There, dozens and dozens of men lounged on benches and chairs, devouring their peas and eggs, swilling ale, playing cards, laughing and carousing noisily until they noticed her and Bash.

Silence fell over them then.

The men had mostly avoided her all day as she worked under the sailing master's watchful gaze, but now they openly stared. She felt entirely exposed, like a rabbit that ventured into a garden party hosted by foxes and owls. Surely someone would notice something that gave her away? Would they spot the binding around her chest or a handkerchief tucked up her sleeve out of habit? Simply smell her and deduce the truth?

"Sounded like you gave quite the tanning, Nav," a big man with salt and pepper hair called out as Bash led Maggie to an empty seat. "Was that before or after you noticed the lady had a cock?"

The assembly roared with laughter and banged their tankards on the table. Maggie's face burned, but she focused on peeling off the shell of her egg.

The instigator picked up his tankard and joined them, dropping down on a bench across from Bash, and casting a discerning eye over Maggie. "Sure and it's a wonder you can sit if your arse is as chapped as your lips. You should go and see the doc about a salve. Aye, O'Riordan?" he added with a conspiratorial wink before glancing back at his mates, where a red-bearded sailor lifted his own drink in answer.

"A salve? For the lips or the arse?" someone called back, to another round of guffaws.

"Drop into sickbay any time, my boy," the red-haired O'Riordan offered. "I'll be more than happy to help. Don't worry. I'll be gentle."

"You try it, Butcher, you'll be needing a surgeon next," Bash said in such a light tone you could almost pretend not to hear the threat.

Maggie shot him a look. Surely being too protective would make them all suspicious of her sex, but to her dismay they were roaring with laughter again, half-drunk already.

"O'Riordan's no physician," Bash huffed. "He's a frustrated barber who likes to hack off limbs."

"It's good to see you taking an interest at last," the instigator across from Bash said, winking at Maggie once more. She was beginning to feel lightheaded. There was too much heat and noise, too many people, and she was suddenly overcome with weariness.

She'd made a terrible mess of her egg, bits of shell littered the table but also covered her peas and half of it still clung to the egg, seeming to crumble instead of peel off as it should.

"The right arse'll do that though. Make you interested," the man was saying.

Why was he still here?

"Fuck off back to your food, Balthasar," Bash growled.

To Maggie's enormous relief and surprise, the instigator offered a salute and returned to his laughing friends.

"They're acting as if—" she began in a whisper. She'd been going to say, *They're acting as if they know the truth*, but caught herself. "As if they think I'm..."

"You've a lot to learn about men at sea," Bash cut her off in a gruff, low voice, and though Maggie was curious, something told her she ought not hurry to unpack every mystery here.

He took the egg from her trembling fingers and replaced it with his own, perfectly peeled and smooth, then he dragged away her bowl of peas, passing her his own shell-free bowl as well, and began to eat hers, shell and all. She watched in shock for a moment before her hunger took over.

After four days at sea with only dried berries to suck on, for she knew the dried beef would make her too thirsty, she devoured every bite, wiping up the remnants with a hard tack biscuit, enjoying the meal all the more for not having to cook it, nor to navigate the crunchy bits of eggshell.

Why had Bash done that for her? It rather went beyond the protection he'd sworn. It was kind.

Belly full, she leaned back against the bulkhead in a drowsy sort of contentment. Her eyes grew glassy as the rowdy pirates picked up more steam. Several came over to speak with Bash, one after another, or by twos and threes. They spoke of navy captains and ghost ships and loot swallowed up by a whale. None of it felt real.

"Do you think we'll finally catch Willy Walsh?" asked a young sailor with dark black skin and big, sad eyes. "Sometimes I reckon there is no Walsh, and no gold neither."

"Sometimes, Samson, I think you could be right. But keep it to yourself, aye?"

The young man nodded, and Bash jerked his head, sending him on his way.

Maggie was impressed with how much authority Bash held amongst the men, though he was younger than most. He must have felt the force of her gaze studying him, for he turned to catch her, and after holding her eyes captive for a too-long moment, he seemed to come to a decision.

She licked her lips, suddenly nervous under the weight of his unrelenting stare after all the bawdy talk.

"You need sleep," he told her, and got to his feet.

"Aw, now, where you going, Nav?" the instigator, Balthasar, called, holding up his cards. "Stay for a hand. You can wager your cabin boy." That earned him another roar of mirth from the nearest men.

"You know it's lights out at eight bells," Bash answered, steering Maggie, who had tripped over her bench, to another round of raucous laughter.

"Yes, yes, Nav, by all means," the barber-surgeon, O'Riordan, called. "Tuck your cabin boy into bed."

The hooting and hollering followed them all the way to Bash's tiny berth near the front of the ship.

When they stepped inside the alcove, he surveyed it as though for the first time. "There isn't room to string another hammock," he observed, like he'd only just realized it.

He scratched his head and looked at her, and she tried to mask her face in stone so he wouldn't guess she hadn't expected to sleep in his cramped quarters with him.

"I can't bed down on the floor," he said softly. "If I'm needed, they'll come to wake me and know something's amiss."

Maggie suddenly missed her straw bed on Orkney as much as she had the feather mattress of her youth, but she knew better than to suggest a hammock in amongst the rest of the crew. "I'm happy to sleep on the floor," she lied, and he pursed his lips but nodded once.

From the same cabinet which had produced her new clothes hours earlier, he withdrew a yellow-and-black length of tartan, which rather caught her by surprise. His accent wasn't pure Scots, and it was such a sentimental thing for a pirate to carry around. Though, as he was a pirate, she supposed it might have been taken off anyone.

"Which clan did you steal that from?" she teased.

His brow furrowed. "D'you want it or not?"

A flash of regret nipped her conscience when she saw he wasn't laughing. "I want it," she said, and tugged it gently from his fists.

The borrowed plaid together with her own earasaid made a cozy nest beneath his fold-down desk, and Maggie lay down to go to sleep, afraid to ask the question she couldn't stop thinking. How long would this ocean voyage take?

She was delighted when Custard, the tattletale cat, padded into the alcove, completely ignoring their privacy curtain, and curled up against her belly purring loudly. Snuggling into the cat's soft fur, Maggie decided she didn't mind the journey lasting a bit longer.

ANOTHER FORTY DAYS AT LEAST. HOW WAS BASH GOING TO survive another forty days in such close quarters with this beautiful, maddening, ocean-eyed girl? Bad enough lying to Dutch, who could read him better than Bash could read the stars, knew him better than Bash knew himself. The quartermaster hadn't pressed him because Mad interrupted, and for once Bash was glad of the interruption. Dutch would have kept their secret, but Bash didn't want his friend and mentor held to account if it all came crashing down. *When* it all came crashing down, more like.

And it would do. Sure as the sun would rise, someone would find out the truth. What man alive could look upon Maggie

Mackintosh Budge and not see the feminine curve of her hips sashaying across the deck in his old breeches? He'd never thought of breeches as erotic until now. What man could dwell on her soft, delicate hands and not imagine those hands cupping his face or unfastening his own buttons? Hell, imagining her shaving him made him hard.

He took hold of himself and then thought better of it—not with her lying there an arm's breadth away.

Staring at the ceiling, he dwelled instead on the terrible realization that she'd hidden in the cargo hold for three whole days without food or water. If the cat hadn't brought him to her, they'd have likely found her dead before long, her pelagic eyes lifeless and cloudy grey rather than flashing cobalt as they had when he'd struck his thigh instead of her.

Shame flooded his belly, shriveling the last of his erection at the memory of her hand, outstretched, demanding a blow, and the scream that had wrenched from her throat as a result. She'd been thirsting away for so long she cried without tears. He'd only seen such a thing once before, when they'd come across a man marooned by his crew so long he was barely a sack of bones when the *Revenge* had found him.

On his honor, Bash would do anything to ensure no such danger ever threatened her, nor any such sound ever escaped her lips again. Not while he was living. Calico Jack once told him the Chinese believed if you saved a person's life, you were responsible for them forever. Bash may not be Chinese, but he was surely responsible for Maggie now, as if she were his own.

But Christ in the desert, it was going to be a long forty days, longer if Mad kept dithering about their direction. Even longer if rumors of the naval ship were true.

There were always rumors, of course. And Bash remained undecided whether it was wise to believe in the eternal threat of Constantin and his HMS *Pursuit*.

He thought back to Mad's twitching eyebrow and tapping

spyglass. The old man was scared of Constantin, good and proper, and not just afraid he'd recover the gold before Mad did. Nothing else got the captain's hackles up, not ever, and the fact he was rattled this time set off alarm bells deep inside Bash.

Why would the *Pursuit* show up now? Had Bash willed her into being with his petulant teasing? Mad was an easy mark, but Bash knew better than to give in to his instinct for deviling the old bastard.

If indeed the *Pursuit* was out there, could it simply be bad luck and timing? They were both sailing away from the British coast, both caught in the same awful storm? Or had the navy caught wind of the tales Bash would swear on his mother's grave had been started by none other than Cornelius MacLeod himself, tales of old Willy Walsh absconding with the missing wealth of some baron or other, stolen from the *Annabel Grace* two decades back as the baron made his way west to govern the rambunctious colonies in America?

The navy had been escorting the *Annabel Grace*, yet somehow Mad distracted them and slipped aboard. They chased him all the way to Port Royal, where he got very drunk, evaded capture by the skin of his teeth, and managed to misplace a hundred-pound chest filled with gold.

Despite Bash not even being born yet, the captain blamed him for the loss, and blamed him still twenty-two years later for not having found it. But the navy didn't know the gold was lost. Had Constantin pursued them for decades, hoping to recover the stolen coins and bring the pirate thief to justice as Mad had always claimed? Hell, they actually christened a newly refitted galleon as HMS *Pursuit*. Why, if not in Mad's honor?

They even came looking for him on Lewis once, missing him by about two years.

Bastian had been out fishing for brown trout all day. Having caught enough to feed his ailing grandparents and Aunt Jenny's brood, he was hurrying home with a basket almost too heavy to carry when a stranger came strolling down the lane. The man wore a fine coat of dark blue serge with shiny buttons and gold braid, and they stopped to study each other.

After setting down the heavy basket of fish, Bastian doffed his cap with a polite, "Feasgar math." The navy man nodded back, then picked up the basket for him and carried it all the way to Granda's house before taking his leave.

"Thig a-steach," Bastian had invited, and on the man's blank expression he switched to English. "Want to come in?" Then he tried his mother's, "Wa fi cum inna?" just for fun.

The man had smiled at him, but patted his shoulder and shook his head, and that was the last Bastian had seen of him, though he painted his laundry peg sailors dark blue, matching the young officer's uniform as best he could.

The next day Bastian heard murmurs among the adults about a naval officer sniffing round the MacLeods' place. Many years later, Bash realized the officer must have been looking for his sire, the infamous pirate of Lewis, bogeyman of bedtime stories and embarrassment to his clan.

Had the officer realized Bastian's lineage, would he have helped to carry his fish? Or would the navy have kidnapped him as bait for a fishing expedition of their own, supposing the pirate captain might possess an ounce of parental instinct which could be turned against him? More fool them.

Maybe it was their proximity to Scotland after so many years making him melancholy, but Bash had the urgent sense his life was all building to its inevitable conclusion. A week ago, he would have said fine. He was tired—of running, of fighting, of thieving—of loneliness stretching out before him like the endless ocean waves.

He loved the waggoner with its pages of colorful maps, loved the sun shining warm upon his face, and the vast night sky. There had even been a time when he embraced the constant movement, the pitch and roll, the never-ending journey, as though each moment were propelling him forward to whatever adventure came next.

But he was older now, and wise to the fact that there was no great mystery unfolding beyond the horizon. A pirate's life would be ended by gangrene or the gallows. He'd long since made peace with the inevitability of his doom.

Before leaving to join the *Ranger* as quartermaster, Calico Jack had been part of Mad's crew, back when Bash was first brought aboard. Most of the men either ignored the pirate captain's boy completely or delighted in kicking him out of their way, but Jack had been kind, slipping Bash the occasional sorghum drop.

He'd been sorry to see Jack leave the *Revenge*, and even more sorry to learn of his execution. Standing there in the shadows of Port Royal's Gallows Point, Bash had realized at the age of twelve what fate lay in store for him and more or less accepted it, because what else was there to do?

But now?

Now a pale face with sun-pinked cheeks and luminous blue eyes left him unable to sleep, clinging to a shard of hope like a splinter of wrecked timber that maybe—just maybe—there was a way out besides the noose. He couldn't see it yet, but he was skilled at charting courses, even through uncertain waters when visibility was next to impossible. If there was a way, he'd find it, if only to put Maggie on another ship and see her returned safely home.

Chapter Six

It took Maggie the better part of a week to finish mending all the torn sails, and between filling her belly, drinking too much rum, and sleeping so deeply in a nest of tangled tartan that she habitually missed breakfast, one day pretty well bled into the next. But she relished the productive, useful work almost as much as the warm sun shining on her shoulders.

Though she felt his eyes on her constantly, Bash had said little over the past week, so it was a surprise when he roused her one morning by shoving a bowl of gruel across the floor. It wasn't homemade parritch, but it looked and smelled almost edible, and was that—?

"Is there milk in this?" she asked, her eyes flying to his and then flitting away from their intensity.

"Just a dash," he growled. "It's not much, but you've had enough hardtack for a lifetime, I'll warrant. Loblolly's about the only thing'll keep you regularish." He punctuated his statement by setting a tankard of the ever-present bumbo down as well.

"Never too early for rum," she muttered, trying not to let her distaste for the drink dampen her spirits.

"Sure you'd prefer tea, but if you saw the state of the water, you'd not wish for anything but this."

She wrinkled her nose, which he seemed to find incredibly amusing, but at least his laughter broke whatever dark cloud hung over him.

He leaned back against the bulkhead, crossing his arms. "You did a good job on the sails. Stick close this morning. May need you to run messages to the captain."

Bash rifled a hand idly through his long, dark locks, a bit wild and curly, but thick and not matted like the few other sailors who hadn't shaved their heads all together.

When he caught her looking, she fully intended to drop her gaze, but she didn't, and it sizzled between them until his lips curved into a small, sheepish smile.

She wanted to tell him that a handsome smile wasn't an apology for a week of grumpiness, but it did funny things to her stomach, so she tried to suppress her own tiny smile and look deeply intrigued by the bowl of gruel.

"Why—" She cut herself off, but Bash looked askance so she tried again. "In the hold Roo called the captain... Mad?"

Bash shrugged. "Well, a fella'd have to be a bit mad to keep choosing this life year after year, wouldn't he?"

Being the youngest of the Mackintosh girls, Maggie knew when she was being given the brushoff, and she'd also perfected the art of the disbelieving glare.

He looked away, rubbing up and down on the back of his neck in a way that made the tiny hairs on her own neck stand up.

"When he first became a captain, he lost a bit of gold."

"Lost?" Maggie asked.

"Aye. Some say he exaggerated the haul and drank it all in the tavern the same night. Others say he gambled it away. Dutch reckons he buried it and forgot where."

"How careless," Maggie said. She'd have thought pirates were a bit more scrupulous than that. If she had any amount of gold, she certainly wouldn't lose it.

"Aye. The frustration of it has eaten away at his mind year after year, making him more than a little mad. That, and being hunted by the naval officer entrusted with guarding the gold—or so he says."

"What do you say?"

He turned thoughtful for a moment. "The sea's been my home more years than it hasn't, but men were made to live near water, not on it. It can do funny things to a fella's mind."

"Has it done funny things to yours?" she asked without meaning to but desperate to know, though she couldn't say why.

"I'm sure it has," he said, brushing her off again, but still smiling. "S'pose I wouldn't know the difference though, would I? Best eat up and get on deck."

So Maggie finished her gruel and got to her feet. Running her fingers down her chest to ensure the cloth binding had stayed in place all night, she turned her back on Bash to adjust it. A large atlas sat open on the desk behind her. It was beautifully illustrated and covered in intersecting crisscrossed lines, as well as perfectly penned letters she recognized forming words she couldn't read.

Had so much sunshine made her addlepated? Or perhaps it was the rum having an effect? She reached out a finger as though touching the words, tracing each letter in turn, might unscramble them in her brain.

"El grande rio de las Amazones," Bash whispered, suddenly so much closer than she'd realized, his breath tickling the back of her neck. "The great river of the Amazon. 'Tis Spanish."

"You speak Spanish?" she asked, a little awed.

"Aye. Spaniards make the best maps."

"You learned Spanish so you could read maps?" she asked, turning to look over her shoulder, and his face was right there, his lips full and pink, only an inch or two away.

"Aye," he breathed, and Maggie licked her own chapped lips. He swallowed, and she watched his throat go up and down.

She turned back to the book. "I was taught French," she said, almost to remind herself that knowing a second language wasn't so remarkable.

"Ah! Je parle français aussi," he said. "And that is Latin," he added, leaning over her shoulder to point out a calligraphed word on the map, near where she'd been touching.

"Show off," she told his forearm.

He shrugged but tucked his arms safely behind his back.

"Are they similar? Spanish and French and Latin?"

"More than not."

His eyes scanned her face and down her neck, and she could feel every bit of skin they lighted on, so she turned back towards the book of maps, flipping to the next page to see if he would stop her. "What else can you speak?"

"Bit of Yoruba. Jamaican. Gaelic. Portuguese. Some Italian. And Dutch."

Now he really was showing off. "Did the quartermaster teach you?"

"Some."

"Does he miss it?"

"Holland, you mean? He's never been there. Dutch pirates attacked a slaving ship, and when they saw how quickly he picked up their language, they took him onto their crew for a time."

Maggie's face burned for having known so little of the world, but she appreciated the way Bash related the tale without the imperious grandstanding her father liked to employ as the smug keeper of the knowledge. Bash didn't make her feel stupid for not knowing, merely uninformed, with no judgment in it.

"Does he miss his real home then?" she asked, wondering the same of Bash, with his warm, tawny skin.

"What good does missing it do?" he asked gruffly. "This ship is his home now. We are his country."

Sensing the conversation was over and Bash's patience had worn thin, Maggie flipped the page back to where it started and turned to face him. He wasn't much taller than she was, merely the distance between his lips and his eyes. She wondered, despite herself, what his lips would taste like—the same sweet spirits and citrus she could smell on him every time he stepped near?

Settle down.

Those were dangerous thoughts, best left to restless dreaming.

"So, messages?" she asked, swallowing a sudden dryness in her throat.

"Aye. And anything else I need done."

"Just for you?"

He smiled, the one dimple popping out below his scar, like a special sort of punctuation mark for his emotions. "Were you looking to take orders from someone else?"

Maggie shook her head and followed him up to the deck.

For a time she stood idle, watching him use his spyglass to examine the water and the clouds as he'd done each day before. "Can you see all the way back to Scotland?" she asked, and he laughed.

"See for yourself," he said, tossing her the glass.

Maggie caught it awkwardly and examined its length, an appealing blend of mahogany and brass, warm to the touch, smooth and sturdy.

"Hold it here," he explained, stepping behind her and moving her left hand down the extended shaft. "Gently. And keep both eyes open."

Hardly breathing, Maggie opened her left eye and relaxed it, peering through the narrow end with her right.

"What do you see?" he asked softly.

"A blur of blue and"—she flinched away from the eye piece—"blinding light."

Taking her shoulders, Bash turned her more to the west so the sun bouncing off the surf would be less intense.

"To focus, expand the middle section." He put his hand gently on hers, twisting the shaft with excruciating patience, and suddenly the wave crests clarified before her eyes along with one —no, two—no, three dolphins leaping out of the water so clearly they seemed close enough to touch. He took his hand away then, and she bobbled the scope, almost dropping it over the railing and into the churning wake below.

She glanced quickly at Bash who stared at her, wide-eyed, and puffed air out of his cheeks, but she couldn't help a giddy laugh as she braced for the yelling and relinquished his precious spyglass.

"Have you never seen dolphins before?" he asked, surprise but no anger lacing his decidedly-not-yelling voice.

"Never so close or so many." There was a whole family of them out there now that she knew where to look, splashing and twirling with glee. "I suppose it's commonplace for you."

He shrugged, smiling softly as he watched the creatures play. "Never gets tiresome though. Even seeing them in Lewis as a boy didn't compare to the first time an entire pod joined us on the open sea."

Maggie grinned at him, delighted to find a kindred spirit and relieved he wasn't going to shout at her for the near miss with his spyglass. She leaned on the railing as far out as she dared, laughing with glee to see the dolphins frolic as if putting on a show just for her.

The sound of flapping canvas brought her attention back to the masts and sails, *her* sails, for they were hers now she'd mended them. They snapped and billowed in the breeze, her stitches holding tight as Bash had assured her they would. Maggie breathed in the mingled scents of citrus and brine and, realized she felt rather content. Perhaps she was born for piracy all along, with her mannish hands and uselessness at cooking.

"Cap should be at his loblolly by now," Bash said, interrupting her thoughts. "Down one level, all the way aft. Run, fast as you can. Don't stop for anyone else, and let him know the wind has shifted again. Then come straight back."

Excitement surged in her stomach at being given such an errand. "Me?"

"Aye," he answered gravely. " 'Tis what cabin boys do, Magnus."

She nodded at his warning and headed down below.

Already she'd forgotten how dark it was inside the ship, and she stood awkwardly beside the ladder, blinking to make her eyes adjust. Then she tiptoed past rows of hammocks, many of which still held sleeping, farting, snoring, naked sailors, and she realized how much better she'd had it curled up on the floor of Bash's alcove.

"Well hello, cabin boy," said Balthasar, the instigator from the canteen her first night. He stepped out of the shadows to block her path. "Lose your way? It can be tricky hereabouts."

When he put a hand on her arm, it made her bowels loosen, and she took a step back, bumping into another sailor who grinned down at her with fetid breath.

She opened and closed her mouth and then forced out her haughtiest tone. "I've an important message for the captain."

"Oh, beg pardon, beg pardon," Balthasar said, bowing but not moving out of her way.

She licked her lips. "Bash says I'm to come straight back."

"Well, we don't want to make Nav unhappy, now do we?"

The other pirate snickered, so Maggie tried another tack, rubbing her backside absently. "I certainly don't," she confided.

"Gave you a good hiding, did he? Must have done, and you still feeling it a week later."

"No more'n the brat deserved." The other pirate spit on the floor. "We run out of drink, it's on your head, younker."

"Well get on 'afore ye earn another," Balthasar said with a little too much glee like he'd enjoy watching her be whipped. Finally, he stepped out of her way, and she scurried off to rap on the captain's door, gulping to try and steady her breathing.

SHE'D BEEN GONE TOO LONG. OF COURSE, BASH HAD TO LET her out of his sight at some point. What use was a cabin boy who didn't run messages to the captain in his cabin? But it made him nervous, which infuriated him. He was accustomed to worrying about the whole ship and her crew as an entity, a living, breathing organism, one he understood and had the where-with-all to tend. He couldn't afford to be constantly fearful about the wellbeing of an individual.

How would it look?

The crew believed the girl was a lad called Magnus. Would a boy be in danger, caught alone in the wrong dark corner with the wrong disreputable sailor? Of course. Would Bash hover and nursemaid a young lad? Or would he trust the men to either respect or fear him enough none would interfere with what he'd claimed and leave the rest to the lad to take care of himself?

Hypotheticals had always made Bash feel stupid. Give him facts and figures, maps and charts, stars and wind. Maybes and what ifs were as useless as chasing hopes and dreams.

"You're a right grumpy bugger today," Dutch observed when Bash glowered towards the hatch for the hundredth time.

He tried to smooth his furious brow before responding. "Hmph," he grunted, and Dutch studied him harder.

"Bit crowded in your berth these days?"

He shot Dutch a look, but the quartermaster was studiously intent on the horizon, unable or unwilling to meet Bash's eye. Time to change the subject.

"Is it a mind game the old man's playing? Veering off course to fuck with me?"

Now Dutch did turn his attention.

"He rejected my plan for the colonies," Bash explained.

"Ordered us back to Jamaica, then deliberately sabotaged our course so we're too far north. Does he want to go to Boston but just can't let me be right?"

"He doesn't know what he wants," Dutch muttered under his breath before turning around and leaning against the railing. "Ahoy, Captain!" he called. "Young Magnus."

Bash took a breath before turning around.

"Cabin boy says you're afraid of the wind."

Maggie seemed nervous, but still in one piece. Her expression turned stricken at the captain's words, but she didn't contradict him. *Good girl.*

"Southerly," Bash explained with a practiced shrug. "Won't carry us to Port Royal, but as you know, I'm happy to see Boston, myself..."

The captain sneered. "We won't find Willy Walsh in Boston."

"Perhaps we'll find he's taken Tew's route from Africa to Yemen," Bash argued sarcastically. A possibility, but they both knew Walsh didn't have Tew's stones.

Mad's wicked grin broadened. "Perhaps I should let you take us there just to prove he hasn't."

"It's no difference to me, sir. Only reporting facts. We're not on course for the Caribbean."

"Well, you're the sailing master, boy. Wear the fucking sails."

"Aye, Captain," Bash said with a curt nod. Then he bellowed, "Ready about," and the men sprang to action like well-oiled cogs.

They swarmed the sails, preparing to turn the tail of the brig into the wind. Bash loved to stand back and watch them in action. He took pride in how smoothly the men worked together.

"Lines are fouled," Duffy called, peering up at the foremast.

And just like that, the magic was spoiled.

Bash's head snapped around to follow Duffy's gaze. Sure enough, the lines were tangled, the sail too tight to make the turn.

"I'll get it," Langley grumbled, starting forward.

"Good lad." Bash cuffed him affectionately, but the captain put out his arm.

"Why not let the new recruit have a go," he asked laconically.

Langley stopped, one hand on the ratline, looking from Mad to Bash unsure who he'd rather please.

"Captain?" Bash glanced at Maggie, expecting her face to have drained of color, but she was simply staring up at the tops, half biting her bottom lip like she was assessing the challenge.

"We each must pull our weight, must we not?" Mad asked, conveniently ignoring Maggie's work repairing the sails.

There was no clean way to argue without Bash showing unwarranted favoritism.

He sidled up to Maggie. "The ropes are all a mess," he explained. "See up at the top there?" he asked, standing a little too close to her, close enough to smell her hair, to catch the faintest notes of rosewater beneath the brine.

She smiled. "Like the tangled-up ribbons of a lady's stays," she muttered.

Bash cleared his throat. If she kept talking like that, their secret would be out in no time. She must have realized it too, for her posture stiffened. "How are they to be untangled, sir?" she asked more loudly.

"Very carefully. Do you know how to climb?"

"Like breathing, isn't it? You just do it?"

A soft laugh escaped before Bash thought to hide it, and she turned with questions in her luminous lapis eyes.

"Hold on to the shrouds," he said, pointing to the angled vertical ropes, "and step on the rat lines. One foot at a time. The wind is stronger than you think."

Completely unperturbed, the girl grabbed hold of the nearest rope and tested her weight on the first rung, then began to climb with an unsuppressed joy that caught Bash by surprise.

"Slow down," he called after her, and she cast an annoyed look over her shoulder at him. She was only about ten feet off the ground, but when she did it, her fists clenched tighter around the rigging, and she tried to grip the rat line with her toes, her face blanching. "Best you don't look down either," Bash cautioned.

Still pale, she rolled her eyes at him before facing forward again as he'd bidden.

Maggie Mackintosh Budge did not like being ordered about. Bash shook his head. She'd make a terrible sailor, whipped constantly for insubordination. What a handful she must have been for her late husband, the lucky bastard.

"Good climber at least," Dutch said, stepping closer as they both gazed up at the rather appealing backside shimmying up the ropes.

"We'll see," Bash huffed, which only amused Dutch all the more.

"Do you remember the first time I sent you up the rigging?"

"Wasn't you who sent me," Bash argued petulantly under his breath.

"I gave the order. And you flew up there like a monkey in a tree."

"Made it to the top, took one look down and lost my footing. Would've fallen the whole way and cracked my skull if I hadn't tangled myself in the lines."

Dutch laughed. "Your face was as red as a radish, time we got you down."

"And my arse soon matched, compliments of the captain."

Dutch stopped laughing then. He'd felt guilty for not arguing when Mad suggested sending a child up the rigging, but Bash had never blamed Dutch for any of it. He knew better than most which way the wind blew on board the *Revenge*.

The girl had reached the topmast, and she paused, looking out at the vast, impregnable vista. Bash well remembered his first time taking in that view. Even the whipping hadn't soured it.

After a moment's pause, she wrapped her arm around the line

and peered down at him again. She looked ill but didn't sway. "Now what?" she yelled.

Now what indeed?

"Has the lad been sailing before?" Dutch asked.

"I rather doubt it."

"Then what are you waiting for?"

Not usually one to require permission, it was all the encouragement Bash needed to climb up after her. It was no more than he'd do for any new recruit not yet dry behind the ears. Proper instruction could mean the difference between life and death, and besides, four hands were better than two when it came to fouled lines.

"You climb very well for a beginner," he said when she and her dangerously round bottom were well within earshot.

"For a—" she started crossly but cut herself off.

"For a beginner," he repeated, close to her ear after grasping the boom on either side of her and pulling himself up to stand behind.

"I don't need help," she snapped, and he was ashamed of how his body responded, rising to follow even as she leaned away. He swung himself to the left of her, as she scooted further to the right.

"You requested it."

"Merely instruction. Up close, I've lost track of the tangle."

She scowled, and Bash doubted she really wanted instructions either. What had it cost her, to call down to him when she'd clearly prefer to muddle about on her own and figure things out?

"It's here," he said, pointing out the loose line which had wound itself around the mast and rigging like the warp and weft of a loom. "Night watch will have to answer for not keeping the lines tighter after you went to such trouble patching the sails."

"What's to be done? Cut it?"

"No, no," he said, showing her how to gently twist the rope back around to where it belonged.

They worked in silence, as the wind whipped their shirts and ruffled her short-cropped hair. Standing close enough to count her freckles in the bright sunshine, he was suddenly conscious of the grotesque scar adorning his own left cheek. She must think him a hideous ogre, and he couldn't blame her. She was like the heroine of a fairy story, trapped aboard a monster's ship.

"I didn't say you were afraid of the wind. Only relayed the message as you told it to me," she finally confessed, drawing him back from his wallowing and perking him right up. Bash knew the captain well enough to guess he'd put words in Maggie's mouth, but for some reason he also liked knowing she cared what he thought.

" 'Tis no matter," he said.

"Was he testing you? Ought you have shouted at me? Or," she swallowed, "or taken me below again? You could have. I wouldn't mind."

"I'm not sure testing is the word. In any event, I don't shout at my crew or punish them when I know they've done no wrong."

"Is that what I am? Part of your crew?" She seemed to hold her breath, anxiously awaiting his reply.

How could he explain that she was and she wasn't? That he protected the crew as a whole but kept himself apart from individuals aside from Dutch? That he didn't care to know most of them in the way he felt drawn to her, or care what they thought of him in the way he desired her good opinion? How could he explain that his crew never drove him to distraction, never made his heart beat too fast, never gave his prick a mind of its own?

"Of course you are. I'm giving orders and you're following them, aren't you?" he asked gruffly, and she bristled—a good thing, because a rough-edged wench was far safer than a soft one.

"Aren't you?" he couldn't help goading, and she set her jaw and turned her face away towards the ocean.

"Look!" she gasped, letting go of the rigging to point but Bash saw only her, as he reflexively leaned out to grab the line she'd released, just in time to catch her when she lost her balance and stumbled.

Her back fit perfectly into his chest, her bottom against his groin, and he was instantly hard once more.

Now she gasped for a whole different reason, and his left hand went to her waist to steady her as she resecured her hold and her footing.

"No," she said.

"My apologies," he murmured, removing his hand from her person and easing back just a little.

"No," she repeated. "I'm not very practiced at following orders, it would seem."

"We'll have to remedy that," he growled, and she swallowed hard.

"Yes," she whispered. "It is I who should apologize. Though I'm not very skilled at that either. I was just overcome by..." She trailed off, scanning the water with a furrowed brow, then pointing more sedately, she sighed, "There."

This time Bash turned to follow her finger, but there was nothing, only the telltale frothy surf.

"What was it?" he asked, studying her rather than the ocean.

"Dinnae ken," she whispered, childlike excitement dancing in her bright eyes. He could happily watch her study his ocean for hours, but he forced himself to turn his attention outward.

Together they held their breaths until a nose breached the surface, and then the biggest fish Bash had ever seen thrust its way out of the water, rolling like a wave on the beach before crashing back to disappear below the surf.

The ship rocked, the crew below equally silent, as though Bash and Maggie were the only two humans in all the world to have witnessed such a remarkable thing, and he was glad she was there to see it.

"Was that a sea monster?" she whispered.

"Some kind of whale, innit?"

The beast breached the surface once more, slapping back down in a spray that reached them all the way in the tops, settling on Maggie's eyelashes like a fine mist of pearls.

"Is it trying to scare us away?" she asked, in a voice that said it wasn't working.

"Nah," Bash explained. "It wants to play."

"Play?" she giggled, leaning forward to watch as the whale leaped and splashed once more, and the men below clapped and cheered it on.

"Mercy," she breathed. "How do you ever grow accustomed to it?"

"Many a fine sailor forgets himself when gazing upon the wonders of the water."

"Not you, I imagine."

Had she heard Dutch reference his ignominious first assent? Impossible, unless she was some kind of witch. She was only teasing, surely. "Ah, but I'm an exception, darlin', born scarred and sea weary from the loins of a mermaid herself."

She laughed, and the sound was something like the tinkling of tiny shells and sea glass.

"Bash?" she asked.

"Yes?" he replied too quickly, desperate to hear her question, even if it was about his past.

"How do we get down?"

Chapter Seven

A man like Bash, Maggie was certain, must be well accustomed to giving orders. He couldn't help it. The life he lived, shouting orders meant the difference between continuing to sail or being swallowed up by some kind of beautiful whale. He was used to giving orders and having them obeyed without question.

They were completely incompatible. Not that she was looking for compatibility.

Maggie might be just a little too much like her cousin Jory in all the wrong ways. She wasn't overly sensitive, but directives chafed at her too-tight skin. Whether a command was common sense, whether aligned to her own desires, the minute an edict was issued, Maggie was compelled to do the very opposite. She'd always been that way—with her parents, her cousins, and obviously with Jeremiah too.

So why, then, did she find something attractive about Bash and his stern commands? Why was some part of her eager to comply, to do his bidding in exchange for a whispered *Good girl*, and not even roll her eyes? It was untenable, and it left her as annoyed with herself as she was with him. At the same time, she'd never lived moment to moment in a life-or-death situation before. It had never truly mattered if she was obstinate or headstrong or rash. Until now. Bash wasn't making demands to exercise his power over her.

When Maggie's father ordered her about, he had an air of detached resignation, like she was a scab he wished to heal for her own good, and with little expectation of compliance. When Jeremiah gave an order, it was always a disgusted dare to defy him. He wanted to fight, so he came in hot and half-angry. He knew Maggie couldn't help giving him a reason for his ire.

In both cases, her father and Jeremiah were demanding power and submission. Theirs were orders rooted in the notion that women should do as they're told regardless of everything else.

Bash was different. He ordered men as easily as women, and he had a way of being instructional. He expected to be obeyed absolutely, and he left no room for trepidation or doubt or disobedience. But he spoke with such confidence, his words sounded like the only logical course of action. It simply made sense to comply. So, as he guided Maggie through her descent from the rigging, she swallowed the desire to push him away and figure it out alone—she had asked him after all—and when she found his instructions at odds with her own instincts, she trusted him to know what he was about.

Once safely on deck, he showed her how to belay the rope which had been tangled and knot it around a long wooden pin so it wouldn't come loose again. Then he ignored her completely to shout orders like, "Helms a lee!" and "Haul wind!" Everyone except Maggie had a role to play in turning the massive ship in a more southerly direction, and she watched with fascination as their muscles bulged and strained to make it happen.

When they finished and the sails were back in place, billowing less fully than before, Bash peered through his spyglass for longer than seemed necessary. Then he sent Maggie to fetch him some rum. So maybe a few of his orders were self-serving.

She was tempted to splash the bumbo back in his face and announce that she wasn't a servant at his beck and call, but as cabin boy, that's exactly what she was, so she filled his tankard to the brim and swallowed her pride.

As she handed it over, her fingers brushed against his rope-calloused palm and heat flared in her cheeks. He stared at her a moment before taking a long drink, never breaking eye contact, then handed the half-full mug back to her.

"Are you drinking enough as well?" he asked, sounding like a school master who knew he'd caught his charge misbehaving.

Maggie licked her chapped lips.

"Finish that," he said, and again she wanted to toss it in his face, except she suddenly felt a powerful thirst which had nothing to do with beverages. "You must drink," he urged, his brows knitting with concern, and this time she drained it, maintaining eye contact just as he had done.

Throughout the rest of the day, she ran a few more messages to the captain and the quartermaster, but much of her time was spent clinging to the rail, gazing out to sea, trying to work out whether this impulsive act of hers had been the silliest thing she'd ever done or, in fact, the bravest.

Would she ever see her family again? Or would she remain a part of this pirate crew forever, pillaging gold from undeserving slavers like a sort of Robin Hood?

The thought made her more melancholy than she might have expected. She loved being able to see forever in any direction, but when she compared the wide-open expanse to home, she found she missed the mountains. The idea of never seeing Ellen or Jory again made tears spring to her eyes, and she even almost missed the patronizing way her father called her *My girl* and her mother managed to turn cooking into a lecture, but only because she wanted to show them both how well she was doing on her own own.

This was an adventure, that was all. An interlude, she resolved.

She'd see them again one day, and with stories they wouldn't half believe.

Peering over the starboard side, she observed the spaces where cannons would be manned in a battle, and she shivered at the thought of them firing one after another, splintering the hull of an enemy ship.

Maggie could well imagine the captain giving orders to attack another vessel. Would she be expected to swing aboard from some hiding place in the top of the rigging and steal away all that was precious to the other crew? Would she be expected to shoot a pistol or slice a man's cheek with her rapier as someone must have done to Bash?

It was hard to even imagine such a thing, especially when there was nothing, not land nor ship, as far as she could see in any direction. How, amidst all this blue—above and below and on and on forever—could they find their way anywhere at all?

"Your face looks mighty fearsome, Magnus. You practicing your pirate scowl?" Bash asked, appearing at her elbow.

"Is it working?"

"Oh, aye. Were I to glimpse you through my spyglass, I would surely turn tail and run t'other way for dear life."

Perhaps she ought to feel insulted, but she laughed instead. It felt good to laugh. She used to do it so often as a girl.

"How would you know which way you were running?" she asked, and his eyebrows seemed to shoot up in surprise at her question. "At home there are roads and landmarks," she explained. "Hills and rivers and towns can be your guide, but out here..." She shook her head, marveling once more at the vast emptiness. "I know you have maps, but can you really map a whole ocean? How do you know you're here until you're there?" she frowned, unsure she was making any sense, but Bash's lips quirked up on one side like he was pleased by her question.

"Out here, it's a bit of dead reckoning, you're quite right. Paying attention to your compass, the current, and the wind."

She tilted her head, trying to decide if he was teasing her. "If you were a woman, they'd burn you as a witch for talking like that."

Now he laughed. "Navigation is a science, not a sorcery." He held up a shiny, circular object, about the size of a man's watch. "Have you ever seen a compass?" he asked, turning the device in his palm so a needle spun around.

Maggie shook her head in awe.

"The tip of the needle will always point north," he explained.

She stared at the compass, recognizing the same directional signs one might find on a map. "It's pointing west right now," she said.

"No, west is merely facing north in my hand." He turned the compass until the needle, which she realized didn't move itself, lay across the N, and a mark between the W and the S was aligned with the bow of the ship. "The compass is pointing north. We're traveling southwest."

"But how does it work?" she asked, furious with herself for admitting her ignorance. She was fully prepared to channel her rage back at him when he scoffed at her feeble feminine mind.

"Lodestone. And magnetite," was all he said.

She stared at him, surely appearing the blankest of fools. Was he speaking in Spanish again, or one of his many other tongues, just to confuse her?

"No one really knows why exactly, but the lodestone magnetizes the needle, and a proper magnet always points north."

"Always?"

She couldn't decide whether to be more amazed by the things he was telling her, the fact that he *was* telling her, or his own admission of not understanding it all. Did Jory know about these magnets?

"Always."

"How do you know it's a proper magnet?" she asked. "And not an upside-down one?"

He chuckled and rocked back on his heels—not like a man giving a belittling lecture, but more the gleeful laugh of a little boy who was proud to share what he'd learned. "For one thing, because I struck it against the lodestone myself just last week. For another, because where is the sun?"

"Dead ahead," she said, realizing her folly. "What do you even need a compass for then, if you can follow the sun?"

He grinned, the nearly invisible scar on his cheek giving a slight twitch.

"For nighttime and cloudy days," she answered her own question.

Bash winked. "The magnet's even more precise than the sun. And knowing where you're going's only half the battle. You've also got to know where you are."

Maggie wasn't sure she'd ever known where she was, let alone where she was going, never more so than right now.

"That's where the astrolabe comes in," he said, placing the compass in his pocket and leading her to a heavy brass ring which hung from the rigging.

The astrolabe was much larger than the compass, etched with numbers around the edge. A double-pointed arm spun freely around the disk.

"You line up the sight with the sun or lodestar. Obviously don't look directly into the sun," Bash explained, turning his back on the sun so a shadow fell across the vane.

Maggie watched in awe, only half listening as he explained how he used the shadows and mathematics to calculate something or other about distance and what all.

"From there you've got a pretty good notion how far north or south you are. We've a backstaff as well, of course. It's best for measuring the noon sun."

"And then more mathematics?" Maggie asked.

"Aye." Bash grinned.

She'd never realized how much learning was required in order to be a proper pirate. "I was never much good at mathematics," she confessed. "I suppose I wasn't meant to be."

The astrolabe felt solid and sturdy in her hands as she studied it and spun the vane. "Do you turn it sideways to do east and west?"

" 'Fraid not. That's where the reckoning comes in," he said with another wink. "Come." He motioned for her to follow. "It's salmagundi tonight."

Though Maggie's head still spun with a million questions, she let him lead the way down the hatch and through to the galley.

"Ho, knave, been swinging the lead?" Roo, asked, tossing Maggie a different sort of wink.

She lifted her chin and said, "I climbed the rigging."

"And back down again in one piece? My, you are brave," Roo said, handing her a plate. Then he eyed Bash cautiously. "An ill wind blows, Bashy," he said.

"Wind'll change," Bash replied, stoically taking his own plate.

"And if it don't?" the cook asked, showing a toothy grin that Maggie suspected was meant to scare her.

"You've been sailing long enough to know it always changes, Rooijakkers."

Roo cackled. Maggie found it quite unnerving.

"And it if doesn't, I've always wanted to raid the colonies," Bash added, motioning for Maggie to head into the dining room, conversation over.

Slouching onto a bench, Maggie could hear her mother's chiding voice reminding her to *Sit up straight, elbows off the table, Miss,* and she did so out of habit. Then she glanced at the posture of the men all around her and slumped back down, resting her elbows where she wanted with delight.

Salmagundi turned out to be a rather nice salad of lettuce and chopped meat, which she supposed must be a delicacy they wouldn't have for much longer, so she relished every bite.

Maggie watched with interest as the others settled into

familiar groups. Duffy, Samson, and Langley played a quiet game with rectangular bone tiles, while O'Riordan, Balthasar, and some others played a rowdy hand of cards.

"Why don't you ever play with them?" she asked Bash.

"What, Ruff?"

"'Acause he doesn't know how, ain't that right, Nav?" Balthasar called.

Bash shook his head at the jibe. "Drink your bumbo."

Balthasar scoffed. "That fucking grog? Rather drink me own piss." But he took a drink all the same, glaring at Bash.

"Don't know how? Say it's not so," Maggie teased to ease the tension.

"It's not. But I don't like how they play," he growled, and the Butcher laughed loudly.

"How do they play?"

"For money," Balthasar answered. "Nav don't like to break the rules. Though, the rules don't forbid wagering the services of your cabin boy," he said, sliding his gaze over Maggie in a way that made her feel sick.

Sensing Bash stiffen for a fight, she nodded towards Langley's group to distract him. "What about their game?"

"Dominoes. And yes, I know how, but it wouldn't be sporting or good for morale."

"Oh, ho, big talk, Nav, big talk," Samson laughed, far more kindly than O'Riordan had.

"Can you teach me to play them both?" Maggie asked.

"Aye, but not tonight."

He looked as bone weary as she felt, and a deep soreness was beginning to settle into her muscles from her adventures in the rigging. How she longed for a hot bath, but she resigned herself to dreaming of one in her nest beneath the desk in Bash's alcove. She was relieved when he ate his meal quickly and stood before the chiming of the bells.

As they neared the companionway, though, instead of turning

towards his berth, Bash made for the ladder to the upper deck. Maggie hesitated, perplexed.

"I've got first watch," he explained, nodding towards the hatch.

Her instinct was to ask what that had to do with her, but she bit her tongue and blinked sleepily.

"You'll accompany me."

For a moment she thought he was joking, but he shifted from foot to foot, impatient for her to climb.

"Sounds like a rare opportunity to enjoy a night of privacy," she tried.

Bash coughed out a laugh but stepped closer to her. "There's not a chance in hell I'll leave you down here alone."

Maggie tossed her head, still not quite used to her short-cropped hair after a lifetime of it trailing to her waist. The move brought her face dangerously close to his. "Surely they'll not trouble me after you said your piece."

"And surely you're not still as naive as you were a week ago," he growled.

Maggie blinked even as a shiver ran through her whole body at the sound his throat made. "I'm exhausted," she said, careful to keep her tone even rather than the plaintive whine she felt to the depths of her being.

"Oh. Well all right then. I'll just tell the captain and the men that I can't take my turn at watch because the cabin boy is sleepy."

"We worked all day," she argued.

"That's life at sea, darlin'," he countered, and what could she say to that?

So, with a sigh that she tried to soften from sounding overly dramatic, she squeezed past him in the tight passageway and, ignoring the little thrill which beset her stomach when she brushed against him, she climbed the ladder hoping to catch her breath in the fresh air above.

FRANKLY, BASH HAD EXPECTED MORE OF A FIGHT. ANYONE could see the girl was asleep on her feet. Of course she'd want to turn in for the night rather than stand watch with his piss-poor company until the wee hours, but if life had taught him anything it was that there's trust and then there's *trust*.

He trusted most of his companions to do their jobs. The majority worked hard and performed well when it mattered and shoddily when they were too drunk. In battle, he trusted every man to do his best to survive, but the list of those he trusted with his life was short indeed.

Not a chance he'd leave Maggie on her own in a quiet corner while he was known to be detained above.

He had little experience with women. None, really, not since the day his sire ripped him from the bosom of his kin. But he'd heard enough stories about the fairer sex—and knew enough young men, as well—to expect her to huff and brat petulantly over his demand. When she acquiesced so quick and easy-like, it left him unsettled and bracing for a counterattack.

Emerging onto the deck, however, he found her once more at the railing, staring out across a horizon of pink and orange hues. In the east, the stars had just begun to appear amidst the inky blue.

"Is it always this beautiful?" she asked, but Bash couldn't peel his eyes off her—the contours painted in honeyed light as well as the features chiseled from shadow.

"I like to think so," he breathed, and a small smile tugged at her lips.

"The island, Orkney, was so different from where I grew up it made me resent the ocean, but I never imagined the open sea could be a world apart yet again."

He grinned. "Wait until you see Jamaica." And suddenly, inexplicably, he wanted to take her there. He wanted to see his mother's homeland through her eyes and to watch her take it all in.

The first and only time he ever set foot in Port Royal, his heart leapt in recognition, as though whatever part of his mother that pulsed in his veins, whatever essence that makes up a human soul, was finally home.

Clearing his throat, he swallowed his excitement. "Where did you grow up then? Inverness, you said?"

"Mostly."

"Landlocked, innit?" he asked, knowing full well that it was. He'd spent his youth pouring over more maps than just oceanic ones.

"Yes. We had a very fine river, but only a thick fog would stop you seeing the opposite shore. Though I'll wager our monster could rival any of yours."

Bash laughed, motioning for her to follow him to the bow. He preferred to keep night watch in the tops, but he'd let Samson or Duffy take his usual spot tonight. The girl really was worn out, and he wouldn't punish her further with a second climb.

"So what do you know of sea monsters, anyway?"

"Besides Nessie, you mean? The Shaw Wretch told a story of one called Cetus," she said, glancing up as if to search for the constellation.

Bash bristled and then batted the jealous feelings away. So what if she'd known other brigands who told stories of the stars to woo her? "The Shaw Wretch?" he asked, in as disinterested a tone as he could muster.

"Finlay Shaw. My cousin's husband. I suppose I really oughtn't call him Wretch now. He's been nothing but worthy and good," she added in a tone laced with something like disappointment.

Bash relaxed. "Then why did you?"

She shrugged. "Everyone used to, until he redeemed himself."

"What made him wretched, if he could be so easily forgiven? Was he an outlaw?"

She laughed. "You know, I'm not actually sure."

"But he redeemed himself?" he asked, annoyed at the desperate hope in his voice.

"He did." She smiled fondly. "He's well respected now."

"How?"

"He helped my cousin Jory save dozens of girls from a terrible fate. And me too, I suppose."

"Then I shall have to thank him," Bash murmured, only realizing he'd said it out loud when her smile grew wider.

The knot in his stomach loosened. "Were you close to your cousin growing up?"

"Yes and no. She lived with us much of the time. She and Ellen were as close as real sisters. I was always chasing after them like a sort of spare leg... a part of things, but unnecessary. Like a harmony that's a little off key," she mumbled, painting a picture that he could see perfectly.

"I never had any brothers or sisters that I knew of."

"Cousins?" she asked.

There had been cousins on Lewis. The youngest MacLeod sister had taken him in after his grandparents died, but she handed him off again a few days after delivering her first child into the world. There was an older sister too. Jenny. She was blessed with far too many mouths to feed of her own. "Not close ones," he said. "Certainly none who knew celestial mythology like your Shaw Wretch."

"When I... left for Orkney, Ellen shared with me something her husband told her—that no matter where we three are—Jory, Ellen, and me—we'll always be looking up into the same stars. It made her feel better."

The sun was fully set now, and the girl turned her face up to the sky once more, speckled like a blanket of shiny jewels. It was a lovely notion, and though Bash wasn't sure the idea made *Maggie* feel less alone, he couldn't bear to tell her the stars actually changed the further south one cared to venture.

"You miss them," he said, instead.

She shivered and he drew closer, lending her some of his heat.

"I miss a lot of things," she answered.

"Then why sneak aboard? Why not go home? You had to know you might never see them again."

She was quiet for a long moment and then she shrugged. "I suppose I missed the illusion of independence most of all."

Christ, she looked young, crowned by starlight. How was it possible for one so unseasoned to have already been both married and widowed? What on earth had ever given her the sense of freedom she was missing enough to board his ship? And what had taken it away?

He cleared his throat again. "Aye, an illusion is all it ever is. We're all of us at the mercy of our fickle mistresses, the winds and tides."

"Is it true the moon controls the tides?"

"Some say so."

"And others?"

"Others say it was the Norse god Thor," he teased. Finlay Shaw, the formerly wretched cousin-in-law, wasn't the only one who could fill her head with ancient tales.

The girl turned to him, her eyes alight with glee.

"What's so funny?"

"Just imagining my mother's face to hear me discussing pagan deities."

He laughed out loud. "That would be her concern? Not the pirate ship in the middle of the ocean and you parading around all but indecent in my breeches?"

"I don't parade!" She dipped her head to hide an elfin sort of smirk. "Go on then, tell me about Thor. Has he a star up there?"

"Nah, he made the stars, innit?"

She laughed and turned the radiance of her smile back to the cloudless sky.

"The story goes, Loki challenged Thor to a drinking contest, but he secretly connected the god's cup to the ocean. No matter how hard Thor tried, he couldn't drain it because, after all, it was the whole ocean, but his efforts created the rise and fall of the tides."

"A likely tale," she said in a dreamy voice, leaning back to tilt her face up even farther.

As she had in the rigging, she fit just perfectly against him. Every hair on his body stood erect as though leaning to meet her, and he fought the urge to rest his chin atop her soft head.

"Jory would say, 'Leave it to men to give the credit to a man,'" she said.

"Ah, but Thor wasn't just any man. He was a god."

She shook, either with a chill or silent laughter.

"Are you cold?" he asked, rubbing his hands along her arms before he caught himself.

"A little," she admitted. "One of the reasons I snuck aboard was to travel someplace warm."

"I recall the isles can be unforgivably fresh."

"Fresh," she laughed. "Spoken like a local. What's the warmest place you've ever visited?"

How could he tell her he'd sailed to many ports but rarely explored them?

"There's nothing finer than to dawdle on the deck as a bright sun warms you from the outside in."

"So you can store it up to keep you going through the long, dark night? You speak as if you know the islands well."

"I was born and raised on Lewis for a time."

"With no cousins or siblings for company," she said sadly.

Bash had never minded being solitary. As a child, it suited him, and when he was taken aboard the ship, he'd been glad not to leave a houseful of cherished brothers and sisters behind. But, despite Maggie's own lonely brooding, something about the way she spoke of her kin, of Jory and Ellen, the Shaw Wretch and the big MacKenzie laird, it stirred a yearning for companionship deep in Bash's soul, one which must have lain dormant all this time.

"Is that why you ran away to sea?" she asked. "Because you were alone?"

"No, but perhaps it's why they let me go."

"Or they recognized you were bound for someplace warm and couldn't deny you the opportunity."

Releasing a humorless huff, Bash shook his head. "It is the irony of my life. My grandparents' greatest fear was that I'd become a pirate. Perhaps not irony. Perhaps it was destiny."

"My father's greatest fear was that I'd become a wanton whore," she said as though it were nothing at all to admit, not painful in the slightest.

Bash's heart caught in his throat. "But my grandparents were proven right," he said softly. "Their fears all came true. I am a good-for-nothing pirate." But not like the captain. Never like the captain.

Maggie nodded, seeming to understand. "Then I suppose my great irony is I went the other way, becoming a... frigid, fatuous shrew."

It sounded as though she were quoting someone.

"I would slit the throat of any man who claimed so," he whispered in her ear, leaning into her so that her next shiver set his groin on fire.

They stayed like that, stock still, until the bells rang at midnight to change the watch.

Chapter Eight

First watch passed far more pleasantly than Maggie had anticipated. With most of the crew in bed and under the shroud of darkness, she could finally let down her guard a little. It was a tremendous relief to speak candidly, almost flirtatiously, without fear of being observed or overheard.

Bash had been terribly forward, standing so close to her. Maybe he'd forgotten she was a lady at all. Or perhaps it was her—a moth responding to a flame she hadn't realized was burning, because she basked in his warmth and his nearness as though she hadn't been held in a lifetime. It made her mind drift to places she oughtn't go.

Frigid she might be, but they hadn't been all wrong about her. She was wanton. She craved touch. Connection. A kind smile, a warm hand—she had shivered from the chill, and his arms around her felt like heaven. Alone in the dark, she wasn't even ashamed to admit it. There was risk in speaking her truth out loud, the words others had said about her, but Bash didn't push her away in disgust. Quite the contrary.

Despite her exhaustion, she would have willingly stood in his arms like that until the sun came up, but when the bells were rung for second watch, he practically dragged her to the hatch, down the companionway, and into his cramped quarters. When she moved to curl up under his desk where she'd slept for the past week, he caught her wrist, stopping her.

"We can both fit," he said, eyeing her uncertainly before glancing back to his canvas hammock.

Maggie very much doubted it, but then she'd never lain in a hammock before. Perhaps it was deceptively spacious, perhaps like sleeping on a cloud. It seemed a very grave waste to sneak aboard a pirate ship and never try out a hammock, and she *was* desperately tired of lying on the hard floor. Even so...

Bash pulled his shirt over his head in one fluid motion, baring not only his bronze chest and the trail of dark hair that led to his waistband, but a ropey scar on his bicep that made her suck in her breath.

"Mags," he breathed, sitting down in the middle of the hammock and drawing her close. "We can both fit."

She stood between his legs, staring into the dark pool of his right eye. Brazenly, she flipped up the patch since he had not, a little surprised when he sat still and let her. Emboldened, she gently traced his cheekbone, avoiding the jagged scar. For days she'd been curious whether the eye was damaged from whatever encounter had scarred his cheek. Now she could see nothing but perfection as both eyes reflected back the starlight shining through a tiny porthole.

As if reading her thoughts he whispered, "It helps me to see," turning his cheek a fraction as if to kiss her fingers.

She reached to flip the patch back down, but he stopped her. "No," he said. "I want to see you."

Something about his scruffy face and earnest voice struck her with a desire to kiss him, too, and instead of being troubled by the notion and dissecting its meaning at length, she gave into the novel urge.

In her younger days, Maggie had longed to be kissed. Every

boy she met was evaluated based on the shape and plumpness of his lips. She had lain awake, night after night, imagining scenarios, tracing her own lips with an inquisitive finger. She'd begged Jory to describe kissing the Shaw Wretch, and though her cousin had been stingy with the details, Maggie gathered Finn wasn't stingy with his tongue.

She'd spent hours scouring Ellen's early letters, too, for details of the MacKenzie's lips, hidden as they were beneath his bushy beard. To her own horror, she'd even once dreamt she let the MacKenzie's younger cousin kiss her. Even more mortifying, her dream self had enjoyed it.

Then, all too soon, her wedding day had arrived, and with it, the moment Maggie had longed for. But when Jeremiah pecked her lips with his, poking her in the eye with his nose, everything changed. His kisses weren't the stuff of daydreams. By turns dry and perfunctory, they were otherwise so wet and sloppy she thought only of drying her face on her sleeve. Every time seemed dutiful and calculated, but poorly executed. Rather than excitement or lust, kissing elicited calculations. When would it end so she could breathe again? Could she wipe the spit away without drawing his wrath?

After Jeremiah's accident, gentlemen came to call. Every bachelor and widower on the island paid their respects, along with a handful of brazen schoolboys. Maggie sent them all away without even a cursory glance at their lips. She had put all manner of romantic notions behind her.

Now, in the dimly lit alcove, Bash's lips looked imminently kissable, even as he licked them nervously.

Quickly, and before she could lose her nerve, Maggie pressed her mouth to his, knowing full well what assumptions he might make, what liberties he might expect to take, knowing—but allowing herself a moment's grace not to worry—and then she promptly sat down beside him on the hammock nudging his thigh with her knee. "Scoot over a bit?"

He pushed her back to standing and swung a leg up into the hammock so he could recline on his back with one foot still on the floor. Then he tugged her hand to him and, bracing herself on his shoulders, she awkwardly straddled him for a moment as she clambered ever-so-gracefully to his side, the memory of his hard length emblazoned on her skin.

The whole hammock rocked so that Maggie fell against him, and they swung wildly until he threw his leg back over the other side to stabilize them while she scrambled to settle in. Were it not for his strong arms around her, she might have flipped right back out onto her head, but soon she found herself lying on her side, head on his shoulder, facing him as they swayed gently in the darkness.

Bash's hand came up to cup her face, and he ran a thumb over her cheek where his own scar would have been. "All right?"

"Mm," was the only reply she managed, though she was desperate to ask how he'd acquired his scar, and when.

He ran his hand down her neck to her shoulder, and he was right there, smelling like citrus and salt, his breath tickling the tiny hairs that framed her face.

"You should unbind," he whispered. "It can't be good to leave that on all the time."

Probably true, but was it worth the risk?

Searching her face, he seemed to know exactly what she was thinking.

"No one will see," he breathed, stroking her upper ribs with his knuckles.

Then he pressed his forehead to hers, and Maggie couldn't stop herself. She leaned forward and kissed him again, the soft, long, lingering sort of kiss she'd always dreamt of.

He was warm and hungry, and his breath hitched as he kissed her back, his tongue darting out to taste the bevel of her lips, until she opened them wider to let him in. He nibbled her bottom lip and then sucked on it tenderly, and dear merciful Jesus, this was what she'd always imagined kissing was supposed to be like, and more.

He kissed along her cheek, her jaw, and down her throat, and then his fingers found the edges of his cravat wrapped around her, and when he loosed it, she gasped in relief over and again, her chest heaving with each breath as he unwound the fabric beneath her shirt.

She threw her head back, drawing each new breath like it was her first, and he continued to kiss her neck and shoulder, leaving her mouth free to gulp in lungfuls of air.

Maggie was dimly aware that Bash had one hand fisted in her sark, but she jumped when the hand traveled to her belly and then up to cup her breast through the linen. Every possible emotion flooded her, leaving her wet and wanting, tears springing to her eyes.

Jeremiah had never touched her like this, like he wanted to worship at the altar of every inch of her with every inch of himself. But when she realized the hardness digging into her leg was Bash's erection, her breathing sped up for another reason altogether, and her vision began to cloud.

She hadn't been thinking clearly—about any of it. Regardless of what her body seemed to wish, she decided long ago she wanted no part in the marital act, not ever again. Not even with Bash. He was still a man, she'd do well to remember, and judging by the rest of him, it would hurt as much as it ever had.

He must have sensed the change in her because he pulled back. "Mags?"

With conflicted tears in her eyes, Maggie turned her face away, into his shoulder, and whispered, "I'm sorry."

He ran his hand over her arm again, then cupped her chin to make her look at him. With an agonized voice he asked, "Did I do something wrong?"

She shook her head and tried to whisper, "No," though she doubted he heard it. "But I can't," she said, trying to sound strong, trying to find the words to explain because even she didn't understand what she meant. She could. She *had*. And just moments ago she'd thought she might again, but she was afraid, and she needed to make him understand.

Bash simply kissed the crown of her head and rolled onto his back, one arm crooked behind his neck.

And just like that, something expanded in Maggie's chest until it burst, and she wanted him more than she'd ever wanted anyone or anything, even as the tears continued streaming down her face.

"Shhh," he soothed. "Just sleep now." He kissed her cheek, chastely, and held her tight to his side. "Just sleep."

With her hand upon his ribcage, she could feel his heart racing deep inside, her own speeding up to keep pace with his.

LYING SO STILL IT HURT, BASH WILLED HIS HEARTBEAT TO SLOW and his prick to stand down. He hadn't brought her to the hammock intending anything more than a restful night's sleep. It pained him to think of her in a pile on the floor while he and every man aboard enjoyed so much better.

He'd sworn to himself he wouldn't touch her, sworn it to Dutch, as well, but then she kissed him, and his brain turned to rum sloshing in a barrel, and he'd pawed at her like a feral dog.

Christ, she was intoxicating. Every brush against her soft skin made him feel like he was caught in a raging storm. And, though he'd never lain with a woman—how could he, when Mad kept him practically a prisoner of this floating dungeon?—he'd found himself wanting desperately to please her.

She had responded to his caress like a dying person, starving for the food of touch, and he'd grown so hard that one errant finger could have brought him to completion.

And then she'd cried.

Because what lady would want to be mauled by a scarred and stormy sailor, especially a pirate with no prospects beyond the hangman's noose? She had trusted him to keep her safe, and now she must surely fear all the strings which could so easily be attached.

Her tears dripped down his neck, tickling him as if they were his own, and he rolled over to face her again, rubbing a hand up and down her back. At least tears meant she was finally getting enough to drink.

"Mags," he whispered, and after a moment she lifted her eyes to greet his. "I'm sorry for whatever it is," he said, and she offered him a watery smile before kissing his shoulder and then his neck, and then his cheek, right where the captain had flayed him with a belaying pin when he was eleven.

She kissed along the scar, a warm trail on either side of skin which was somehow sensitive yet registered no touch. Then she found his lips again, and he kissed her back, hungrily, greedily, trying not to press his starving prick against her belly. He ran a hand lightly down her back once more and she shivered.

Christ. She was going to be the end of him, he had not one single doubt.

"How did your husband pleasure you?" he asked, shy and confused, but eager to learn, to understand, quite willing to follow her lead.

She stopped kissing him then and pressed her forehead into his chest breathing heavily. If he weren't lying in a hammock, he'd kick himself right in the arse, bastard and fool that he was for bringing up her dead lover now.

But she surprised him once more, this girl, so full of depths and eddies. "How? He didn't," she whispered. "Not even once."

Was that why she'd cried? A sick sort of rage flooded through Bash at that cold pronouncement, that he, a fumbling gelding, might have more concern for her pleasure than the man sworn above all to cherish and keep her. If the man wasn't already dead, Bash would steal her away and challenge the bastard to duel.

"Never?" he repeated, and she shook her head, burying her face as though she had aught to be ashamed of. "Then it's high time someone did," he breathed, stifling his rage as far down as it would go. "If you'll allow me?"

She faltered again, just a little, her lips pressed to his heart. "How?" she whispered again, her voice almost imperceptible.

"Is that a yes?" he clarified.

"Yes," she said, and then, "Yes, please."

"I'll stop at your command," he whispered, and then pushed up her shirt to suckle her breast, licking circles around the little pebble, while stroking her hair, her back, her perfect, round arse.

She responded at once, gasping and arching to meet his lips and his touch, and when he brought his hand around her pelvis and dipped into her waistband, her breathing sped up and he had to kiss her to sequester the tiny moan that escaped.

Over the years, his shipmates had told innumerable tales of lovers and whores, of women who liked it rough and those who required a gentler hand. Bash had listened to it all, learning to distill truth from fantasy. With the softest touch his calloused finger had ever attempted, he petted and stroked his way to her center.

The girl was wet, which he understood to be crucial, and he listened closely for changes in her breathing as he explored, searching for the magic spot men liked to brag of finding, like buried treasure all their own. When he grazed it, she arched into his hand, and he kissed her fiercely to swallow her cries, holding on tight lest she roll right out of the hammock and bring the crew crashing in on them.

He teased her soft curls and the slit beneath them, always returning to the treasure, then receding again when her whimpers grew high pitched, lapping at the spot like a tide-washed shell on the shore. All too soon she began to tremble, and he cupped the heel of his hand against that same delicious pearl, maintaining pressure as she shuddered in his arms until finally she lay still, breathing heavily against his sweaty chest.

Only then did he notice her arm around him and the raw burn from where she must have clawed his back. The sting was a delicious reminder of the ecstasy they'd just endured.

"Is that what it's supposed to be like?" she gasped.

Bash knew well enough some men were callous and others were fools, but even the selfish ones knew that attending to a woman's pleasure would only increase his own. How could any husband be so inept with a wife this pretty and full of life?

Had she lied about being married and widowed in some misguided effort to protect her virtue? Was she actually as inexperienced as he, and more so? For his mind was hardly a virgin. A tiny, dangerous thrill fluttered in his stomach.

When her breathing finally returned to normal, she kissed his cheek again and turned to wiggle out of the hammock. Would she sleep on the floor after all that?

"Stay," he whispered.

"I assumed you'd want..." She trailed off, running her hand down the outside of his breeches. His prick jerked in recognition and she drew back, momentarily startled by the ferocity of his need. *Want? Fuck yes.* But he'd done that for her and no other reason.

"Stay," he said again, moving her hand away before he could embarrass himself and foul his breeches.

He could hardly look at her, but her eyes were piercing holes in his skin, so he turned to meet their curious gaze. And then he kissed the hand he'd removed from his very disappointed prick and turned her gently so he could cuddle her close like a pair of perfectly matched spoons, tucking himself away between his legs.

"Mrow," the cat murmured, padding past his curtain and right up next to the hammock. Bash reached a lazy hand down to stroke the wee beast and pretended to sleep, hoping to conjure a way to keep up their charade forever instead of putting her on the first ship back to Scotland.

Or they could find some remote and uninhabited island. He'd have to consult his waggoner to find the perfect spot. After he fashioned a shelter out of fallen trees, and with no pirate hunters to bother them, they could spend their days fishing and their nights making love upon the sand.

He would teach her the name of every star in the sky, and she could teach him the name of every member of her extensive family, and then they could begin a family of their own—and keep going until they ran out of names of either stars or Scots.

It was a beautiful sort of dream, the kind that physically ached to wake up from, the kind you could never cling to for long before reality rose up to punch you in the jaw.

She was an educated girl with a family and a home. She wouldn't wish to trade one island prison for another, even if he would promise her the warmth she was chasing. And besides all that, neither the navy nor Mad MacLeod was likely to let him sail away and start a life someplace new.

The sooner he put her on a boat back to Scotland, the better off they'd both be. Best he could do was offer her safety on her adventure and open her eyes to the sort of pleasure she should demand from her next husband.

Chapter Nine

Strangely, Maggie had never felt more rested than she did each morning after spending the night wrapped in Bash's arms, swaying with the swell of the sea.

After a week of sleeping side by side in the hammock, she still marveled at the fact that she didn't feel crowded out by him. The canvas expanded to cradle them both, and his body heat provided the cozy warmth she'd been longing for. He didn't kiss her again or touch her in the way he had the first night, but his arms around her kept her safe and still, so she never once feared she might tumble out.

How many times had she woken in the bed she shared with Jeremiah, squeezing herself so close to the edge one flinch might send her sprawling to the floor? It wasn't necessarily because he took up too much room, but even her unconscious mind had been desperate to put space between them. How strange then, to find comfort in proximity now. She tried not to dwell on what it might mean.

The truth was, Maggie didn't like to think too hard about her marriage. Usually, such memories brought a headache and a queasy stomach, but it was growing harder to keep from comparing the past with her present situation. Jeremiah had been her husband. He had touched her everywhere, but he'd never touched her in the way Bash now had. He'd also called her every insult under the sun, and now perhaps she'd earned some of those epithets, for she'd finally indulged her most wicked desires.

Perhaps her soul was damned to hell, because Maggie didn't feel wicked, and she certainly didn't feel sorry. No, she felt amazed. She felt worshipped—like a goddess in a temple surrounded by men whose sole purpose in life was to pleasure her and only her.

Had she actually died? Was this ship some kind of strange bacchanal limbo?

He was there now, hard behind her, as he'd been each morning since that night a week ago. She wondered, not for the first time, which other activities might be possible within the confines of a hammock.

Who even was she, to consider such things? These were the naughty musings of teenage Maggie, who had long since been replaced by the version in a cage. By professing to the world that she was a child of fourteen, had Bash spoken her naive lust back into existence? A year ago, awareness of Jeremiah's arousal made her sick to her stomach, but not now. Not with Bash.

No, Bash the pirate was going to be trouble.

As he came awake, he nuzzled the back of her neck, sending a shower of shivers down her spine, then he moved his braw arm off her, brushing the side of her breast in the process, murmuring, "Sorry."

Maggie hoped he wasn't actually sorry. She never wanted to leave this cozy cocoon.

His hand came to rest on her hip bone, and he whispered as he had each morning, "Best you sit up first, and get your feet under you, else we'll both wind up on the floor." The fantasy was over yet again. Time to go back to being pirates, the sailing master and his obedient cabin boy.

She'd like to show him just how obedient she could be. *Settle. Down.*

Maggie did as he'd instructed, snatching up his cravat to rebind herself. When she peeked over her shoulder to ensure he wasn't watching, she noticed faint red scratches on his back. A reminder of their time together a few nights ago? Beneath those fading marks was a crisscross of old, healed-over scars.

She opened her mouth to ask, but then he cast a glance back at her, catching her looking, and she swallowed her questions. In the next moment, he pulled on his shirt and stepped out of the alcove, giving her privacy to finish dressing. She tucked some dried beef into her pocket for later and headed above deck after him.

Each night after the first, there had been no discussion or negotiation. Bash simply pulled off his shirt and nodded towards the hammock before they tumbled in together and fell asleep. Each night she had hoped to revisit their nocturnal activities, and each night she could feel the restraint in his taut muscles as he tucked himself away and lay stock still.

Her disappointment had been tempered by exhaustion, along with the peacefulness of simply being held as the ship rocked her to sleep.

Last night they had once again taken the late watch, and Maggie savored the time alone with him outside under a magnificent cloak of stars.

"Do you ever get homesick?" she had finally asked.

"For Scotland, you mean? Not as such."

"You don't consider yourself from there?"

"Sometimes I feel like I'm from nowhere," he admitted.

She wanted to ask him all kinds of questions then, but before she settled on the right one, he went on. "In some ways, home is more of a person than a place, innit?"

"How do you mean?"

"Lewis was only home because my Ma was there. Once she

was gone, and my grandparents not long after, there was no one left who wanted me. It stopped being home."

It had broken Maggie's heart to picture him as a child, unwanted and alone. "It's kind of strange, when you think about it," she mused. "Not enough people wanted you, and too many want me—potential husbands, I mean. And yet we're sort of the same. All alone."

"Will you marry again?" he had asked softly.

"My father wishes me to. He has another bridegroom all picked out and ready to stand up in a kirk."

"What do you want?" Bash had asked, and Maggie inhaled sharply.

Had anyone ever asked her that before and really meant it?

"I just want to be someplace warm."

Lorna had scoffed at that answer, but Bash nodded as if he understood everything the dream encompassed. Perhaps they were even more alike than she realized.

WITHOUT MAGGIE NOTICING A CHANGE DAY TO DAY, THEY HAD finally reached *someplace warm*. The atmosphere felt different when she joined Bash on deck with a tankard of rum for each of them.

It was a little humid and sweaty, as though the very air was reflecting her mood and secret desires.

"Good—" Bash rumbled when she offered him the drink, but he cut himself off and accepted the mug, raising it in toast. "Good idea, Mags. Best way to start the day. Stick close, aye?" he added.

Did he feel the frenetic undercurrent in the air too?

"Has the wind changed?" she asked. "Do we still head towards Boston?"

"No. We're right on course." He squinted past her, his tongue poking out like a cat tasting the air.

The pink of his tongue made her wonder—did the tips of his

ears burn the same color when he grew embarrassed like her brothers-in-law? And what would embarrass a man like Bash, used to living cheek by jowl with this bawdy lot?

She was still staring at his tongue when a shadow fell over them, and with it, a chill. Maggie glanced beyond his shoulder in time to see a magnificent black creature flopping back into the brine.

"Jesus, Mary, and Joseph," she exclaimed, running to the forecastle so she could peer over the side at the wide, diamond-shaped shadow floating in the water.

"Another whale?" Bash asked, joining her at the railing.

"I don't think so. More like a... I don't know, a giant oyster outside its shell, all floppy and wide? There it is!" She pointed at the dark shadow, nearly as broad as the very deck beneath their feet, floating like a shawl carelessly tossed overboard.

Bash frowned into the water, throwing an arm protectively in front of her to make her step back.

Flapping its fins like the wings of a seagull, the creature flew from the water once more in a perfect arc, this time exposing its white belly to the sun before diving back into the water and then coming back again for another go. Forward arc, backward flip, and then forward arc again, the creature leaped and dove with balletic precision, almost as though someone beneath the surface were tossing it to and fro.

"Did you see it, Nav?" the junior sailor, Langley, called, pounding up to them with a look of horror on his sunburned face. "It's an ill omen, that," he panted, stopping at the edge of the forecastle, hesitant to come any nearer. "Should we shoot it?"

"You've seen a devil ray before, surely," Bash said, exuding a calm that belied the way he'd pushed Maggie away from the railing.

"Never one so monstrous big, have you?"

"Maybe not this big, Langley, but the sea is full of all sorts. Despite its name, it means no harm."

The ray continued to dance alongside them, as though it were performing a sort of magic meant to mesmerize, and it was working. Maggie was certainly spellbound.

"Never saw one do that before, neither. Doesn't have to mean evil to bring it," Langley protested, then he lowered his voice to a fast whisper. "Your adversary, the devil, prowls around like a roaming lion, seeking someone to devour." He made the sign of the cross, and then for good measure crossed himself a second time.

"It's neither roared nor prowled, and last I checked, rays don't eat people. Man your post," Bash chided, eyeing the creature warily.

"You never saw one that size before, you said. Fella that big would need more'n prawns to keep its strength up. Maybe it'll open its gullet like a snake and swallow the whole brig in one giant gulp."

Bash sighed and shook his head, while Maggie bounced on her toes and grabbed hold of her elbows to keep from clapping with delight, refusing to let Langley's fear infect her.

"Devil ray," she repeated, shivering, as the giant beast cast them in shadow and sea spray once more. She liked the way its name sounded like devilry, something she'd been accused of plenty throughout her childhood. "I think it wants to be friends."

Langley scoffed but Bash laughed. "If anyone could achieve such a feat, it's surely you."

She feigned a skeptical expression, though she still didn't take her eyes off the leaping ray. "Because I've some great knack for charming the devil?"

"I believe you could charm anyone you put your mind to, Mags," he rumbled in his deep, growly voice, making her stomach do backflips just like the flying fish out there, which continued to frolic, though somewhat less enthusiastically as the *Revenge* continued on its course and out of the ray's territory.

It was simply magical. "You've seen such creatures before?" she asked, wide-eyed.

"Aye, big ones, and tiny wee ones, too. Their skin is soft as buttered leather."

"What a strange and wondrous place this ocean of yours is," she murmured.

"Aye," Bash agreed. "And it's playing all its best numbers just for you."

Maggie beamed, but she still couldn't bring herself to break her gaze as the ray grew smaller and smaller in the distance. If she glanced away even for a second, she might never see another such creature again.

With all Jory had encountered in her travels, Maggie bet she'd never even heard of a devil ray or seen such a breathtaking sight. They wouldn't believe the stories she'd have to tell.

Maybe this adventure hadn't been such a terribly rash misjudgment after all. She was certainly richer for having taken it.

"I'm telling you, Nav, it's a sign, and not a good one," Langley said, daring to step closer now the beast was far away. Maggie had forgotten he was even there.

"Return to your post, Langley," Bash said again with a slightly irritated tone that suggested he'd forgotten too.

"Middle watch claim they may have seen sails."

"May have?" Bash repeated, stern but not unkind.

"Everyone's saying."

"Who saw it?"

Langley scratched his head. "Dunno, but they're saying it's the *Woebegone*. They're saying we've found Willy Walsh at last!"

Bash's eyes darted to Maggie, and he took out his spyglass.

"Willy Walsh, is it?"

"Aye, Nav. Sure as beans the devil means to trick us somehow."

"Did you also reckon it was a sign when we encountered the whale last week?"

"Aye, Nav, course. Meant we'd find him, and now we have."

"But we didn't find him last week, did we?" Bash asked, turning the glass out to scan the water.

"No, but you know how these things—"

"So even if the ray was a sign, might have naught to do with Walsh."

"It's a sign, sure as beans, and not the only one."

"Who was on second watch, Langley?"

The young man's face fell. "Dunno. Balthasar and Samson, maybe."

Bash's eyes flicked to Maggie and away so fast she thought she had imagined it. "Balthasar was on watch with Samson?"

Langley shrugged. "Traded with the Butcher."

Bash set his mouth in a firm line.

"Spread the word, aye. Anyone who glimpsed the *Woebegone Whale* should come and speak to me, understand? Now go on back to your post."

"Aye, Nav," Langley said, looking out towards the ray and crossing himself once more before he hurried off.

Maggie had overheard bits and pieces about Willy Walsh since coming aboard, but she couldn't reconcile the excitement of most sailors with Bash's present agitation.

"Who is he? Willy Walsh?" she asked, peering earnestly up into Bash's dark, stormy face.

"No one, if he knows what's good for him," Bash replied.

"I take it you've heard?" the quartermaster asked, coming to lean against the rail on Bash's other side.

"Ravings of drunkards, nothing more. Wishful thinking. What would Walsh be doing all the way out here?"

"Captain told them he returned to Scotland. As far as they're concerned, he's but one step ahead of us and losing ground."

"You and I both know the value of that story," Bash grumbled.

Dutch merely shrugged. "Maybe you and I were wrong."

The two men exchanged a dark look that Maggie couldn't

interpret, and then Bash turned back to scan the ocean again. "Well there's no sign of him now."

"You think it was a ghost ship?" Dutch asked in a voice so low Maggie wasn't sure she heard correctly.

"Or our old friend from the navy. He does so love a game of cat and mouse."

Dutch's mouth was drawn, but he nodded in what looked like agreement.

Maggie wasn't sure which she preferred between a ghost, a whale, and the navy. She'd much rather dancing devil rays and stolen moments below deck in a certain navigator's hammock. She didn't know if she believed in signs good or bad, but the air still felt different today, and that made her ill at ease.

"Gentlemen," the captain called, striding up the deck with an unusually energetic gait. "I understand we dine on whale tonight."

Bash's heart sank. If there was no ship, the men would be all riled up with nothing to do. And if there was one, how was he going to protect Maggie as they went charging into battle, cannons blazing?

He was third in command of a ship of one hundred men, the only expert in navigational science, and yet he'd never felt so powerful as he did when she allowed herself to come apart in his arms—when she allowed him the chance to take her to that height. He wanted a thousand more chances and a thousand after that. He was far too distracted to face the likes of Willy Walsh or an angry mob of his own men, either one.

" 'Tis a rumor, Cap. You know the value of that," he protested, but Mad ignored his words, as well as the presence of Dutch and Maggie, stepping up nose to nose with Bash.

"That would be a personal disappointment, boy," he said. "You know I've a very fond taste for whale meat."

"We'll double the lookouts up top," Bash assured him.

The captain's lips curved into a sneer. "Double zero is still zero."

"Zero?" Bash craned his neck to scan the platform at the top of the foremast, then, seeing no one, he stepped around Dutch to glimpse the main mast. Both empty. "Where are the watchmen?"

The captain jerked his head towards a nearby circle of sailors hurling eggs up at the mast shouting and being shouted at by Roo.

"I'll fry up your liver and loins when we run out of grub, you rutting kloothommels!"

"Attempting to de-kestrel the tops," the captain explained gleefully. And sure enough, a bird flapped and squawked around them. But a kestrel?

The Butcher stepped up with a blunderbuss, took aim, and fired, the lead ball tearing right through the recently mended main sail. Furious, the bird flew directly at him, flapping its wings defiantly in his face, dodging the men who attempted to hit it with shirts and neckcloths they'd stripped off to the purpose.

"Stop!" Maggie yelled, and Bash felt the color drain from his own face just as hers reddened.

She was an enigma, too bold and brash by half, blustering into his life like a hurricane, with a glare that could grab any man by the balls. And yet the other night, she had grown soft and fearful in his arms, then come back to him again under his touch in a way that gave him life. Now she seemed determined to be the death of him.

The captain turned his cold, beady gaze and lascivious grin on the girl. Had she somehow just earned herself a legitimate flogging while Bash was woolgathering?

"Your cabin boy has a tender heart," Mad sneered, not taking his eyes off Maggie, who licked her lips and swallowed, but didn't back down. "That infernal crow has made a nest of my tops. It attacks any man who tries to take the watch."

"Isn't killing it bad luck, sir?" she tried, her voice low and raspy, stoking the lust already burning deep in Bash's loins.

The captain pinned her with his gaze, and Maggie lifted her chin as though the unconscious gesture might keep her from shriveling before the madman.

"Worse luck not to," Dutch reasoned, "what with rumors of ships about."

"The child could be right," the captain shouted to get the crew's attention, and Bash's gut twisted. The captain's agreement never ended well for whatever poor soul Mad had in his sights.

The Butcher shot at the kestrel again and feathers rained down on them as the bird darted safely away.

"Stop," the captain ordered as Maggie rubbed her ears, no doubt to ease their ringing after the gun blast. "What would you have us do, Magnus?" he asked her almost kindly, laying a trap. There could be no right answer.

"Since when do we seek guidance from the cabin boy?" Bash jumped in, sacrificing himself in her place. Mad cut him with a glare so sharp he could almost feel the lash of the cat across his tender back, but he refused to shrink. "You said yourself, he's a child."

"I seem to recall another cabin boy who was full to bursting with opinions you thought worth sharing," Mad sneered. "Though I suppose, under Dutch's guiding hand, you eventually grew up."

"Still full of opinions, though." Bash tried to lace his words with levity instead of venom. If Mad could hear the difference, he didn't let on. They were both all too aware of their audience, and Bash could swear the phantom stings of long-healed scars burned as sweat trickled down his skin.

Then Mad turned to Maggie. "A ship was spotted which bears the colors of my old nemesis, a man with no scruples, who stole my property and has been on the run these twenty years. Such fortune as we might all retire and live out our days in splendor. Surely that is worth the life of one obnoxious bird? Righting old wrongs after all this time must cancel out any ill the bird's death might herald."

Maggie blinked at him like he was speaking in riddles.

"What would you do, if you were boatswain instead of him?" the captain implored her, goading Bash, trying to create a rift.

She swallowed again and licked her lips, which, to his imagination, still looked bruised from kissing even all these days later. She glanced at Bash, almost as though she were seeking permission, and when he nodded, she took a deep breath and nodded back.

"I suppose, sir, I would try to bring it down alive," she said, and Bash silently cursed.

Bugger Mad, and bugger luck, and bugger that buggered bird.

"It's only protecting what it perceives as its own, same as you."

They all turned towards the kestrel—why the blazes was there a kestrel this far out to sea?—then they were forced back a step as it shat at them. Very like Mad, indeed.

Maggie cleared her throat. "That way, you won't cancel out your good fortune in finally locating the thief who wronged you."

The deck had never been more silent as a collective breath was held, waiting to see how the captain would react.

Mad clapped her on the shoulder, drawing her to his side, jostling her roughly, but patting her on the back, though Bash still half expected him to slit her throat in the same motion.

"Cap?" Roo called from the circle of men still awaiting orders.

"Magnus will go up," Mad replied, turning an expectant smirk on Maggie.

Christ. She was well and truly caught in the trap he'd so artfully laid, its jaws springing shut.

Mad tossed her his spyglass. "Have a look around while you're up there."

She turned to Bash once more, and on his grim nod, she set her shoulders and walked into the circle of men.

Langley stepped forward and handed over a small basket on a long strap, now empty of eggs, and she hung it crosswise over her shoulder, as the others moved back to give her room.

She was a good climber, and canny. Even with that beast diving at her, she would probably be fine, but Bash stepped closer all the same, calculating where she'd land if she did fall, where he'd need to stand so he could catch her.

He should volunteer to take her place, but Mad would find a way to punish them both. A real man would stand up to the captain, sacrifice himself while still protecting her. But if Bash knew how to do that, he'd have done it a hundred times over.

All he could do was trust her to remember everything he'd taught, hope for a good outcome, and try not get hard watching from below as she climbed—try not to envision her climbing him. *Stand easy, sailor.*

She truly was a marvel to behold, despite the angry bird circling her, and not just because of her marvelous arse. She climbed with a skill that belied her inexperience, and Bash was pleased she didn't go too fast or look down. She was a quicker student than he'd ever been, may God have mercy on them both.

Chapter Ten

After the initial shock of being up so high her first time in the rigging, Maggie had enjoyed the climb. Her muscles had ached for days, but the good kind of ache, from having done something new and helpful. The view alone was worth it, unlike anything she'd ever imagined. Now, as she climbed once more, her body came alive with excitement. From all the way up in the tops, would she be able to catch one last glimpse of the giant devil ray with its white belly and flapping wings? The way it soared, perhaps it should have been called an angel ray instead.

Her neck prickled with the weight of so many eyes, but she would show them. She'd show them all.

Less than a dozen feet into her ascent, however, the angry kestrel flew right at her, forcing her to duck, and she almost lost her grip despite being careful not to look down. Then something smacked into her cheek and out of instinct she jumped away, letting go with her right hand to cover her face. She swung dangerously by the other hand as her feet scrambled for purchase, yanking her shoulder almost out of place.

Down below, a few men guffawed, but another roared in fury.

Catching her breath, Maggie rubbed her stinging cheek, and her fingers came away sticky with dark yellow yolk.

She chanced a look down and saw Bash shouting in the face of a shameful-looking pirate, Bash's own face livid and red as beetroot. She didn't need him flying to her defense, but her traitorous heart swelled at the sight. Who else but Jory had ever done as much for her? Grinning, she wiped the egg off her hand onto the ropes and resumed her climb.

A few minutes later, the kestrel squawked, diving again, and Maggie closed her eyes and held on tight, burying her face in the crook of her arm. She was only just discovering the beauty of this big, wide world. It wouldn't do at all to have her eyes pecked out so soon.

The bird came back for another pass, and this time Maggie felt a sharp sting where it must have pulled out a few strands of hair.

"Shh, shh, shh," she whispered as either of her brothers-in-law might soothe a horse.

Whether comforted by her shushing or not, the bird laid off its attack, so Maggie continued to climb until the kestrel grew agitated once more. Again, she wrapped her arms around the ropes and ducked her head, trying desperately not to fall. "Shh, shh, shh," she said again. "Don't you know I'm the one stopping them from shooting at you?"

When it flew back to its perch at the very top, Maggie took a moment to gaze out across the ocean, where aqua water met azure sky on a vanishing blue horizon. She must have stared at a similar, if greyer, view on the boat over to Orkney, but stared without seeing, for this was entirely new. It was worth the climb, worth the danger, even worth the angry kestrel, for who could ever tire of such a sight?

Lucky bird, she wanted to tell it, *to see this from your perch every day. If only you could coexist.*

Not realizing how lucky it was, the kestrel grew more frantic about her intrusion, flapping its wings in her face and squawking angrily in her ears.

What would Jory do? she wondered. *Or gentle Wee Ellen?*

When Maggie was a very little girl, storms upset her terribly, and she would rage as though she could outscream the thunder—as though if she kicked up a bigger fuss than the weather did, she could chase the lightning away. Her parents were at a loss. They tried consoling her, and they tried birching her, and eventually they gave up and left her to destroy the furniture in her chamber all alone, flying at anyone who entered, talons bared, not unlike this poor bird.

But Ellen couldn't stand to see her little sister so distraught. She came to Maggie, singing some made-up wordless hymn, and somehow it had settled her restless soul when nothing else could. The melody came back to her now, and she offered her voice to the kestrel, which finally returned to its perch. Maggie hummed louder as the bird bobbed up and down, not in time to the music, but sizing her up for its next attack.

She sang louder still, hoping the men below wouldn't hear her and guess by her voice that she wasn't actually a boy, not that she really need worry. Jeremiah liked to say she sang like a dying duck.

The kestrel watched suspiciously as Maggie reached the top platform, pulling herself up and grabbing hold of the railing. It cocked its head and blinked, but Maggie kept singing softly and it tolerated her approach.

Catching it, however, would be a whole other thing.

She stared out across the water once more, and the bird hopped down onto the railing, casting so much side-eye in her direction that it reminded her a little of her cousin Lennox.

"I'm sorry, Kes," she cooed to the bird. "I know you've found the perfect spot, but it won't do. Not if it gets you shot for your trouble."

The bird stepped to the left, then the right, moving closer, bobbing its head again.

"You know men," Maggie sighed. "They'll have their way, and like as not, eat you for dinner now they've wasted half the eggs."

Her stomach growled, and she remembered the dried beef in her pocket.

"I suppose you eat fish," she said, taking out a strip of beef and holding it flat on her palm the way Finn taught her to feed carrots to his Clydesdale. "Don't imagine this will interest you?"

The kestrel bobbed its head once more and snatched the meat from her hand, gobbling it up.

"That's a good girl, Kes! You're a pretty girl, aren't you?"

Kes trilled in reply.

"I don't actually know if you're a girl or a boy, but you're pretty all the same."

She offered another bite of beef, and Kes took it without hesitation, scrutinizing Maggie's every movement. She held out one more piece to distract the bird, and caught it with her other hand, letting it snag the beef before she settled it into the basket Langley had given her.

"Shh, shh, shh," she crooned. "You'll be all right."

Standing on the platform, leaning out over the rail, she took one last longing look for her big grey and white ray, this time through the captain's spyglass.

She almost missed it—would have done if not for the way the sunlight glinted off the sails. Not her ray, but way out almost as far as she could see, there was a ship, sailing fast. It flew a black flag with a white blob.

She squinted through the spyglass, relaxing her left eye, and twisted the shaft as Bash had shown her. The white blob morphed into a fish, not unlike an illustration of Jonah's whale, with a cutlass beneath. After the rumors of ghost ships that circulated like currency, Bash would want to know about this straight away.

Maggie climbed quickly back down holding the guide rope as Bash had taught her, an angry squawking bird rattling the basket at her side.

The moment her feet touched the deck, a rousing cheer went up from the circle of men, and Bash picked her up and swung her around.

"Careful," she exclaimed, holding the basket out of harm's way, until he set her down again.

"Well done," the captain said in a cold, begrudging tone.

"How'd you do it, Magnus?" Duffy asked.

"Magic," Bash whispered, nodding at her reverently, and Maggie felt hot all over.

"Magic," Samson grinned, nodding along with Bash.

"Huh?" Duffy asked.

"Sorcery, innit?" Bash teased. "Forenoon watch," he bellowed, jerking his head toward the tops. "Man your posts, you lubbers. Double up!"

"Wait," Maggie called, a little breathless. "Sails," she said, and the deck fell silent.

"You saw sails?" Dutch repeated.

"How many masts?" Bash asked.

"One. A sloop, I think."

He smiled at her and she practically melted into a puddle of wanting.

"What banner did she fly?" he asked, darting a glance towards the captain.

"Black. With a white round fish or whale and a sword on it."

Another silence fell, this one palpable. The air practically hummed with excitement. And then the men erupted into more cheers, jumping up and down, pushing and shoving, and tossing her about. Samson did a back flip. It was quite the stramash.

Bash waived the men up the rigging, and then hovered as the captain approached Maggie. She offered him his spyglass, but he pushed it back to her chest.

"Keep it." Then he patted her shoulder and walked away.

"Shall I take the hen for you?" Roo asked, nodding at her basket of kestrel with a toothy grin.

"No!" she exclaimed. "If you thought it was bad luck to shoot her, you don't want to see what will happen if you eat her!"

"Found the *Whale*," Roo pouted. "Seems like good luck to me."

"What will you do with her?" Bash asked.

"I was hoping to let her rest in a quiet corner below deck," she said, and Roo guffawed.

"Looks like your pet has found a pet there, Bashy."

Bash glared at the cook but gestured for Maggie to lead the way below deck.

No sooner had they entered his alcove, however, than Bash pushed her against the bulkhead, surprising her so she almost dropped the basket she was taking off her shoulder.

She looked up at him, searching his eyes, and he took her face in both hands, staring at her in a way that made it impossible to breathe, running his thumbs along each side of her jaw. Then he crashed his lips against hers, frantically, hungrily, like if he reined himself in any longer he'd burst.

His whole body was so close, as though he would climb inside her skin if he could, and Maggie wanted him to, even as she felt his heartbeat through the bulge hardening against her stomach. Then, just as abruptly, he ripped himself back, pressing only his forehead to hers and breathing heavily.

She didn't remember grabbing him, but there were fistfuls of his shirt balled in her hands, which she released, noting how crumpled the fabric had become.

"I messed up your sark," she said, still gasping for breath after such a thorough kissing.

"No matter," he replied in a rough whisper.

Kes squawked grumpily.

Just within reach, there was a small ledge where the bulkhead and the upper deck met, and she stood on her toes, stretching to place the basket and open it before stepping back.

Bash watched, frowning, as the bird hopped out of the basket, tossing them both a dirty look, then hunkered back down quietly in her new nest box.

"Why are you glaring at her like that?" Maggie asked, noting Bash's wary scowl. "Did you really mind bringing her in?"

He shook his head. "Kestrel," he said, frowning even more deeply. "This far out on the open sea? Where the devil did she come from?"

Now it was Maggie's turn to frown.

"So you do believe in omens? Like Langley and the rest?"

"Dunno what to think," Bash admitted, drawing Maggie back against his chest with one arm, kissing the top of her head as they watched the bird settle in. "Perhaps the fool thing snuck aboard in Scotland, same as you."

Yet again, she couldn't dodge the desire to stay right there in his little alcove for the rest of forever.

THE LOOKOUTS CONFIRMED MAGGIE'S SIGHTING, AND A COURSE was laid for a furtive interception. The evening's revelry was unlike anything she'd yet experienced.

Prevented from cooking the kestrel, Roo killed the last two fat hens instead. It was an optimistic move, but Maggie supposed they would soon capture the *Woebegone Whale* and be inundated with whatever livestock and provisions were aboard.

The cook stuffed his birds with corn and who knew what all, and roasted them up, before making the men arm wrestle for the chance to snap apart the collarbones for luck. Everyone was joyous and rowdy, finishing off the dregs of bumbo and starting in on the Scottish ale.

She, too, felt tipsy and thirsty, with a thirst no amount of drink could ever quench. She finally fit somewhere, never mind it was amongst pirates, passing as one of them, assumed name and all. They loved her for having spotted the *Woebegone Whale*, not to mention ridding them of the pesky bird, and they made it clear, offering her tankard after tankard.

Only Bash seemed reticent about the coming days. He sat apart, quietly observing the celebrations like a glowering figurehead on a forbidding prow. His mood was the only thing to temper Maggie's spirits, reminding her of the battle and bloodshed looming on the horizon.

When they grew too drunk to continue dancing around the tables, several men began tussling over a deck of cards.

"Oh!" Maggie remembered. "You were going to teach me how to play!"

"Aye," Bash said.

"Now's good a time as any, Bashy," Roo said. "Shall we deal you in?"

"Not tonight," Bash answered, steering Maggie through the rowdy throng, muttering, "Friends don't let friends wager when they're in their cups."

"Is that what we are?" Maggie asked, smiling giddily, warmth spreading through her that was wholly unrelated to the ale. *Friends.*

She hadn't had one in so very long. Lorna had been the only person on Orkney she'd have called a friend, and the woman was more of a conveniently located acquaintance—a neighbor who tolerated her because of the only things they had in common: their gender and their proximity.

When they finally snuck away from the celebration, Maggie was thankful there was no detour to the upper deck. The last thing she wanted to do tonight was keep watch.

A million different questions swirled through her mind now they were finally alone. Bash, however, still seemed disinclined to speak, so she crossed to the bird's basket and delivered some corn she'd stashed away during dinner.

"Hello, beautiful Kes," she crooned, and the bird squawked at her, gobbling up the corn immediately.

"Reckon she'd rather have a go at the rats," Bash suggested. "The mouser won't be happy to share."

When she turned around again, Maggie found herself faced with the glorious sight of a shirtless Bash. As he bent over a bowl to wash his face, the muscles in his back rippled under the patchwork of crisscrossed scars. In their tiny alcove, he was close enough she could reach out and touch those scars, and this time she surrendered to temptation.

His skin was warm and soft, but he jumped at her touch, so she snatched her hand away. Turning swiftly, he caught her.

"Like ice," he growled, and her stomach did a little flip. "Shall I warm them?" he asked, entwining her fingers with his.

"Yes, please," she whispered, and he pulled her close, drawing her into an embrace.

"Always so polite. A proper lady," he murmured.

She stroked his back hesitantly. "Does it hurt?"

"Not anymore," he said, shutting down further questions. "Were you really married?" he asked, and she froze.

She didn't want to think about Jeremiah right now. "Briefly," she said.

"How brief?" he rasped. "A day?"

"A year and a bit."

"And in all that time, he never tried to seduce you?"

Maggie didn't know how to answer. A flood of memories came crashing forward, threatening to drown her, and for some reason she began to tremble. What did she know of seduction—she who had never enjoyed a single moment in her husband's bed?

"I'm sorry," Bash whispered. "I'm beginning to suspect your husband was—"

"He was real," she snapped, pulling back, and he cocked his head.

"I'm beginning to suspect he was a fucking fool."

A laugh bubbled out of her, surprising them both, and he held her tighter, running a hand gently over her short-cropped hair.

"Why?" she managed to say. "How do you seduce the ladies you meet at port?"

When he didn't answer except to still his hand, she drew back again to study him, and his eyes flashed, recognizing her challenge. Then he looked away, at the floor, pink creeping up his neck and tinging his cheeks and the tips of his ears as deliciously as she'd hoped. He leaned against the opposite bulkhead, putting as much space as possible between them in the tiny berth, and shoved his hands in his pockets.

The chill that settled in that few feet of space made Maggie immediately sorry for her question, and she searched the room for something else to say to make it better.

"I could show you," he answered softly, "what I would do were I ever allowed to leave the ship."

She didn't quite understand his admission. Was he more or less a prisoner? The very notion broke another wall within her, and she flew into his arms, kissing him with every bit of pent-up yearning she'd ever felt in all her twenty years of living.

After a moment, he broke the kiss and held her at arm's length. "Is that a yes?" he asked, peering intently into her eyes.

"Yes," she said, trembling for a different reason this time. "Please."

She gazed up at him, and he offered her the most roguish of smiles, and Maggie's breath caught in her throat.

He stepped forward and for some reason she stepped back, brushing against the hammock. She couldn't imagine what he had in mind, and she was both terrified and not. It made her dizzy.

"Sit," he whispered in her ear, and she sat on the hammock. "Lie back," he added, taking his yellow-and-black plaid from the corner cabinet and kneeling before her so his chiseled jaw and that roguish dimple were at eye level.

When she didn't move, he stretched the hammock around her to support her back and head, pulling her forward so she sat right at the edge, sure to tumble out in the least ladylike of puddles.

"You're shivering," he said, draping the plaid around her.

"I'm not," she lied, and his dimple deepened.

"What will you say if you want me to stop?" he asked, leaning towards her on his knees.

"Stop," she whispered, and he drew back, hands in the air.

"Go," she giggled, and this time when he grinned, he transformed into a mischievous schoolboy with ridiculously tousled hair.

He tugged at the string securing her breeches, and then lowered them, his eyebrows lifting in delighted surprise when he found she'd fashioned a pair of smalls for underneath. He grinned naughtily, reaching for the next drawstring.

"Will there be another pair, I wonder?" he teased. "Even smaller than these?"

"Stop," she said, and he froze. "Will you be disappointed if there isn't?"

"Nothing about you could ever disappoint me," he said earnestly, and what was left of Maggie's bones melted right out of her body.

"Go," she whispered, and he lowered her drawers and clicked his tongue with a smile.

"What a shame."

Then he slipped her legs over his shoulders and ducked his head under the plaid, kissing up her leg and behind her knee and along the crease of her hip, all her most ticklish places, making her squirm.

"So impatient," he murmured, placing a steadying hand on her low belly. She tried to be still—so still that he poked his head out from under the plaid. "Understandable, when your pleasure's been ignored for so very long. Were I your husband, I'd attend to you every day. Twice on Sundays."

Maggie had the vague thought that such a promise might get her to a kirk on Sundays again. Her stomach flipped over and over, as though the hammock were swinging wildly instead of being held still by Bash.

And then he kissed her where he'd touched her before, and she heard herself whimper as her eyes rolled back in her head.

"Shh," he whispered, nipping at the inside of her thigh, and she put an arm over her face to smother her moans just in time, for the next moment he licked up the length of her and she gasped aloud.

With one gentle hand he spread her while the other ventured up to find her breasts, which she quickly unwrapped beneath the plaid. As he licked lazy circles around her most sensitive spot, he mirrored the motion with a featherlight finger around each breast, and she pulled the blanket tight against her face to muffle her panting.

The same tingly tension which had built within her the prior week began to hum inside her head and inside her core, and she pushed herself wantonly against him, which seemed to encourage him for soon he was holding onto her bucking hips, flicking her torturously with his tongue until she was jerking against him, vibrating from tip to toe, riding the crest of an endless wave and drifting far out to sea.

Chapter Eleven

Tasting Maggie was better than Bash had ever imagined, and he'd imagined it plenty—first in theory, with nameless, faceless women from the docks, and then approximately fifty different times with Maggie since the moment he found her hiding in the hold.

It was amazing, but it was also a careless, stupid thing to do, especially so early in the night with the ship all in an uproar and the lantern still lit.

At first, he thought he heard the nosy cat coming to investigate, and he chuckled against Maggie's bucking pelvis. Then his brain caught up to his ears, recognizing the tread of man-sized boots. Eager to bring the girl to her peak, he dismissed all caution and simply hoped the boots would pass on by.

When his curtain was yanked unceremoniously aside and a second lantern shoved in to blind him, he had blinked up into the disappointed face of his mentor. Thank Christ he'd had the foresight to throw his tartan over Maggie, or else Dutch would be in on the greater part of their secret, instead of merely disgusted by his lack of restraint.

After a painful moment in which he took in the scene and

digested it, Dutch had whisked the curtain closed once more leaving Maggie none the wiser, and Bash had channeled all his adrenaline into finishing her off quite thoroughly. He was grateful she'd been too deep in the throes of passion to register the interruption, because apart from that, it was ecstasy made flesh.

He shifted her boneless form ninety degrees and joined her in the hammock, tucking his aching prick away from her and drawing her bottom into his lap, her naked, sweaty back against his chest. He'd never thought of himself as starved for touch, but he craved the contact with her and burrowed his face into her neck as she recovered her senses, reveling in the feel of skin on skin.

Guilt lapped at his conscience for lingering in bed with her when it was past time they planned tomorrow's raid, but he would rather pretend it wasn't happening for just a little while longer. Dutch wasn't shy. If he felt strongly about it, he'd have stayed, no matter what Bash was doing.

"Thank you," Maggie panted, and it made him smile all over. Even his toes were smiling.

"My pleasure," he murmured, and she giggled. "What?"

"Mine actually, I think," she said, arching her neck to kiss his shoulder.

"Ah, but your pleasure is my pleasure, darlin'," he said.

If she wasn't already a widow, he'd have liked to make her one, ending whatever worthless sot had failed to see the perfection lying next to him night after night for a year and a bit and failed to worship her with everything he had.

She snuggled against him, but he could sense her turmoil as though his own restless soul were drawn to hers like magnetite.

"What is it?" he whispered, nosing the back of her neck and running a hand over her belly.

"How did you learn to do that, if you never leave the ship?" she asked.

Oh, was that all? He kissed her neck again to make her shiver. "I'm a very good listener."

"Oh, aye?" she teased.

"Aye. You've a sister called Ellen who wed the big Laird MacKenzie and has two mischievous bairns. And you've a cousin, Jory, who fell for the Shaw Wretch. No children those two, but you reckon they tup every chance they possibly get."

He pinched her bottom and she wiggled it against him, setting him on fire anew, so he had to run a hand over her hip to still her.

"Jory studies medicine disguised as a man. The women in your family must enjoy wearing breeches."

She shook with laughter and then said with a prim and proper air, "It was you who ordered me into the breeches. And I have more than one cousin."

"None who matter," he guessed. "While the breeches certainly suit you, I must confess I like you best out of them." He gave her a light smack and she wiggled against him again. Christ.

"Cousin Lennox would've married me, if my father had let him."

"Why'd he refuse?" Bash asked, not sure he wanted to hear the answer.

She was silent for a moment. "I suppose because he thinks he's better than everyone else. My father, not Lennox. Well maybe Lennox too, I don't know. Do you really never go ashore?" She stroked a lazy finger along his forearm, causing his mind to judder.

"Alone? Once. A decade back. Dutch will take me now and again if he needs help with something."

"But the others all come and go freely?"

"Aye."

"Then why?"

Bash sighed. "When I was a boy, I think Mad feared I'd find his lost gold."

"Were you so good at solving puzzles?"

"Suppose he thought I'd have beginner's luck."

"And now?"

"Now it's about power. And the illusion of power."

She paused her idle stroking, and he wondered if she saw similarities between their situations.

Rolling onto his back, he crooked an arm under his head and considered. "He's afraid I'll leave," he explained, "and there won't be anyone left to navigate this old wreck."

"Why don't you?" she whispered in a small voice. "Will he beat you with that whip if you try to go ashore?" She shivered, and he wrapped his arm around her once more.

"Possibly. But I submit so he thinks I accept his authority. That way, when the time is right, it'll be easier to slip away. Keep your enemies close, as they say."

She snuggled against him and murmured, "Maybe he'll get struck by lightning."

"Lightning?" he asked. What a very specific notion. But her breathing had changed to the soft, slow rhythm of sleep, so he kissed the top of her head and closed his eyes, determined to steal every last possible moment of peace until dawn.

By morning, he was antsy—not ready to leave the pleasant cocoon, but eager to have the next twelve hours over and done so he could return to it.

Maggie rested languorously in the hammock, still basking in last night's glow as he performed his daily ablutions. When he caught her watching, he smiled warmly, and she slid down under his plaid, peeking out at him with a shy, smug expression that stirred his arousal.

The kestrel squawked at him, waking the cat, which had slunk in during the night and curled up under his desk as Maggie used to do. It watched the confounded bird with interest, sitting up on its hind legs for a better view.

"Now Mouser, that bird is the cabin boy's pet, mind," Bash

scolded quietly, offering the cat a bit of dried beef instead. "You'd do well to leave it be."

"Mrow," the cat replied, snapping up the beef and washing its own face as he'd just done.

Then Bash sat on the edge of the hammock, still watching the kestrel and the cat instead of Maggie.

"His name is Custard," she said, nodding to the cat.

"Custard? What kind of a name is that?"

What kind of a name is Bash? he half expected her to retort.

But she shook her head and said softly, "It's just his name." Then she hesitantly reached out to trace the old scars on his back like she had almost done the night before.

He grew very still under her touch, and she retracted her hand, but he said, "You can ask."

"The captain?"

"Dutch. The captain rarely administers his own beatings."

"What could you have possibly done to deserve such cruelty?" she asked, tears springing to her eyes.

"That," he said, pulling his shirt over his head and letting it fall like a shroud over the past, "was the only time I ever snuck ashore."

"You must have been a little boy," she gasped, the tears finally wetting her cheeks. "You must have been so scared and lonely and betrayed."

He'd felt all those things and more when Mad ordered Dutch to take the cat o' nine to him, but he didn't like to dwell.

Bash leaned over and kissed her cheek. "Don't cry, Mags," he said, wiping a tear away with his thumb. " 'Twas a long time ago. I'm all grown up now."

He tried to smile as he searched her eyes, but they just clouded more, so he pulled her into his chest.

"It breaks my heart to think of you—of no one taking care of you."

"Shh, don't cry," he said again, stroking her hair. "Don't cry, else I shall have to go back on my knees, and we've neither of us time for that now."

A little thrill ran down his belly and straight to his groin at the notion, but he meant what he said. There wasn't time, not today. Such was life at sea, after all.

"Why are they all so excited about the ship with the whale?" she asked. "And why aren't you?"

"Ah." He rose from the hammock and paced the few steps back and forth to the porthole. "Mainly because they believe it will be our redemption, whereas I believe the captain is full of shite. Begging your pardon," he added.

She nodded her pardon, and he continued.

"I told you about how Mad came into that gold."

"Plundered it. And then lost it."

"Aye. He was boasting in a tavern in Kingston that he buried it as his baby son's inheritance."

"He's a father?"

"Of a sort, aye," he said, feeling strangely gratified she didn't notice any resemblance between them. "When Dutch and the lads found him passed out in his own piss, there was no sign of the chest, but the navy was hell bent on recovering the loot along with whoever stole it. So the men dragged him back to his ship and set sail. By the time he sobered up, he couldn't remember what he'd done with it, and he's been chasing that memory ever since."

"Afraid you'd find it first?"

"Aye, well, afraid anyone would."

"How long has it been?"

"Decades. Then a few years back someone told a tale of Willy Walsh, Mad's old nemesis and captain of the *Woebegone Whale*. Legend has it they fought the night his treasure went missing, and there's some who swear Walsh made off with the gold. But he hasn't been seen for years now."

Bash ran a hand through his hair, trying to put into words just exactly why he didn't believe the story. Walsh was a rabbity little man, brave enough to plunder fishermen or unguarded merchants, but far too skittish to consider crossing the likes of Madman Neil MacLeod.

Before Bash could put his feelings into words, however, Maggie chewed her bottom lip in a seductively distracting sort of way, and he completely lost his train of thought, leaning over to kiss that lush lip instead.

"You don't believe the rumors?" she asked when he stepped back again. "About Walsh?"

Ah. Right. Walsh.

"No. I thought he was out of the game completely. But the lads were growing restless. So Mad told them he'd heard Walsh went home to Scotland, and we chased the figment all the way there and back again. He's no reason to be out here in the great wide middle, but unless someone else is flying his standard, we'll have to fight. And when he doesn't have the gold..." Bash trailed off, but he didn't want to frighten her with dire predictions of mutiny.

"Our ship's bigger than his. If we fight, will we win?" she asked.

Something about the way she said *our* and *we* tugged him in two different directions at once, just like memories of his mother did.

"The brig is fast," he said. "We're sneaky and we probably out-gun them. But I don't like it. There's nowhere to hide out here. Why's he even here? We're only here because of Mad's last-ditch charade."

"Could he be up to his old tricks?"

Bash shrugged. "I always heard Walsh took the pardon back in 1717 and retired, as we all should've done." Then again, Calico Jack took the pardon too, until he got bored or hungry or both. "Once a pirate, always a pirate, I suppose," he added.

"The ocean seems to feature more drama and changes of fortune than a Greek tragedy."

Bash laughed sadly. He doubted she could really comprehend the danger.

"You mustn't join the raid," he said, stroking her face and hair. "Even if ordered, you must slip away in the chaos and hide. Promise me."

"Wouldn't such cowardice see me flogged? And exposed?"

She wasn't wrong, but he could only cross one bridge at a time. "On my life, I'll protect you. Do you promise?"

Maggie nodded, and his chest eased the tiniest bit.

"Good girl," he whispered. "If we're boarded by Walsh's crew, you must continue the ruse—you're Mark Magnus of Orkney."

"Mark?" she laughed.

Bash shrugged. "Whatever name you like. But if the navy ever catches us, you must reveal yourself at once and beg saving, else you'll be hanged."

"The navy?" she asked, confused.

"Repeat it back," he ordered, and heat flared in her cheeks.

"Keep playing the game unless we're taken by the navy, in which case, I should become a damsel in distress."

"Aye," he agreed, though he doubted she could ever allow herself to be that.

"You think it's a trap," she said, suddenly understanding his reticence.

He shrugged, but it was the only justification for Walsh's being out here that made any sense. "Perhaps I'm no more sound than Mad, but he swears the same navy man who pursued him to Kingston after the heist has never given up the chase."

She licked her lips, doing an almost passible job of hiding her nerves. Anyone who spent less time studying her mouth might not have noticed. He was scaring her, but on his life, he would die to keep her safe. She may not think she needed him to, but he'd do it all the same.

"And if Walsh does have the gold? What would you do with that much coin?" she asked with a sultry smirk.

He'd never allowed himself to ponder overmuch. When he did, something like hope flared within his chest and he couldn't bear it. Today that hope looked very much like him and Maggie sailing off with their fair share to make their own way in the world together.

It was a preposterous notion. She was a scholar's daughter, ken to clan lairds by blood and by marriage. He was no more than the bastard of a bastard, living his life one step ahead of the hangman.

What did it matter if she could make him laugh? What did it matter if her smile made his fractured parts feel whole?

"Would you buy your own private island? Build a castle on the beach and call yourself laird?" she pressed in a teasing tone.

Bash leaned against the bulkhead. Her enthusiasm was contagious, but it was also dangerous, this game of pretend. "He doesn't have it," he said. When her smile faltered he added, "Why, what would you do?"

"I'd finally be independent," she said firmly. "Isn't that all any of us wants?"

"Certainly can't disagree. Come," he said, squeezing her hand and nodding to the deck above. "I'll see you up there."

A deep, sick dread roiled in his gut as Bash climbed to the upper deck. He'd thought he was doing a decent job of burying it, but Maggie had seen right through him. The *Whale* wasn't the only reason he dragged his feet this morning, however. At some point, he would have to face Dutch. If there was to be a skirmish, there could be no mistrust between them, and the quartermaster was already awaiting his arrival at the forecastle.

"So we engage the *Whale* today," Bash said, gazing out at some distant storm clouds and calculating their progression in his head.

"We do. Hopefully Walsh has the sense to surrender."

"And if he doesn't?"

"Then we force him."

"He doesn't have the gold," Bash muttered.

"Then we can finally put this fiction behind us for good," Dutch replied, ever sensible.

Bash nodded, but the truth of another fiction still hung, palpably, between them.

"Last night," he began.

Dutch pierced him with a rapier glare, and Bash rubbed his ear, the traitorous words sticking in his throat.

"You pledged your protection—the same protection I once swore to you."

"There was consent," he protested feebly.

"How can there be? You are the sailing master. Magnus is a cabin boy. You hold all the power," Dutch growled, and Bash's very soul shriveled. "Was it the same when you stepped in for Langley?" Dutch asked, his voice ice cold.

"No!" Bash exclaimed, shaking his head emphatically. "No," he said again, and Dutch held his gaze a long while before he was satisfied.

But the quartermaster was right. Bash was scum. Even if Maggie had wanted him, he didn't deserve her—could never deserve her.

Had he been in her position, he might have said yes to avoid the repercussions of saying no. He'd allowed himself to pretend they were equal, because the plain fact was she held his heart in her two lovely, capable hands, and along with it, the power to destroy him. But he was still her superior according to the chain of command. He barked orders and she obeyed them.

Dutch cupped the back of Bash's neck, forcing him to meet the older man's gaze.

"You're better than this, Bastian. You are not your father. Remember that and treat the child as I treated you."

When Bash had been brought aboard *Auldfarrand's Revenge* at the age of nine and a half, the captain had waited two hours after setting sail, just long enough to be certain his son wouldn't risk swimming back to Lewis. Then, before the entire crew, he ordered Bash to drop his trousers, and he whipped him with his own belt, proclaiming that after nine years growing up coddled, he had it coming.

Because Bash had cried, he did it again the next day, and the next—every day for a week—until Bash learned how to take it stoically *like a man*. It had been Dutch who quietly comforted him, teaching him to dissociate and making it clear to all aboard that he'd slit the throat of any sailor who laid a finger on Bash. After that first week, Bash became very good at doing as he was told and otherwise keeping out of sight. He also never shed another tear.

It had been Dutch who looked out for him and saw he was fed. Dutch who found out he could read and asked the previous sailing master to tutor him in navigation. Dutch took care of him when his sire didn't seem concerned whether he were beaten or buggered or starved.

"I've never properly thanked you," Bash rasped, and Dutch shoved him away.

"Fuck off, son. It's time to ready the cannons."

He pointed to the specter of the *Woebegone Whale* coming into firing range on the starboard side.

"We'll speak no more of this," Dutch added, granting a sort of absolution which Bash didn't deserve—one only she could offer.

And now he was leading her into war.

He'd been ten the first time he'd seen battle, and he spent its entirety cowering in a secret hiding place below deck. That was where she needed to be right now.

By eleven, the captain insisted he run gun powder from the magazine to each artillery station, and when his pace slowed after what felt like hours, Mad had come at him with a belaying pin, bestowing his first battle scar upon his left cheek.

Weeks later, Dutch began teaching him the sword.

There had been many fights in the intervening years, and Bash was hardened to them now. He did the job by rote, his training taking over, but his stomach never felt easy before or after, and this time there was an extra layer of dread, like that same ill wind blowing from the south.

He glared up to make sure false colors had been raised and saw a Dutch flag snapping in the breeze.

Beside him, the quartermaster who acknowledged no flag nodded with a smirk.

"Ready the grappling," Bash ordered young Langley. "Every man to his post," he bellowed.

The men sprang into action at once, eager to take their stations and unleash a bloodthirsty hell.

Chapter Twelve

Just as it had a week and a half ago when the men had converged on their stations and worked as a single organism to turn the ship through the wind, everything happened all at once.

Pirates swarmed around the brigantine, like busy ants intent on their work, adjusting the sails and readying the cannons, preparing themselves for war. The crew of the *Woebegone Whale* would have easily spied them by now, just as surely as the *Revenge* had marked her prey.

The trick was to pretend to be a Dutch merchant vessel with no interest whatsoever in Willy Walsh as they sailed calmly past his sloop until they were close enough to hoist the Jolly Roger and demand surrender.

Unlike last time, Bash didn't ignore Maggie to focus on the horizon, nor did he observe his men with a close and careful watch. This time he only had eyes for her, as a battle seemed to rage within himself, the muscle in his jaw twitching beneath his scar, where the dimple Maggie loved so much ought to be.

"What shall I do?" she asked, desperate to be useful. "Shall I climb the rigging to keep watch? Bash...? Sir?"

"I'm thinking," he replied, though to Maggie it looked like he was merely glowering into her soul.

"Not the rigging. I forgot," she corrected. "The gun powder. Langley said when the cannons come out, it's my job to keep the powder bags full."

Bash sighed. "It should be. Aye."

She nodded. The task sounded simple enough. She could be quick, as long as it wasn't too dark below deck. She certainly wouldn't be permitted to race around with powder and a candle lantern together. "I can do that," she said. "Show me to the magazine and I'll get to work."

Bash cast an assessing gaze over her whole person making her tingle with anticipation.

"Come with me," he said, grabbing her hand and leading her swiftly to the hatch, his face the fiercest she'd ever seen.

"Langley said it's already apportioned in flannel cartridges?" she asked, but Bash neither confirmed nor denied Langley's words. "How many do you think I can carry at once? One per cannon? Or must I try to carry more? I'm strong. I can do it."

Still no reply.

Maggie couldn't make out a thing as he led her on a winding path through the belly of the ship. The magazine was certainly well hidden, but then she supposed it would have to be, to protect it from the blast of a well-placed enemy cannon.

"How many guns on a brigantine?" she asked, hurrying to catch up, unsure how she'd ever find her way out of this labyrinth again, let alone quickly enough to suit the gunners.

"The *Revenge* has fourteen," he answered gruffly, "but someone else can worry about all that."

"What do you mean?" Maggie asked, stopping short, though he kept walking. When he didn't break his stride or even glance back at her she called, "Stop," and just as he'd promised in his berth last night, he froze right where he was standing. Oh, to be back in that cozy alcove now, with none of this pirate business to get in the way. "It's my job to carry the powder, Bash," a reminder for herself as much as for him.

"Your job is to stay safe," he growled in a strained voice.

Maggie made her way to him like a salmon upstream as she tripped over the corners of boxes and crates like her first day in the hold. "I'm not a child. I can help."

"This isn't a game."

"I never meant it was."

"Lead balls. Expandable bar shot. Swords—they pierce through skin like it's nothing and thirst for blood. You are flesh and bone," he pleaded.

"So are you."

"This is my lot," he muttered, taking her hand once more to continue on.

"Then it's my lot, too," she protested. "Did I not choose it when I signed the articles to become part of the crew?"

"You don't know what you're asking."

"Then explain it to me. Where are we going if not to the magazine?" she asked, hating how small and needy her voice came out.

He was silent for a moment, filling the chasm between them with the sound of ragged breathing.

"I swore an oath to protect you," he finally said, his voice the same low tone that betrayed his lust last evening. "So far I've done a piss-poor job of it. Christ. I will see you safe."

Nothing made any sense. How would hiding with the rats keep her safe if the ship sank because she hadn't been there to pull her weight? "I'm safest by your side," she said, reaching out towards his voice in the darkness and finding his cheek, her thumb stroking the length of his scar. "Don't you think there's even the smallest way I can help?"

He turned his face to kiss her palm.

"I'm taking a party aboard that ship," he whispered. "You're safest as far from me as possible. You promised me you wouldn't fight."

He had tricked her into that promise, and she wanted to rage at him, but then he gently, lifted her hand away from his face, pressing his lips to the pulse point inside her wrist, before lacing his fingers through hers, and she allowed him to lead her forward once more.

Maggie's skin burned where his lips had touched her, bringing back the flood of sensation and emotion that had surged through every limb as he tasted her last night. Then he'd seemed eager to be as close as possible, never parted. Now, in the face of imminent danger, he would push her away while he ran headlong into the fray? She may have promised to hide only an hour ago, but the notion was completely untenable now.

"I rescind my promise," she said.

"That's not how promises work," he countered with an eerie, almost detached calm in his voice. "Elsewise they wouldn't be promises."

Finally, he stopped walking and released her hand to run his fingers along the bulkhead, fumbling with some sort of latch. Then a door popped open, a priest hole hidden deep within the hold, and he pushed her inside.

Maggie swallowed. "Have I done something wrong?" she asked, unable to hide the quiver. Was he angry that she'd told everyone about seeing the *Whale*, when he alone hoped to avoid engaging with the vessel? "Is it because—"

"I need you to trust me," he said, following her into the too small space and pressing his forehead to hers, and somehow that was all the answer she needed.

Trust? She owed him that much after the way he'd risked his neck to save her. How could she not honor such a request? Trust —he might be the only person in all the world who she trusted with her whole heart. She couldn't let him go out there to face battle with any doubt on that front.

Raising up on her toes, Maggie crushed her lips against his, and he kissed her right back, hungrily, desperately. She wrapped her arms around his neck, tangling her fingers in his hair, trying to get closer, to climb inside him if she could and never let him go.

He ran his hands down her face, her sides, up her back. He caressed her bottom, her belly, her breasts, still frustratingly bound.

Maggie let go of his neck to memorize the shape of his taut arms and the ridges of his chest. Emboldened, she went further, grazing his crotch, rubbing the steel-hard length of him through is breeches, and he hissed.

Catching her right wrist, Bash moved her hand away from his erection, so she reached out with her left, but he caught that one too, pinning them both above her head with one strong hand as he pressed her against the bulkhead.

"May God forgive me," he seemed to sigh, as he kissed down her throat and then up again to suckle her ear. With her arms still pinned above her head, he dipped his other hand into her breeches, right past her smalls, to cup her so his palm pressed deliciously against her favorite spot, and as she squirmed wantonly, he thrust a finger inside.

Maggie was shocked by how easily he entered her, how deliciously wicked it felt to welcome him in. Keeping pressure against her outside, he began to stroke her on the inside, and tiny little gasps escaped her lips, a pressure already building and begging for release.

Rocking against him—finger, palm, and shaft—Maggie found herself moaning as loudly as she wanted to, a surprising sound that almost seemed to come from someone else's throat. Then her moans became a high-pitched sort of mewling the likes of which she'd certainly never uttered before, as her cheeks burned and tears trickled down her face.

So deep inside the ship that even the noisy chaos of battle preparations couldn't reach them, Bash didn't try to swallow her whimpers, but instead, buried his face in her neck, kissing everywhere as her panting grew more desperate until she shook, body and soul, and he finally released her wrists and held her in his strong arms, keeping her upright despite her legs having turned into jelly.

Slowly Bash eased her to the floor, where she sat like a puddle, and pressed one last kiss to her forehead.

"I will come back for you," he swore.

"You promised to teach me the rules of Ruff," she rasped.

He nodded, and as he closed the door, a shadow slipped in and settled, warm and purring, in Maggie's lap.

"Mrow?" Custard asked, licking her arm with his rough tongue, and Maggie held the cat close and waited.

LEAVING MAGGIE BEHIND WAS THE HARDEST THING BASH HAD ever done, and his regret was only tempered by his self-loathing. Had even an hour passed since he swore to Dutch he wouldn't touch her again before his control had fled like smoke on the wind?

His only intention had been to stow her in his secret hiding place, safe from dangerous orders as well as ruthless men. But then she had kissed him like she knew there was no tomorrow, like she, too, felt the heavy cloud of dread that this would be the last time they'd meet in this life, or certainly the next. He couldn't leave her down there with any doubt about his feelings—feelings that were almost too big and too powerful to name.

Back on deck, he tried to push her from his thoughts. These next few hours would be fraught, requiring every ounce of his attention. He must be at his best in order to make good on his vow to return for her. By God, he'd do it or die trying, and that meant no lingering lust nor guilt nor regret, there wasn't space or time.

The *Revenge* drew within firing range, but the *Whale* gave no sign of concern. She gave no sign of anything much at all.

Indeed, when Bash peered through his spyglass, he could make out not a single soul on board. The sloop seemed almost adrift, and his nerves jangled like alarm bells sounding a fire.

They raised the Jolly Roger, but no white flag was hoisted in response, nor did the ship attempt to flee.

"Anything?" Dutch asked.

Bash shook his head. "She looks like a ghost."

"You don't believe in ghosts."

"I don't."

"But?" Dutch asked, reading his mind or his mood. Maybe both.

"But if I were a certain naval captain, I would think this a mightily clever lure to catch old Mad MacLeod."

"Now you believe in his persecution fantasy."

Bash put his spyglass away and turned to Dutch. "I don't know what I believe. Six years ago, when we made the run up to New Orleans?"

"I remember."

"The *Pursuit* came out of nowhere. Like she was waiting for us. Like she knew where we'd be."

"Could have been waiting for anybody," Dutch reasoned. "We were just the anybody who happened along."

"Aye. If it had been the French navy, I might agree with you. But a British ship right there? So far into French territory? Mad's paranoia didn't seem so mad to me after that."

"And now?" Dutch asked.

"Outside New Orleans, I stood at the railing and looked through my glass, and I'll swear to my last breath I saw the bastard Constantin staring back at me. He lifted his cap like he was saying hello. Maybe he's as mad as the captain. Maybe he just enjoys the chase." Bash's words voiced a line of thought which had haunted him for half a dozen years, finally given form as he spoke them out loud.

But Dutch didn't look at him like he was crazy. "You think it's a trap."

"It would be a brilliant strategy, would it not? Especially if Walsh took the pardon as we always believed. And these rumors floating around like sardines? Send him out on his own. Reel us in. Hell, maybe Constantin started the rumor about Walsh finding Mad's gold in the first place."

"You put a great deal of faith in the navy man," Dutch said, taking Bash's spyglass to have a look of his own.

"Maybe. Could be I'm as mad as old Neil, but I'd believe it's a trick before I believe there's a single coin on board that sloop. And you know as well as I do what'll happen when there's not," he mumbled.

"You're a fortune teller now?" Dutch quipped, and Bash looked at him hard until his old friend tilted his head in acquiescence. "Would it be the worst thing for the crew to decide there's no bounty to be had?"

Now Bash shrugged. "Suppose it depends."

"Why have we not fired?" the captain bellowed striding up the deck. "What are you waiting for?"

Bash and Dutch exchanged a glance.

"What?" Mad asked when he drew even with them.

"Have a look," Dutch said, tossing him the spyglass.

Mad swept his gaze across the abandoned deck, then collapsed the scope. "Excellent," he said, slapping it against Bash's chest. "Take a party aboard and check it out."

"Aren't you even the slightest bit concerned it may be a trap?" Bash countered.

Mad shrugged. "You're trained for battle. Don't get caught with your breeks down. It's only a trap if you let yourself be trapped." He grinned the charming grin that probably won over his ladies in each and every port. Bash was immune. He hated everything about the man, including his smug smirk.

"Can I ask?" he pressed the captain, feeling reckless. "What's the end game? If we find no gold?" His challenge was clear. They both knew there was no gold.

The grin stayed in place, but Mad's eyes hardened. "Best hope you find something," he said dangerously.

That was a threat too. Come back with something of value or don't bother coming back at all.

Bash eyed Dutch once more. "Ready the pirogue," he called, moving aft with the quartermaster on his heels. "I'll not take us close enough to tether. Duffy, Samson, Langley, with me."

His vanguard was comprised of the three youngest aboard, but they were loyal to Bash, and together with Dutch, they were the men he trusted most in all the world. As they fell into step behind him, though, Bash couldn't help feeling like one was missing. Maggie was hidden away in the hold where he'd left her, God willing, out of harm's reach. Her absence was like a hole in his armor, he realized too late, but he couldn't worry about that right now. She was safe.

They collected cutlasses and daggers and settled into the pirogue to row silently over to the *Whale*.

"Why's she so quiet?" Langley whispered, but no one had an answer for the lad.

Bash braced himself for cannons or pistol fire as he pulled the oars, but none came, which only made him grind his teeth harder. He tried to lose himself in the rhythm of exercise, but his scalp tingled with anticipation, and all too soon he was putting out a hand to still the rowboat from banging against the *Whale*'s hull.

Duffy threw a grapple expertly over the side of the sloop, and they shimmied silently up and over, but the deck was as empty as it had looked from afar. No pirates hid behind barrels or up in the rigging. There was no one, only a few pigeons cooing in their cages to greet them.

Bash had never heard of pirates carrying pigeons. He shivered in the noonday sun.

"Those to eat?" Samson whispered, and Bash put a finger to his lips, demanding silence, cutting off further discussion of the paltry amount of meat on a pigeon.

The sloop was in pitiful condition. Sails hung slack and torn, the lines hopelessly fouled. Bash glanced back and Dutch nodded his agreement. Something wasn't right. A ghost ship indeed.

They continued to scour the deck for secret hidey-holes, and then had no choice but to descend into the damp, slippery bowels of the ship, flipping their eye patches up as they went.

Her ghostly emptiness gave Bash the sense of retreating deep into the belly of an actual whale. It was far more unnerving than an armed resistance would have been, with iron exploding overhead and swords flashing out of every corner.

The galley was filthy, the larder nearly empty except for a few sacks of moldering oats.

"Sure as beans they all died of something catching," Langley whispered.

"If there were sickness, we'd be stepping over bodies," Duffy replied. "This here's some kind of *Flying Dutchman* shite."

"Stay vigilant, lads," Bash reminded them so they wouldn't let their guard down. "There's no such thing as ghosts."

"We'll see," Duffy murmured.

The cargo hold, like the larder, was also empty but for two bone-dry rum barrels and some more rancid grain. Samson looked at Bash askance, and he shrugged at the young man.

"Wouldn't keep a hoard right out in the open, would you?" he muttered. Samson just shrugged back at him. This was new for everyone.

The crew area was likewise deserted, with dirty hammocks still strung as though waiting for their earthly occupants to return. Chill after prickly chill ran down Bash's sweaty spine like warning shots.

They cleared the entire deck, searching for any sign of secret compartments or dusty old chests shoved innocuously into cobweb-covered corners, but there was nothing and no one. Even the rats had fled.

"Captain's quarters?" Bash suggested and Dutch nodded.

With his guts roiling, Bash led his little party back the way they'd come, Dutch pulling up the rear. He was proud of how stealthily the lads prowled through the dark, barely allowing a single creak in the unfamiliar passageway. Hopefully they'd reach the captain's quarters and find old white-haired Willy passed out drunk where they could truss him up and deliver him to Mad. Even better if he were sat atop a pot of gold like an Irish fucking leprechaun.

Silently, they turned down another passageway and Bash's nerves went on the highest alert. Someone or something else was here with them, hiding in its own familiar darkness.

He froze, and Langley tripped into the back of him with a grunt. Then a blinding flash flew out of the shadows accompanied by a shout and a searing pain the likes of which Bash had never fathomed. He fell back onto Langley, who stumbled into someone else.

The party became a tangle of limbs and shouted curses.

Sweat pouring down his face, Bash extracted himself from the jumble and got to his feet. Then the flash of a blunderbuss temporarily lit the passage, blinding him just as he caught a glimpse of wild, white hair careening away.

Then nothing.

Chapter Thirteen

Maggie snapped to attention, straining her ears against the deafening silence. Had she heard a gunshot or dozed off and dreamt it? She tried to take one of Jory's calming breaths, in through the nose and out through the mouth, but the air felt too close, and her lungs refused to expand.

Though her eyes had adjusted somewhat to the darkness, she could see nothing but walls—walls which seemed to be closing in. They'd soon crush her and she'd suffocate twice over. Where was Bash? *How* was Bash?

After he left, she had pictured him in her mind's eye, leading Langley and the others stealing over the side of the *Whale*, then creeping through the ship searching for stolen treasure. Had they found it?

Her skin was crawling with the not knowing, and remaining locked away, deprived of every sense, for two more seconds was bound to drive her as mad as Captain MacLeod.

Custard scrambled off her lap as she struggled to her feet, legs numb with pins and needles.

"Mrow!" Custard grumped, but Maggie shushed the cat and listened.

How long had it been since Bash had left her down here? She wasn't hungry, so it couldn't have been a terribly long time. She tried hard to read the ship beneath her, and it felt... sedate. Not tossed about in a storm or the turbulent waters of war, but not moving either.

It was still, too still to be engaged in battle. Still was good. Still was fine. Probably. Promises be damned, she was going to see what was happening above.

But when she reached for the door, the wall before her felt smooth and solid. Swallowing her mounting panic, Maggie stamped her feet to stop the tingling and ran both hands along the wall, turning in a small circle. The only sound besides her ragged breath was Custard squalling when she accidentally stomped his tail.

Maggie bit back the urge to scream for help and pressed the wall a bit more firmly as she circled her tiny cupboard once more. At last, her fingers snagged on a vertical crack in the wood, and she was able to shove the door wide and stumble out into more darkness.

It would be impossible to get her bearings down here.

"Do you know the way out?" she whispered to Custard, but the feline had already fled, leaving her behind as punishment for his poor tail. "Right," she whispered to herself. "This is fine. You're a pirate, Magnus. Figure it out."

Shoving her way forward, Maggie bumped into a stack of crates and barrel after barrel as she went, like the cattle who once got loose inside a London porcelain shop. Lucky the ship didn't have much in the way of fragile cargo. Bruised knees and shins were nothing if it meant escaping this infernal darkness.

It felt as she imagined being buried alive might feel, and now it seemed she was wandering in circles. She'd be lost down here forever, and even if Bash came back, he wouldn't find her. She laughed a little hysterically at the thought of his smug, annoyed face, turning in circles looking for her even as she faded into a specter, doomed to wander the sea for all eternity.

Just when she was ready to weep in despair, she heard muffled shouting, and dim rays of light began to infiltrate the hold. She finally reached a companionway as Dutch stumbled down backwards supporting someone's shoulders while the barber-surgeon followed holding the legs.

Bash.

His face was ashy, beautiful eyes closed and hair matted down with blood. More blood was smeared across Dutch's cheek and shirt—Bash's blood. Everyone was sticky with it.

In that moment, Maggie's heart stopped, and she wasn't sure it would ever start beating again.

"To the infirmary," the Butcher was saying. "Keep pressure on the wound."

Dutch cursed, but Bash lay still and silent as stone.

Swallowing her tears and squinting against the daylight, Maggie fell into step behind them as though she belonged there. They picked up speed as they neared the infirmary, and Langley ran ahead to sweep a pile of odds and ends off the operating table and onto the floor so they could lay Bash out properly. None of them paid Maggie any mind.

"What happened?" the Butcher asked.

"Bastard was hiding all alone down there, innit? Came at us from the shadows," Langley practically yelled, twisting up the front of his shirt in his nervous, fretful fists. "Cut Nav and pushed him over, then shot at the lot of us and ran off into the dark again, laughing like a fiend."

The Butcher pushed Bash's eyelids up with rough, meaty fingers, then scraped back his hair to see the bloody mess around one ear.

"Was he hit by the gun? Knocked out?"

"Couldn't see," Dutch said. "Walsh carried a blunderbuss in one hand and a cutlass in the other. Did he hit his head when he fell on you, Langley?"

"Yes. I mean, no. I mean—"

"Quiet," the Butcher snapped. "The ear's not completely severed, but I'll have to remove it and cauterize with powder. Hold him down, Dutch. If he's anything but dead, this'll wake him, mark me. Langley, fetch my powder bag."

He meant to light gunpowder in Bash's ear?

"No," Maggie said, but no one heard her, as the men scrambled around, and though she forced herself to look, she couldn't make out the extent of his wounds for all the blood.

The barber-surgeon rummaged through a pile of instruments and, finding his bistoury blade, inspected it, then spit on it and wiped it on his shirt before turning back to his patient.

How many times had Jory insisted that medical equipment be kept clean or that some learned men in Edinburgh tended to cut first and ask questions later?

He's a frustrated barber who likes to hack off limbs, Bash had said in disgust. Maggie had to stop him.

"No," she said again. When still nobody listened, she grunted, "Men!" to herself and, taking a deep breath, she stepped in between the Butcher and Bash. "Leave it," she demanded as though she had any right.

The Butcher gave her a patronizing eye roll. "He loses the ear or he loses his life," he said. "If he doesn't bleed to death first, the tissue will become necrotic and kill him anyway. Slowly. That what you want, cabin boy?"

His words sounded educated and terrifying, but in her gut, Maggie knew they were wrong. She couldn't have explained how she knew, only the idea of lacing Bash's beautiful face with gunpowder and setting it alight sent a deep chill of dread to her very core. There had to be another way.

She racked her memory for anything Jory might have taught her. Vinegar and clay plasters and willow bark. Leeches. Jory had once shown Maggie the amazing healing properties of leeches, and, as though her cousin were with her now, every fiber of her being was telling her that leeches could help save Bash's ear as she'd seen them do with the Mackintosh of Borlum's necrotic toe.

"Have you any leeches, sir?" she asked the Butcher, but he ignored her, shoving her away and tilting Bash's head into position.

Maggie glanced to Dutch for help but found him completely inscrutable. Desperate, she turned to Langley next, but he stared through her, yanking fistfuls of his own hair.

"Stop," she said with all the authority she could summon, sliding her hand over Bash's ear, cupping it protectively, her palm brushing his cheek. Had his eyes fluttered just then? Would he thank her for this or be angry at her interference? Would he get the chance for either?

"Do you wish to lose a finger, child?" the Butcher growled.

"I wish to know if you have any leeches."

"Leeches," Langley said at her elbow, offering a large stoneware jug full of the slimy creatures.

Maggie practically laughed with relief.

"Leeches will not—" the Butcher began.

"They'll keep the ear alive until it can heal itself," she said, channeling every ounce of Jory in every drop of their shared blood.

The barber-surgeon shifted uncomfortably. "*If* such a thing were possible, it would take weeks."

"Is it possible or isn't it?" Dutch demanded, his eyes flicking to Maggie.

The Butcher's face flashed like angry lightning. "You would question my expertise over the experimentation of a cabin boy?"

"Is. It. Possible?" Dutch repeated.

"Theoretically. But if it doesn't work, he could lose more than the ear. Do you know how to read those star charts of his well enough to find your way back to Jamaica for MacLeod?"

"How long before the ear must be removed?" Dutch asked.

"Twenty-four hours. Maybe less. It's already beginning to lose color."

"Then we have time. Give the leeches one night."

Tears sprang to Maggie's eyes as she reached for the jug Langley offered.

The Butcher raised his hands in surrender, stepping back as if to say he'd have no part in this witchcraft. And let it be witchcraft, then. Maggie could use all the luck and magic in the world to see this right.

Tenderly, she brushed the soft brown curls away from Bash's right ear, careful not to let any of the dry, sticky blood pull against his wound.

There was just so much of it, and more purple ooze filling the area all the time, seeping down his neck to soak his collar. The Butcher was surely right about the need to staunch the bleeding.

She took a steadying breath. "Is there any clean linen?" she asked, suddenly nervous about simply dropping a leech down his ear canal.

"Bandages," Dutch said, fetching a roll. "How much do you need?"

"No more than an inch," she guessed, and Dutch sliced off a bit with his knife.

Hoping the knife was cleaner than the Butcher's blade, Maggie wadded it up and tamped it gently into the canal, careful not to disturb the ragged cartilage. Then she selected a leech from Langley's jar, trying not to grimace, and placed the little worm in the curve of Bash's ear.

Instantly the creature began to feed, but Maggie realized she'd have to keep the ear in place somehow while it healed.

"Will you stitch it up?" Langley asked, as though reading her mind.

"Suppose I should?" she asked, but both men simply stared at her, waiting for her to decide. "Suppose I should," she repeated emphatically, and Langley rummaged in the cabinet until he found a needle and thread.

As she'd observed Jory do on more than one occasion, Maggie held the needle tip in the flame of a candle lantern for a moment. Then she leaned forward and ever so gently pinched the skin behind the ear and stuck the needle through. Bash didn't so much as twitch, so she carefully pierced the soft, fleshy part of the upper helix and then brought the needle back down to where she started, making one quick knot. Just one tiny loop to hold the ear where it ought to be.

She released a shaky breath, and Dutch clapped her on the shoulder, nodding in approval when she dared look his way.

"Is it me eyes, or does it look less purple and puffed up already?" Langley asked.

Maggie couldn't be certain it wasn't wishful thinking, but Bash's ear did look a little more normal than before.

"How long will it drink?" young Langley asked, leaning over to inspect the leech, his nose wrinkled in disgusted delight.

"Until it's full," she replied, desperately wishing Jory were there to guide her, but Langley nodded, apparently happy with the answer.

And though she'd probably go to hell, she prayed to Jory to be right. After all, if the Virgin Mary or even Jesus Himself had any experience with leeches, the men who wrote the Bible forgot to mention it.

"Now what?" Langley asked.

"I'll stay with him," Maggie said, as if anyone could have made her leave without carrying her bodily from the sickbay. "Before long that one'll drop off and he'll need another." Then she pulled up a stool to sit a vigil at Bash's side.

She didn't notice when Dutch left. Only when Langley sneezed did she realize time had passed, because the candle had burned down so low. She glanced around, confused.

"Butcher says if he wakes up, he can smoke some hashish for the pain."

"The Butcher?" she asked, scanning Bash in alarm. "Did he come back?"

"Couple hours ago," Langley replied. "I didn't like to wake you, and he seemed to prefer it that way."

Maggie bit her lip. She'd fallen asleep when Bash needed her most. He never would've done such a thing if their positions were reversed.

"He didn't try to cut him or anything. Honest. He looked sort of impressed with your stitching and the color of Nav's ear."

"If he returns—if anyone at all comes—will you promise to wake me no matter how tired I look?"

"On me mother's grave," he agreed solemnly, and Maggie's heart broke just a little. Were all pirates deep down just a pack of lost, motherless boys trying to find their way home?

"D'you think them things'll really work?" Langley asked her.

"Yes," she said confidently, instead of the desperate *I hope so* she felt inside.

The leech in question, however, had swollen to about three times its original size and rolled itself onto Bash's cheek. His ear was already beginning to swell with blood once more.

"That one's done, I think," she said, picking it up and dropping it into an empty jar before selecting a new one to continue draining away the awful mess.

"Always gave me the willies, leeches," Langley said with a shiver. "But if they save Nav's ear, I reckon they're all right in my book. Even if it is a bit of witchy stuff."

"It's not sorcery, it's science," she said.

"You sound like him. How d'you know so much about doctoring anyway?" he asked, wiping his nose on his sleeve.

"My cousin's a physician and the smartest person I know."

"Why not follow his footsteps, then? Be a prentice 'stead of running away to sea?"

Maggie had never once in her life thought about trying to emulate Jory or imagined she'd be any good at it if she tried. After all, she hadn't even been able to properly care for Jeremiah when he was well. Complaining about the leaky roof made him climb up on the fool thing in a lightning storm. And come to think of it, Bash wouldn't need her help now if she hadn't announced to God and everybody that she'd seen the damned ship, igniting the fervor of both captain and crew.

She'd opened her big mouth like always, and now she had to make it right.

"I don't have the temperament for it," she told Langley honestly. "And I wanted an adventure. To prove myself away from home."

Langley shook his head. "Reckon you got more than you bargained for, then."

And wasn't that the truth?

"Did you at least find what you were after over there?" she asked, hardly daring to hope.

"Christ, no," he almost laughed. "It were naught but pigeons and one crazy old man. The ship weren't even in good enough shape for Dutch to claim it. Shame, too," he said dreamily. "He'd make a good skipper, him. You saw how even the Butcher listened to him. There's not many alive'd dare cross our Dutch."

"How long have you sailed with them?" Maggie asked.

"Five years, since I were your age. I worked on a merchant ship they took, and they gived me the choice of stay and drown or join the crew. Easy choice." He grinned.

Easy choice indeed.

"Ain't been all bad. Nav's been good to me. Food's better, too, and the rum's endless." He shrugged. "Used to be endless."

Maggie smiled.

"Speaking of, I'm a bit dry. D'you want some ale?" he asked, before disappearing to the galley for two tankards.

Maggie looked down at Bash and squeezed his hand. When he awoke, he'd be glad she was drinking at least.

And he *would* wake, because Maggie refused to live in a world in which he didn't. Ridiculous though it may sound, he was the best friend she'd ever had, and even if it meant becoming a real pirate and spending the rest of her days in disguise, she wanted to do whatever it would take to be near him, to continue to know him.

Maybe she had always been destined to become a pirate, seeing as how she had no real skills to recommend her as a lady. She knew, theoretically, how to do a great many things, but she always managed to bungle the execution. And though he was a rough-and-tumble sailor—with a dark past and no real prospects for the future—somehow they fit, like two halves of a coin, like a sail and the wind, as though together they were enough to take on the whole world.

It would be madness to allow a friendship like that to sail away and become nothing more than a watermark upon her history.

So yes. He would get better, even if she had to drag the whole ship to Jory back in Edinburgh, rowing the oars herself the whole way home.

BASH WAS FLOATING ON A CLOUD OF PAIN, DISCONNECTED FROM space and time, trying his hardest to sever awareness from his physical self as Dutch had once taught him to do. But each time his eyes fluttered open, nothing quite made sense—not where he was, not why the world sounded muffled and underwater, not the fire burning his head and down his spine.

The only right thing was the hand holding his, and the other hand occasionally mopping his sweaty brow and pressing an ale-soaked rag to his lips. And eyes like the watery sea.

Chapter Fourteen

Below deck, even outside the priest hole, day and night had little meaning. Each time an engorged leech fell off Bash's ear and rolled down his cheek or neck, Maggie noted that another couple of hours must have passed. The bells rang to change the watch, but she didn't heed them. She only had attention for Bash.

Would removing the whole ear have been less painful? Was she prolonging his torment only to meet the same outcome in the end? Would he thank her for interfering if he had the chance, or be angry because she'd chosen for him when he'd have preferred the quickest solution?

She hoped he'd be glad, but either way, Maggie wasn't sorry. She doubted she would ever be sorry, unless he died as the Butcher had threatened, and that she would not allow.

If the Butcher had returned to spy on her patient's progress, she hadn't noticed him any more than the bells. She dozed in fits and starts when Langley's snoring would permit it, stirring every time Bash so much as twitched.

He was still running a fever, and as often as she could, Maggie rinsed a linen cloth in the bucket of cool water Langley had brought in for her to mop Bash's clammy brow. When his eyes fluttered open, there was no recognition in them, only an agony that made her ache with second-guessing. His breaths came in rapid, shallow gasps, and once, when she leaned forward to wipe his face, he grabbed her wrist with surprising strength and begged, "Put a bullet in me."

"Langley," she snapped, and the boy bolted up in his hammock, completely alert. "The hashish?"

He grinned and went straight to a cupboard, quickly returning with a small, rolled cigar which he lit off a nearby candle.

"Here you go, Nav, suck that in nice and slow."

It smelled foul, but Langley patiently held it to Bash's parched lips, and his breathing seemed to ease after a few excruciating minutes.

When it was clear Bash had passed out again, Langley rocked back on his heels and took a drag of the tiny cigar himself. "Seems a shame to waste it," he explained. "Good stuff, hashish. Ever tried any?" He offered it to Maggie, but she shook her head.

"No," she said with a self-conscious laugh, wiping Bash's hair off his forehead and smoothing the creased lines between his brows. Mercy, she hoped this treatment worked and didn't add to the patchwork of scars he already carried.

Langley giggled to himself, enjoying the hashish. She only hoped that in his oblivion, Bash was feeling half so fine.

He would still be beautiful with or without the ear, with or without another scar, so long as he was hers.

Hers.

Even without imbibing, the medicinal smoke seemed to be turning Maggie's own nerves to confidence. As every new leech drank its fill, the angry, purple swelling abated and the ear shrank down to size, leaving Maggie more convinced she'd done the right thing. Her plan would work because it had to.

But would it work before the Butcher or the quartermaster called time up?

. . .

Wʜᴇɴ ᴍᴏʀɴɪɴɢ ᴄᴀᴍᴇ, sʜᴇ ᴋɴᴇᴡ ɪᴛ ᴍᴜsᴛ ʙᴇ ᴍᴏʀɴɪɴɢ because Langley had fetched her a bowl of Roo's infamous loblolly, and Maggie was grateful to scarf it down. After having missed at least two meals already, her stomach was burning with a ravenous hunger.

"Kind of funny, innit?" Langley said, digging into his own breakfast with gusto. "Even on the merchant ship, I ate better than home. I'm the youngest of twelve, and anyone who thinks a girl won't throw a punch over the last crust of bread ain't never met one of my sisters."

Maggie smiled, trying to imagine Ellen fighting her for anything. Eleven sisters like Ellen wouldn't be so bad, but eleven little Maggies would add up to a reign of terror. "I hope all eleven weren't sisters."

"No, but four was enough."

"Are all your brothers sailors?" She said sailors, but she meant pirates.

"Mostly, though I ain't been home in a while, mind. Ben and Charlie were 'prenticed to a ship builder. And the youngest 'afore me was sent to the Virginia colony. But for the rest of us, it was the army or the sea."

"I despise Red Coats," Maggie sighed with a ferocity she hadn't even realized she possessed. At Langley's curious head tilt, she added, "No offense."

He grinned. "We chose the sea."

She nodded, marveling at how little the Scottish versus English divide seemed to matter here, aboard the ship.

"Do you miss them?" she asked. She missed Ellen and Jory something fierce and couldn't imagine the loss of nine more siblings in the bargain.

Langley pondered the question with a wistful expression. "Not so much during mealtimes," he concluded. "Truth, in some ways

Nav here's been more a brother to me than my real brothers ever were. He's about the same age as Isaac there in Virginia. Better temperament, though. 'Levi,' he always said—that's me Christian name—'you're a scab, but you're my scab, and I'll crush anyone tries to pick you.'"

"I never had any brothers," Maggie admitted. "I used to wish I did, but now I'm not so sure." She laughed, and Langley laughed with her.

"Well... they're good for learning to fight. But if you had sisters, you probably learned just as good as if you had brothers."

She shook her head, and his eyes widened in surprise.

"No one would knock you down faster, but if anyone else tried it, there'd be blood."

"Sounds like my cousins. Lion, Logan, Lennox, and Lodie. Suppose you'd fit right in with them, Levi Langley."

Langley found the whole thing especially hilarious and slapped Maggie repeatedly on the arm to emphasize it as he laughed. "Cor, we start counting cousins, we'll never finish!"

"Do you ever think about what comes next?" she asked him.

"If that poxy Walsh'd had the captain's bounty, you mean?"

"Aye."

Langley leaned back against the bulkhead, his chin tilted up in thought. "Like to go back to Hull and set me oldest sister, Annie, up proper so she never has to wash another frock or stocking again, including her own."

Maggie couldn't help grinning at such a selfless dream from the young pirate. The riches of the world, and he wanted to look after his sister.

"Sure the others must have half a dozen brats apiece by now. Someone ought to look after Annie."

"She's lucky to have you."

He snorted but preened a little. "Mind telling her that?"

"I'll drop a message in a bottle."

"Probably reach Yorkshire before I do." He said it with a

laugh, but she couldn't help wondering what would become of them all.

"So did Red Coats steal your sheep or something?" he asked, with none of his usual cheek.

"No." Maggie shook her head. "But they turned clan against clan. Without them, I don't think Simon Fraser would have ever marched on Inverness, forcing entire families to flee their homes. I was only little. What I remember most is that I didn't really understand."

"Did they burn your houses down?" Langley asked, setting down his half-eaten breakfast to listen to her tale.

Maggie shook her head again. "We got lucky. Twice. We had somewhere safe to go until the Rising was all over with. But they quartered soldiers in our house while we were gone. I'll always swear they stole my favorite doll."

Langley burst out laughing at that, and Maggie realized her mistake. Her face heated furiously as she tried to stammer an excuse.

"You must have had sisters, besides all them boy cousins," Langley cackled. "Did they make you play with the ugliest one?"

"Exactly," she agreed. "Every single time. It wasn't fair."

Langley collapsed in another fit of laughter, and Maggie smiled, her heart starting to beat again because mentioning the doll didn't seem to have given her away.

"You two scallawags are just about loud enough to wake the dead," Dutch said, stepping into the infirmary, but there was no anger in his voice.

"Seemed like the thing to do," Langley giggled. "To make sure Nav stayed with us."

"How's he doing?" Dutch asked, stepping close enough to see for himself, but looking to Maggie for confirmation.

"His fever hasn't broken yet," she admitted, praying he wasn't here to say her time was up. "But he's easier than he was, and the ear doesn't look any worse."

"No," the quartermaster agreed. "I dare say it looks better."

She exhaled in relief, tears springing to her eyes, and she bit her lip and nodded her own agreement.

Dutch studied her intently. "Keep up the good work, Magnus."

"Aye, sir."

To Langley he added, "But keep it down. This is supposed to be sickbay, not shore leave."

"Aye," Langley echoed, sitting up a little straighter.

"Fetch me if anything changes."

Maggie nodded, laying the back of her hand against Bash's cheek to check his temperature once more.

BASH'S MOTHER WAS RADIANT IN A DRESS OF GREEN AND GOLD. HER skirt flapped in the wind as she stood on the white sandy beach, gazing out to sea. She didn't look like anyone else on their island, and she didn't love like anyone else, either. She loved Bash with her whole heart and nothing held back in reserve.

The breeze carried her voice to him, where he perched on a rock watching her. It was an old familiar tune and Bash hummed along, trying to dredge the words from the back of his memory. She sang them, but they were gobbled up by the surf, so he hopped down from his rock and went to her.

Skipping along until he grew tired, Bash slowed to a walk, and then a trudge, his feet growing heavier and heavier with caked-on sand. It was like sailing into a headwind, he fought and fought but never got any closer, so he broke into a run. She turned, squatted down, and held her arms out for him to fly into, so Bash ran harder until he tripped over his own feet, landing facedown with a mouthful of sand, slicing his ear open on a sharp shell.

After scraping his eyes clean, Bash glanced behind him to see how far he'd come. His boulder was miles away, an almost indiscernible speck. When he turned back towards his mother, she was gone.

Bash began to cry, rubbing his burning ear, trying desperately to remember the words of her song as though singing it might bring her back to him.

The king once built a town so fair.
Red hibiscus lined the square...

HIS EYES SNAPPED OPEN. HE WAS ON A SHIP, THE FAMILIAR creak of timbers a comfort in his discombobulation. His head pounded, the whump, whump, whump of his heartbeat so loud it was almost deafening, and his ear burned like fire. He reached for it, but someone caught his wrist, then entwined their fingers with his.

"You mustn't touch," his mother scolded. No. Not his mother. Maggie. He blinked, and she came into focus. "Do you need more hashish? I can rouse Langley."

Ah. Hashish. That explained the vivid dreams.

"I dreamt of my mother," he said, and his voice sounded strained and scratchy to his own ears, too loud and too close by half. "What's happened?"

"Have something to drink," she urged, tipping a tankard to his lips, and he tried to sit up, but she pushed him back down with a firm yet gentle hand. "Tiny sips. What do you remember?"

His vision swam and he closed his eyes. Waves, on a beach. Why did his head ache so badly? Even his hair hurt. How on earth did one's hair hurt?

"I was on a beach."

"A beach?"

"She was singing this old lullaby she used to always sing."

"She?"

"My ma."

"Before your dream, Bash. What do you remember from before?"

He tried to think, but it was all a blank of blinding, searing pain.

She knelt before him so they were eye to eye and licked her lips. He'd kissed those lips once, he remembered that, kissed them and grown lost in them. He wished he could kiss them now, except he firmly believed even his lips would hurt to touch. They felt as dry and cracked as hers had been the day he found her.

"Do you remember boarding a ship?" she asked. "With Langley and Samson and Dutch?"

Dutch. He'd been standing with Dutch, feeling small and disgraceful as a whipped pup.

You're better than that, Bastian, Dutch had scolded. *You're not your father. You must treat the child as I treated you.*

Shame washed over him, and his eyes burned as though full of sand like in his dream. "Can you ever forgive me," he whispered. A tear tickled down his cheek like the slow, fiery slice of a knife. Was he crying fire?

"It's all right," she soothed, stroking his brow. "You've been injured. Your memory will return."

"I took advantage of you," he said, his heart ripping open. "I never meant my protection to be contingent upon... upon anything else."

"What?" she asked, glancing around nervously.

"I didn't think. I'm no better than the captain, no better than your husband. I hope you can forgive me. I should never—"

"Shh, shh, shh," she whispered as though he were the silly parrot. No. A kestrel, that was her pet. "You mustn't upset yourself. You'll wake up Langley."

"I am upset. Dutch was right. I preyed upon your trust and let myself believe you wanted me to—"

"Bash," she said, taking his face in both hands, and they were soft and cool against his fevered skin. They felt like heaven must surely feel. "You did nothing wrong."

"I did everything wrong—"

"Please, listen to me. I don't know what Dutch said—" Fear flickered across her face, but she schooled it into a determined calm. "I never once felt like anything less than a queen."

He closed his eyes against the tears. Christ, what was happening to him? He hadn't wept since he was nine years old, not even when the captain ordered Dutch to flog him for leaving the ship to search out his mother's old place in Kingston. The pain had been unbearable, only rivaling his disappointment at not even managing to leave Port Royal, but still, he hadn't cried.

The king once built a town so fair. Red hibiscus lined the square...

Ma's song drifted back to him again. Would she be ashamed of him as Dutch had been for his treatment of Maggie?

"You have my word and my honor," he whispered fiercely. "I will protect you no matter what—even if you send me away, you'll have it from afar."

He meant to swear he wouldn't touch her again, but it seemed a hollow promise when something was so obviously wrong with him. He tugged hard at his forelock and then reached for his ear again, but as before, she took his hand so he couldn't rub away the pain.

"There was a ship," she explained, her brow creasing. "The *Woebegone Whale*? You feared it might be a trap."

A trap. Of course. How had he forgotten? "It was deserted," he said. "Nothing in the hold to even keep the rats alive."

She nodded, encouraging him to continue.

"But someone was there."

Blinding pain shot through Bash and he closed his eyes, recalling the flash of a cutlass. His hand jerked up again, but she held it fast, pressing it instead against her heart.

"Did I lose my ear?" he whispered.

She bit her lip and shook her head. "Not yet."

"The Butcher wanted to, but Magnus here insisted it stay attached to your ugly mug, Nav," Langley said, grinning from a nearby hammock.

Maggie released Bash's hand and turned to the lad. "He might need more hashish," she said. "Did you save any?"

Langley jumped up still grinning, but Bash tried to shake his head and instantly regretted it. "No," he gasped, closing his eyes. "Not just now."

"You sure?" Langley asked with a disappointed tone. "It's the good stuff."

"I can bear it," Bash said. He didn't want to lose a moment's consciousness with Maggie, nor did he want to chance any more nightmares.

"Then I'm to run and tell Dutch you're proper awake," Langley said.

"Ask Roo for some cheese, while you're at it?"

"Cheese, Nav? How hard was you hit?"

"You know Roo. Why do you think we've a cow and no milk?"

Langley's eyes widened and he scampered off, twirling to avoid running into a stack of supply crates on his gangly legs.

Dance a waltz, then dance again...

"What does that mean?" Bash wondered.

Maggie winced. "About your ear? It's ah... still attached at the bottom. The Butcher wanted to make a clean cut of it and then stop the bleeding with gun powder." She shrugged. "I... strongly suggested an alternative. It was Dutch who made him let me try."

Bash blinked, having trouble following her words through the throbbing pain. "An alternative? What alternative could there be?" he asked. "Magic?"

She bit her lip and his prick stirred, and he wanted to scream, *Really? Now?* But he didn't have the energy to even feel ashamed anymore.

"Leeches," she said, closing her eyes and then peeking at him through a half-opened one.

She was so adorable that for a moment he forgot to be horrified. He even forgot about his pain. Then his brain caught up with her words.

"Leeches?" he rasped.

"They're quite remarkable, honestly. Jory taught me."

He was silent for a long moment, contemplating the little marvel. Every ship, pirate or otherwise, should be as lucky in their selection of cabin boys.

"Are you angry?" she asked.

"That you single-handedly kept the Butcher from blowing my head off? Livid." Why had he ever thought she needed his protection from the Butcher or Balthasar or any of them?

"I told you, it was Dutch who—"

He stopped her. "I'm grateful."

"Still might not work."

He reached out blindly for her hand, and when she met him, it felt like coming home. "I'm grateful," he said again. "Somewhere around here, the Butcher keeps a bit of mirrored glass."

"You want to see it?" she asked, uncertainly.

"Please."

She released his hand once more and it pained him, as she and her light and her warmth left his side to rummage through the barber-surgeon's supplies, finally returning with the mirror in hand.

"Are you certain?" she asked.

He swallowed. "No. But show me anyway."

She held up the glass and somehow it was both shockingly grotesque and intriguing at the same time. "How does it work?"

"I don't know," she confessed. "But the Butcher gave me twenty-four hours to try and, bad as it looks, it was worse yesterday."

"You should've seen the kid standing up to the Butcher," Langley exclaimed bursting in with Dutch and inspecting Bash's ear for himself with a shudder.

"Reminded me of you, in point of fact," Dutch agreed, clapping Bash on the shoulder and shaking his hand.

Langley offered Bash a small hunk of cheese. "Roo says fuck you, by the way, for ratting him out, but enjoy. I only took a tiny taste on account of you're convalescing."

Bash sniffed the cheese, and it smelled divine, making his stomach rumble. He hadn't realized he was hungry, only wanted Langley gone long enough to ensure a few more minutes' privacy.

"Color looks better," Dutch observed to Maggie, who blushed, making Bash's prick stir once more.

Christ, he was going straight to hell if he could be so prurient while in this much pain.

"Was it Walsh?" he asked, to take his mind off Maggie and her lovely face.

Dutch nodded. "Half out of his mind with starvation. Said his crew abandoned him when they realized the rumors about the gold weren't true. There's an odor to his story, but I believe that much."

"Thought he retired?"

"Maybe he un-retired. Wouldn't be the first," Dutch said with a shrug.

"The lads tore up every inch of his ship searching for Mad's bounty," Langley added. "While the old bastard sat in a corner cackling at his pigeons. Samson and Duffy were desperate to see you didn't get sliced up for no reason."

"What did they do with him?" Maggie asked. "The other captain?"

"Left him to it," Dutch told her. "Ship wasn't worth taking, and he wasn't worth a bullet."

"Have we laid in a course?" Bash asked. Maybe it was the injury or he was still unnerved by the whole encounter, but something felt off. The ship was too still, and he didn't want to loiter in these waters.

"We found ourselves becalmed," Dutch said. "The men are rowing on alternating shifts. Wind'll pick up in a day or two."

A shiver ran down Bash's spine. "Feel that in your bones, do you?"

"Don't get cheeky with me, son," Dutch warned, but the relief in his face was evident, and Bash flooded with affection for the old quartermaster, though he was still uncomfortable with the close eye Dutch was keeping on him and Maggie.

"Mad?" Bash asked. He could well imagine the captain would be raging if he really believed his own fairytales about Willy Walsh, and whether he did or he didn't, the crew would be simmering with their own discontent.

"There's nothing for you to do but heal," Dutch said. "And you," he added, turning to Maggie, "if you're planning to stay aboard the *Revenge*, perhaps you should consider apprenticing with the Butcher. Or just taking over for him all together."

Maggie's blush deepened at the compliment, and Dutch turned back to Bash, nodding once. "I'll see that you're not disturbed," he said, and Bash blinked his acknowledgment rather than move his aching head. He was grateful to have cheated death out of a few extra days, but he needed to make the most of them, get back on his feet as soon as possible, and find a fair wind to carry them to safe harbor.

Chapter Fifteen

The doldrums which had caught the *Revenge* dragged on for more than a week, though the crew took turns at the oars so they weren't completely stranded. While the Butcher wouldn't go so far as to admit the leeches had worked wonders, he grudgingly agreed Bash's ear wasn't getting any worse. Still, he offered to cut it off and have done. Bash told him in no uncertain terms precisely where he could shove his blade, which Langley found hilarious.

After that, the barber-surgeon had abandoned his infirmary entirely, which was fine with Maggie. She quite liked their little world of just the three of them—her, Bash, and an oft-snoring Langley.

No one questioned the need for a cabin boy to remain at the sailing master's side, nursing him through the worst of it, and doing whatever was needed. She had saved Bash's ear, maybe even his life, and that was good enough for them.

They were almost forgotten, tucked away out of sight as they were—even Langley. Maggie suspected Dutch had ordered him to help her at first, but as one of the youngest sailors on board, he seemed to genuinely enjoy her company, and while she'd have rather been alone with Bash during his waking hours, she did enjoy Langley's kinship and chatter.

With each new day of his confinement, however, Bash grew more and more restless. Long accustomed to an active lifestyle, lying still, cooped up indoors and in darkness was making him surly. He was a creature of the ocean—requiring sun and brine to thrive. Honestly, Maggie wouldn't have been surprised to learn his mother, Amoy, really had been a mermaid or that saltwater flowed through his veins.

His ear was steadily improving. They'd run through about a hundred leeches so far, and both the color and swelling were dramatically improved, along with the pain. So, once he felt like sitting up, Maggie wrapped his head with a clean bandage and relocated him to a more comfortable position in a hammock, which at least improved his disposition a little.

Though exhausted, his sleep was fitful, and several times he awoke singing long forgotten lyrics with a wistful look in his faraway gaze. Late at night, after Langley had helped himself to the medicinal hashish and passed out with Custard the cat for a pillow, Maggie and Bash would speak in low, murmured tones—about their youths and their youthful dreams.

He sang for her, what he could remember of his mother's song. It was the only tune he could recall her ever singing, though her voice was strong and fair.

"How old were you when she passed?" Maggie asked.

"Five," he answered. "Or six, maybe. She was the whole world to me. She sailed from Jamaica to Lewis to find my sire, but instead she found his family. They took her in, loved her, and she looked after them... after all of us."

Maggie played with his hair absently as he reminisced, just happy to be near him. She didn't ever want to stop touching him.

"Nothing gave her more joy than the fruit and flower garden she kept beside the house. She could coax any old seed to thrive, no matter the soil."

It made her smile to hear the brash, brave pirate speak so lovingly of his mother. In turn, she shared more about her brother-in-law, Silas, who liked to study plants as they grew upon his windowsill. She told him stories of growing up with Jory and Ellen, how she used to torment them as only a little sister or cousin could, and how much she had learned from them about becoming a woman. She even showed him the little folding frame with their likenesses and flushed with pleasure when he noted the family resemblance.

One night, he opened up about life after his mother's death: being passed from grandparents to aunts to neighbors until one day his pirate sire came to take him away.

"Dutch?" she asked, laughing ruefully.

"Not Dutch."

"Oh. Only I thought—"

"Understandable," he said, catching her fingers and kissing them so she forgot to feel embarrassed by her mistake. "Dutch has been more of a father to me than my own flesh and blood ever could."

In a way, Maggie knew what he meant. "Mine tried," she said. "But it was hard, I suppose, when his sole mission in life was to find someone to take each of us off his hands."

"Explains your husband, then," he murmured. "A foolish man found you an equally foolish man."

She was silent for so long that he reached out to brush her arm.

"I apologize," he said. "I shouldn't speak ill of—"

"Jeremiah wasn't foolish. He was cruel."

She hadn't always realized it. Maggie had thought it was just how men were—thought perhaps she'd been deceived by the kindness of Finn and Si. She convinced herself they, too, would have shown their true natures eventually had Jory and Ellen been less perfect. But over the last month and a bit, living amongst pirates, she had begun to realize that some men were cruel and some were kind. Even if she had been more capable like her sister and cousin, it still wouldn't have been enough for Jeremiah.

"He hurt you," Bash said, and a knot formed in Maggie's throat. No one had ever asked. She'd never allowed herself to say it either—even to think it—only to excuse it.

He was just a man. She was just his wife. There was something wrong with her for not desiring him, for not enjoying what little he offered, just as there was something wrong with her stitching and cooking and the way she scrubbed the floor.

There was something wrong with her for wishing he would fall off the roof, even as she shouted at him that it could wait until morning, as it had waited weeks already. There was something wrong with her for feeling relief when he died.

"Mags?" Bash asked, running his thumb along her shoulder.

"You should drink," she said, getting up to fetch them both more ale.

In the galley, she took a moment to gather herself.

Jeremiah hadn't hurt her undeservingly, she told her brain, squashing down the tears. She had picked every fight with him because she was impulsive and far too dramatic, and he was right to be disappointed with her. He had needed someone capable and level-headed, a mother for his children, not a seemingly-barren child of his own.

She took a deep breath and then another and then filled two tankards with watered-down ale. The barrel was dangerously close to empty. She had to stretch to reach deep inside.

"Well, if it isn't the cabin boy turned personal nursemaid," a voice said, and a prickle of alarm shot down her back, making the tiny hairs on her arms stand on end. She pulled herself back upright, slowly, determined not to show her fear, and turned to see Balthasar grinning lasciviously behind her, with an upturned smirk and a glint of Jeremiah in his eye.

"Pity," he said, clucking his tongue and stepping closer. "That was the perfect position."

"I should get back to Bash," she said loudly, hoping anyone might be around to hear and intervene.

He drew closer. "Should you, now? And do your attentions extend to the whole crew or just our fearless Nav?"

She swallowed down bile as he sidled even closer. "By helping Bash, I'm helping all of you," she stammered, as though she didn't understand his meaning.

"I can think of much better ways for you to help me, cabin boy." He leaned in and sniffed her, and she jerked back, splashing warm, sticky ale down her front. It made him roar with laughter.

"Excuse me," she said, trying to duck away, but he put a hand on her waist to stop her.

"Oh, I'll excuse you—once I've decided whether your mouth or your arse would be the more pleasant fit."

A faintness threatened to overcome Maggie as she tried to calculate whether splashing the remaining ale in his eyes would give her ample time to get away—and if so—where she could run. Leading him back to a weakened but enraged Bash was a terrible notion.

"Magnus?" Langley called. "All right?" he asked, stepping into the galley.

Balthasar shuffled back a step. "Just updating me on Bash's miraculous recovery," he said, winking at her.

Langley drew even with her, standing up straight and shoving his hands in his pockets. "Ain't miraculous," he said. "It's science."

Balthasar threw back his head and laughed. "All grown up now, are you, Lev? Big man of science?" he laughed again before slinking off into the shadows.

"All right?" Langley repeated, the slightest tremor in his voice.

Maggie nodded, but she couldn't speak. Bash had been right. She was still as naive as a newborn babe. If Langley hadn't been looking out for her... she shuddered.

He took the tankards from her quaking hands and topped them up before guiding her back to the infirmary, where she retook her seat on the stool beside Bash, clutching her own drink so tightly her fingers glowed white in the semidarkness.

SOMEHOW BASH HAD FUCKED UP YET AGAIN. HE NEEDED TO remember, no matter his tender feelings, he was nothing but a pirate brute, and he shouldn't be allowed within ten feet of a lady, even one pretending to be a tough pirate boy.

She'd practically flown from the room after he mentioned her late husband, and when Langley brought her back, she looked even more upset than he had realized. No doubt she was sick of being trapped in the dim and stuffy sickbay—would much rather take some sunshine and spend the night in a hammock alone. He couldn't blame her there. His skin was beginning to crawl and not because of the leeches.

He resolved that no matter how dizzy it made him and despite his cabin boy's orders to stay put, come the dawn he would leave his sickbed and resume his post. The crew were exhausting themselves with rowing in God-knew-which direction, and he needed to ascertain their location and find a wind to carry them back to Jamaica.

Between his confinement, the stagnation of the ship, and dreams of his mother, he felt like he was going mad. She haunted him, as though calling from beyond the veil, warning of imminent disaster. But like the rest of her song, he couldn't remember her message when he surfaced from those vivid dreams.

Maggie, however, didn't seem to ever sleep. No matter the hour, day or night, each time he awoke he found her eyes boring into his. For a moment he drowned in the fantasy of waking up to swim in their azure depths every morning for the rest of his life. But that was a dangerous line of thinking. His life was wherever the winds took him, and hers was in Scotland as soon as he could see her aboard an eastbound vessel.

At the same time, the life of a pirate could be all too brief. Somehow, he'd never been less troubled by the notion of death—not if it meant waking beside her until it was his turn to dance the hempen jig.

"How do you feel?" she whispered.

"Ready to get back to work."

She sat up straight, incensed. "The Butcher said recovery would take about three weeks."

"The Butcher also claimed your idea would never work at all, Mags. It may seem like one long nightmare, but it's been two weeks already, and I'm long overdue on deck."

She frowned, and he pushed himself to sit up, pretending it didn't make his head swim. As long as he stayed off the rigging, he'd be fine. Probably.

"Come now," he whispered. "Your treatment has worked wonders. It's time I earned my salvation."

"There's nothing to earn," she muttered.

"I'm going above," he said gently, but firmly. "Will you come with me and make sure I don't fall overboard?"

She smiled at that and offered him a reluctant nod, and Christ, how he longed to kiss her. But Langley was just stirring a few feet away and there was work to be done. Kissing would have to wait, heaven help him.

"Fine, but you must promise—"

"Anything."

"Swear you'll continue your treatment. The leeches still need replacing every few hours."

"Is that all? I'll be the model patient."

But he was far weaker than he realized after the whole ordeal. Just climbing the ladder to the deck nearly wiped him out. He almost asked Langley to help him back to bed, except whatever pride he had left wouldn't allow it. Now wasn't the time to appear weak, not when the ship was adrift and tensions coming to a boil.

He only hoped they were out here alone. If he had to lead this divided lot into battle, he'd be done for.

"Well, well," the captain greeted, a manic look barely hidden behind his lazy mask. "Finished swinging lead at last, have you, boy?" he asked, tapping his spyglass against his leg.

"Aye, Captain. Reporting for duty. Still no wind?"

"As you can see," Mad said, nodding to the slack sails, his eye twitching.

Bash blinked up at them and almost stumbled backwards.

The leech in his ear was affecting his balance more than he'd anticipated, and the sunlight was blinding. But Maggie was there, slipping under his shoulder so he could lean against her.

"Thank you," he murmured.

"Yes, I understand you're to thank for keeping my sailing master out of commission all this time," the captain said, turning his attention on her.

"Keeping your sailing master out of the grave, sir," Bash said. "I'm here now. Do we still make for Kingston?"

Mad sneered at him. "You're here now. You decide."

Which of course meant any decision Bash made would be the wrong one. Same as it ever was.

Enjoying the warmth of Maggie tucked under his arm, he walked to the bow, took out his compass and watch, and squinted up at the sun.

The men were rowing more or less in a westerly direction, but they made slow progress against the current. There were no clouds overhead, though in the distance, his spyglass revealed the speck of a vessel. Perhaps merely the *Whale* they'd left behind, but it ignited a familiar tingling in his scalp, intensified by the damage to his ear.

"What is it?" Maggie asked, reading his posture and expression as plainly as he read maps and charts. How did she know him so well after, what, a little more than five weeks? What other secrets had he failed to keep hidden?

He collapsed the spyglass and dropped it in his pocket. "Nothing to worry about," he told her. "Can you find Dutch for me?"

She nodded once. "Of course," she said, and he rested against the railing as she hurried away.

"Langley," he shouted in no particular direction.

"All right, Nav?" the boy asked, dropping from the rigging.

"In my quarters, there's a book of maps. Bring it to me?"

"The one with all them squiggly lines?" Langley asked nervously.

"Yes... why?"

"I were feeding the blasted bird, and well, it got out of its nest and shat all over your book when no one was looking."

Bash closed his eyes. When he opened them, Langley had gone, but Maggie was heading back with Dutch.

"Should he be up?" the quartermaster asked her, eyeing Bash's bandaged head warily.

"Either way, he is."

Bash ignored them and began growling out orders. "If we turn the gib lines, we might tack a little more southerly and pick up wind."

Dutch nodded and turned away, to relay the orders so Bash didn't have to exert himself, but Bash caught his arm.

"Magnus," he called. "You should check on your bird."

A look of faint surprise crossed her face, guilty, like she hadn't thought about the kestrel in days, and Bash was more pleased than he ought to be, knowing he was the reason.

"Are you sure?" she asked, clearly torn between eagerness to do as he suggested and trepidation at leaving him behind.

"Go on. I'll be fine. See, I've Dutch here to look after me."

She nodded warily and took off once more.

"What's the temperature?" Bash asked Dutch quietly, not wanting to alarm Maggie as she walked away.

"Hot," Dutch replied just as softly into his good ear. "Three skirmishes yesterday. Just fisticuffs, not much blood. Reports from the night watch claim ghost ships appearing and disappearing on the horizon."

"Fata morgana?" Bash asked, the Italian term for a mirage some less experienced sailors took for phantoms.

Dutch shrugged. "Who can say?"

"Could it be Walsh coming after us?"

"With what wind?"

"Which direction would the *Whale* be now?"

Dutch pointed to port, as Bash would have expected. At least his instinctual sense of direction remained intact.

"What did you see?" Dutch muttered, and Bash realized he was frowning.

He handed Dutch his spyglass and indicated the starboard side, where he'd spotted the ship a moment ago. Now it was Dutch's turn to frown.

"Could be anything," the quartermaster said, handing back the glass.

"Aye," Bash agreed uncertainly. "Could be."

"You think it's him? The navy man?"

"When's the last time we saw him?" Bash asked struggling to remember. "Sixteen—eighteen months ago?"

They might all joke that the captain was a madman with a persecution complex, but he'd come by it honestly, after twenty years of cat and mouse with Constantin. "There were pigeons on that boat. You ever known Walsh to fuck about with pigeons?"

Dutch shook his head and looked through the glass again.

"Navy uses pigeons."

Dutch didn't comment.

"Does he know?" Bash asked, glancing over his shoulder towards the captain's quarters.

"It's a speck on the horizon, son. There's nothing to know."

But Bash could sense trouble in his tingling scalp. "Tack the sails to port," he said. If there was any wind to be found, they'd better do it.

"We need to talk about your cabin boy," Dutch said.

Bash's gut twisted. Had he figured out what transpired moments after their last conversation, before everything went to hell?

"Saved my life," Bash said.

"May have at that. Were you ever going to come clean?"

" 'Bout what?" Bash asked, squinting out at that speck in the middle of the ocean.

Dutch huffed. "You're a terrible liar, son. I'm almost impressed you made it this long."

"I don't know what you—"

"You got sloppy. She got even sloppier," the quartermaster whispered, confirming Bash's fear, and his mouth went dry. "How the hell did you think you could pull off such a stupid stunt?"

"I didn't know what else to do."

"Well it was quick thinking, I'll give you that."

"How—?" Bash began, but Dutch cut him off with a look.

"Aside from that?" Bash asked, rolling his eyes.

"A million broken pieces eventually make a whole."

"Do you think anyone else knows?"

Dutch shook his head once, but stopped.

"Dutch?"

"The day after..." He gestured to Bash's ear. "She and Langley were chatting over loud. She mentioned watching Simon Fraser march on Inverness."

Bash stared at him blankly, the name ringing some vague, distant bell.

"Not many books on this boat for a man learning to read, but the captain always did like his Scottish history."

Bash nodded, holding his breath. He'd avoided the captain's favorite books, preferring to memorize his maps instead.

"The siege of Inverness was in 1715."

Bash remembered now, part of the Rising to restore the Scottish king. "Fifteen years ago," he said.

Dutch nodded. "Arithmetic doesn't quite add up," he said. Not if Maggie was supposed to be a lad of fourteen.

Bash swallowed. "What else?"

Dutch looked away then, almost embarrassed.

"What?"

"She was leaning forward stitching you up. I was crowding in to see. Looked down and well... most men don't wrap their chests in linen, do they?"

Ah. "Christ."

"Who is she?"

"She's just... a marvel. Just..."

"Magic?"

"Aye," Bash agreed, cheeks burning.

"Are you in love with her?" Dutch asked, and Bash slowly nodded his head. "Well. Seems like so far she's brought pretty good luck," he said, cupping the back of Bash's neck.

Exhaling with relief, Bash nodded once more in agreement. She was the best kind of luck.

"Promise me you'll be careful."

He nodded at that too, seemingly all out of words.

Dutch put one arm around him in a quick, sideways embrace.

"I wanted to tell you," Bash whispered.

"Well. Now you have."

Chapter Sixteen

Maggie was fairly certain she wasn't actually going to die, no matter what her body was telling her. And that was almost too bad, because she really kind of wanted to. If she'd been less impulsive, if she'd stopped to consider anything beyond her immediate desires for more than five minutes, she might have made some sort of plan for this eventuality. Instead, running around pretending to be a boy had allowed her to forget.

Until she awoke in the hammock alone, after Bash had insisted he sleep on the floor for the sake of his ear. She was roused by the sensation of being repeatedly stabbed in the gut with the Butcher's filthiest knife. Her courses, which had never been predictable, had finally made a most inconvenient appearance.

"Is it dysentery?" Bash asked, searching her face when she emerged from the head.

"No, of course not," she assured him.

He wasn't convinced. "Scurvy then?" he asked, baring his teeth to make her do the same, gently tugging down her lip to check her gums. "Honestly, you look quite peaked."

She patted his arm. "I am well," she said, and then tried to drink the ale he offered, but instead raced to the railing and vomited over the side.

"Mags," he said plaintively, "you're not well."

"I'll be fine," she snapped and walked away from him, wanting nothing more than to curl up in a heap with Custard purring warmly on her abdomen until it was her turn for the watch.

Because the captain was getting restless.

Bash hadn't taken a night watch since the incident with Walsh, which meant neither had Maggie. But with more rumors than ever flying about ghost ships, the captain had put everyone on high alert, and since Maggie had been first to confirm sighting the *Woebegone Whale*, he was insistent she spend tonight looking out for any kind of vessel, friend or foe—and who was a friend to pirates?

A little surprised when Bash let her walk away, a thrill of fear ran through Maggie the moment she descended below deck on her own. Was Balthasar occupied above? Or lurking somewhere, waiting to catch her unawares with no Langley to intervene this time?

She shuddered, but no bogeymen jumped out of the shadows as she swiped bandages from the infirmary to line her smalls. She fed Kes a bit of dried beef and eventually Custard joined her in the hammock, glaring hungrily at the bird from Maggie's lap.

Bash roused her with a bowl of bland fish soup not long before the second watch bells.

"It was supposed to have a touch of milk in it, but they ate the cow last week," he said sorrowfully. "I've never seen Rooijakkers so devastated on account of his cheese."

"Poor Roo," Maggie agreed. "It's delicious even without the milk, thank you," she told him, hoping gratitude might make up for her earlier crabbiness.

She wasn't terribly hungry, but she forced herself to eat every bite. As rations had grown tighter each day, Bash tried to hide the fact that he was taking even less than his allotted portions so Maggie could have more—she, who had stolen onto their ship and by rights should not have any portion at all, while he was still recuperating and needed every ounce of nourishment. When questioned, he pretended not to know a thing about it, but she knew.

The others had not lately been so kind. They glared daggers at her across their bowls of gruel. She may have spotted the *Whale* and saved Bash's ear, but the *Whale* held neither treasure nor food, and the ear could not be eaten, and now she was just another mouth they could ill afford to feed.

If they saw land before they all starved to death, they'd probably vote her off the ship whether a port was available or not. She couldn't bear to think about ports and ships and Scotland. She wasn't sure she could bring herself to leave.

She squeezed Bash's hand, and he rubbed his thumb along the back of her knuckles.

"How are you?" he asked.

"I'll be fine. Promise."

"I'll go with you tonight," he said.

She was glad of the offer. She wanted him there, but he shouldn't be climbing yet, not with his head still leeched and bandaged. "You don't have to do that. I'm capable."

"You're more than capable, darlin', but I miss the tops. No argument. Cabin boys mustn't get cheeky with the sailing master."

He must be feeling better to put his bossy breeks on like that, and Maggie liked to think maybe it wasn't just the tops he was missing.

When the bells rang, they made their way to the main mast and began to climb just as they had on her second week aboard only seven weeks ago now.

"It's not just a ghost ship tying the captain up in knots, is it?" she asked as they huddled side by side on the platform, looking out into a star-covered night.

"No," he said after a moment. "Ghosts aren't real. But the navy is."

Maggie didn't know what to say to that. An encounter with the military could mean death for them all. As pirates, the navy was their natural sworn enemy. And just as she'd known it when the Butcher wanted to cut off Bash's beautiful ear, Maggie knew she couldn't lose him. Whatever was coming, she was powerless to stop it, but she could also never allow it to happen. The Royal Navy couldn't have him. He was hers.

"Wind's picking up," he sighed with palpable relief.

That had to be a good sign, didn't it?

A wave of cramping crashed against her belly, making her knees almost buckle and she hunched forward holding onto the railing for life. In an instant, Bash's arm was around her.

"I wish you'd tell me what ails you," he said.

But ladies did not speak of their courses with gentlemen, not even their fathers or their husbands. Most especially not with pirates.

"Should I fetch O'Riordan?" he asked, and he really must be worried to suggest such a thing and use the barber-surgeon's proper name.

"No," she gasped. "I'll be fine. It's only..."

"Only what?"

Maggie studied his face. His intense brows were packed with years of dread, his dark amber eyes swirling with both anguish and innocence. He would either empathize with a pain he couldn't quite fathom or he'd shy away in disgust and revile her for the sin of being a woman. She couldn't bear the latter, though it might ease their inevitable parting, the one she refused to contemplate. Either way, he had trusted her with his ear. It was time she trusted him with this.

"Only my monthly courses," she whispered.

"The blood of Eve?" he asked, and when she nodded, "Do you need to sit down?"

"No." Curious concern was not the response she'd expected, but perhaps it should have been.

He rubbed her back. "It hurts a great deal?"

"Sometimes more than others."

"Will anything ease it?"

"No. At home I might brew a cup of willow bark or raspberry tea and warm a stone on the hearth to wrap in a blanket and hold against my belly, but as I'm not home and have no stove or hearth or willow bark..."

"My hands are warm," he said, low in her ear, and her breath sped up for a different reason.

Bash moved behind her, almost shy despite the intimacies they'd shared thus far. Slowly, he ran his large hand up under her shirt to cradle her stomach.

His hand *was* warm, and she nudged it just a bit lower to span from hip bone to hip bone. The cozy pressure helped her relax muscles she hadn't realized she was clenching.

They stood that way for a long time, as Maggie absorbed the relief his warmth provided. His breath tickled her cheek but he held himself impossibly still, even while growing hard against her.

"I apologize," he finally whispered.

It was one of the things she loved most about him, his inclination to address any awkwardness rather than pretending it away while it festered into rot.

"Don't," she said, and he seemed to hesitate, to draw back, so she put her hand over his, holding him in place, and repeated, "Don't... apologize."

Then he drew her closer and nuzzled into her neck, and she wished she wasn't menstruating because she'd never longed to be as close to another human being as she did right then with him.

"Is it true," he began tentatively, "an orgasm can alleviate the pain? Or is that just tales men tell?"

Maggie didn't know the word, though she felt an inkling of

what it meant. When she didn't answer he mumbled, "Forgive me, I—"

"What is orgasm?" she blurted out.

"Oh. Er—climax. During relations."

So her inkling had been correct, and that indefinable moment of bliss had a name.

"I don't know," she admitted. "I only ever felt it with you."

For a moment she could sense him swell with pride, and then he kissed her neck, making her shiver.

"Would you like to try?" he asked.

Maggie froze, momentarily unable to breathe.

Responding to her rigid posture, Bash froze too.

She braced herself for the next part. He was Bash, he wouldn't shove her away or shout at her. He wouldn't demand to know why she was such a cocktease.

"I'm sorry," he whispered. "Was that the wrong thing to say?" And by God, if he could address it head-on so casually, then so could Maggie.

She turned to face him. "I don't... typically like to be entered. Especially back there."

Back there, his lips moved as if to say, but he frowned, not understanding.

Her cheeks burned, very much regretting her decision to be bold.

"In the arse?" he asked suddenly, his eyebrows shooting up to his hairline.

She could have both laughed and cried. "Yes."

"Is that a requirement? I only meant in the regular way."

Did he not understand how it all worked? "My courses. I'm unclean," she explained, and now his brow furrowed.

"Maggie, you're only you."

Love flooded through her, fierce and pure, washing away her doubts and fears like a tidal wave unleashed, leaving her newly raw and vulnerable, a scallop stripped of its shell when it washed up on a sandy beach.

"I only thought there might be extra—ah—lubrication," he fumbled to explain, and Maggie buried her face in his chest, squeezing him tight.

For the first few months of married life, her courses had been her only reprieve from Jeremiah's attentions. He wouldn't come near her, as though she were so filthy her blood would stain his appendage forever. But then the more he drank, the more creative he got, and he began to insist she offer her bottom, so he could still hump to his heart's content while keeping his precious cock *clean*.

"It was a foolish thing to suggest," Bash murmured. "Forgive me, Mags, truly. As I've said, I've no real experience, only the stories of bawdy sailors. It's not always easy to tell fact from fiction."

For some reason, as he mumbled his apology, Maggie had never been more aroused.

"It doesn't repulse you?" she asked, giving him one last chance to disappoint her.

He tilted his head, confused, then shook it and she raised up on her toes to kiss him, a heated, bruising kiss, and he hardened against her stomach once more.

"Will you show me? For science?" she asked, running a hand over his length, making him shudder deliciously.

He peered down at her, his face a mixture of lust and concern. "But you don't like—"

"Maybe this time I will."

"I've no wish to hurt you," he said.

"Then go slow."

He searched her eyes, and finding the truth there, he kissed her again, thirstily, like a man who'd been deprived of water for weeks, and Maggie kissed him back, just as thirsty, a woman who'd been deprived of love.

Gently, he turned her back around so she could grip the railing and whispered, "Hold on. I won't go in your arse, and I won't let you fall. Keep your eyes open, you might see a shooting star."

Then he lowered her breeches just enough to grant access, and her smalls as well, and her bottom felt the nip of the chill sea air for only a moment as he touched her like he had that first night in his hammock. She gasped.

"Try to keep your voice down, Mags," he whispered, kissing her cheek, and the inside of her neck, and her shoulder, and then closing the chilly gap, pushing up close behind her, his erection bobbing eagerly between her legs.

She stepped her feet further apart.

"Are you certain?" he whispered.

"Yes, please," she replied, and he entered her only a little, just the tip. This time he gasped, which made her wetter if such a thing were possible.

She had closed her eyes, but she wrenched them open as he kissed the back of her neck and circled her with his finger, all the while drawing in and out at a torturously slow pace.

Maggie clenched the railing and leaned lower, deepening the angle and he hissed, speeding up just a little. The friction was exquisite, as Bash panted, stifling his own moans by burying his face in her hair, while she turned into her shoulder to keep quiet as she rode crescendo after crescendo until at last she broke apart and became one of those shooting stars.

HOLY FUCKING HELL. BASH WAS A LITTLE PUT OUT THAT NOT A single story he'd ever been told of the act had come close to living up to the real thing. It was sacred and incandescent, St. Elmo's fire made flesh.

He'd known for weeks that Maggie's body fit perfectly against his own, known too that her mind and spirit were his perfect counterweight. And though he'd dreamt of their coupling more than one dark night, he'd never dared hope such a thing might come true, let alone fill him up, body and soul, all the empty, broken parts made new.

Now he sat with his back against the mast, and she rested between his legs, leaning into his chest, as though they were cut from the same piece of wood.

"Thank you," she murmured sleepily, and he chuckled.

"Did it work?"

"I believe it did."

"Good." He kissed the top of her head. "Let me know if you need another."

She giggled softly, and he wanted to bottle the sound to hear again and again after she was gone, like the ocean waves inside a shell. His stomach sank, and he deflated a little. Soon they'd reach Jamaica and she'd sail away home forever, leaving him lost and wandering without compass or lodestar to guide him.

Once she was safe, he would dedicate the rest of his life to making an honest living for himself so that someday he might actually deserve her.

"Dutch was looking at me funny this morning," she said softly. "I'm afraid he might suspect."

Christ. Bash considered his options—lie, deflect, or be honest —and he decided on the truth. "I should have warned you, but I didn't want you to worry," he admitted.

She stiffened in his arms but didn't pull away.

"He would never betray me," he swore.

"But if he knows, surely others—"

"I don't think so. Dutch is the most perceptive man I've ever met. Especially where I'm concerned."

"He loves you."

Her statement made him warm all over, such a simple

pronouncement of fact, and yet one Bash had never allowed himself to put into words lest he be mistaken.

"I could see it," she went on. "When he visited the infirmary. Langley, too."

Bash smiled. He'd often felt unlovable after his mother died. Strange to think the actions of a man who never wanted him had led him to this other family, aboard a pirate ship no less.

"We've been through a lot together."

"Mmm," Maggie chuckled.

"What?"

"It's just funny how that works. You know Finn?"

"The erstwhile Shaw Wretch?"

"Mmhmm. He had two brothers. One still lives, but I believe Silas MacKenzie is more of a brother to him than his own flesh and blood even now. It's just... it's like God gives you a family, but if that one doesn't fit, He leaves you the pieces to make one of your own."

Bash had never thought of it quite in that way before, but he was getting used to seeing a new world through Maggie's sea-blue eyes. "And which do you have?"

"A little of both, I hope," she whispered.

He was glad for her to say so. It would make their parting easier for her. "Will you go to Ellen? Or to Jory? When you return home."

"If I were to return, Langley thinks I should apprentice to be a physician," she said, and he could hear the smile in her voice.

"You must return. I'll write you a letter of reference," he agreed.

"I'll be the most sought-after ear reattacher in all of Scotland. Pirates and highwaymen will be lining up in droves for my services. They'll pay me in golden teeth and stolen jewels, and the leech houses will soon be empty."

Bash snorted and rested his scarred cheek against the crown of her head. He almost hoped she would hang up a shingle. It might make her easier to find if he was ever respectable enough to track her down.

Maggie snuggled against him and sighed. "Honestly, I could get used to this life," she said. "This freedom."

"It only feels like freedom," he reminded her. "Because you've never been free. This ship is just a different sort of cage."

"I'm sorry, Bash. I didn't think."

"You've nothing to apologize for. You're like the Pleiades. He pointed up to the brightest stars in the sky.

"What are they?"

"The seven sisters: Sterope, Merope, Electra, Maia, Taygeta, Celaeno, and Algone," he said, lifting her arm to point out each star. "The daughters of Atlas. He couldn't protect them," he said, frowning. "He was too busy holding up the sky." Did that make him Atlas, then? Distracted by a task so colossal that he'd fail in the one that truly mattered—keeping Maggie safe?

"A valid reason," Maggie said. "I'm sure they understood."

"To save them from the hunter Orion, Zeus transformed them into stars and fixed them up there for eternity."

"Mmm," she said sadly. "Turned seven innocent women into stars rather than shackle one man."

Bash couldn't argue. If he could place her amongst the stars to keep her safe, he'd like to do it, but what right did he have?

She pointed back up at the stars. "Jory, Ellen, Maggie..."

He followed the line of her long, lovely finger. Would it bother her, comfortable as she was, if he kissed all the way down her arm and back up again?

She dropped her pointing finger lower. "That's not a star."

He tore his gaze from her hand to the speck she'd identified on the horizon. "Sails," he breathed, as she took out her spyglass for a better look. Of course it was. He was as cursed as the captain, not deserving even a breath of stolen peace.

"What do we do?" she asked.

"We sound the alarm and get the hell out of here."

Chapter Seventeen

Bash left Maggie to keep an eye on the approaching vessel while he shimmied down the rigging to alert the other lookouts. Within minutes, the sails were turned into the wind, and oars were manned to speed up their escape.

The bells were not rung to change the watch, and no one came to relieve her, so she stared into the distance until her eyes burned, until she had to blink to keep from seeing double, as the naval ship slipped further and further behind them. When dawn came, she could see nothing at all in their wake.

Finally, Langley arrived for the forenoon watch a little after eight and greeted Maggie with a serious nod. "Nav says it were you spied the devil out there. Well done, Magnus. Go and have a rest."

"What'll happen if they catch us?" she asked, to which Langley gave a studied shrug and extended his spyglass. "I mean," Maggie pressed, "will they fire on us? Or will they wish to take the ship in one piece?"

What she meant was, *destroy us or take us alive, so they can execute us one by one?*

"Nav won't let it happen, don't you worry," Langley assured her, but he refused to meet her gaze.

Maggie squeezed his shoulder and then clumsily descended the rigging and stumbled below deck. She wasn't surprised to find Bash's quarters empty but for Kes, who squawked a greeting. Maggie tossed the bird a bite of beef before collapsing into the hammock and falling instantly to sleep.

She awoke sometime later, disoriented and thirsty, so she crept to the galley where Roo was clearing up.

"Beans is all," he said, and she nodded while he dished out a bit of what he'd just packed away. Then from a chest he took a small wheel of cheese. "Isn't aged long enough, but as you saved Bashy, enjoy."

"Cheese?" she asked excitedly, almost unable to believe her eyes.

"Cheese, pah!" Roo scoffed. "Not just cheese. Dutch gouda!"

"Thank you," she said, her mouth practically watering.

Roo shrugged. "Makes the beans almost palatable," he said, but she knew a gift when she saw one, and she took a tiny taste of her prize. It was a sweet, nutty heaven.

She carried her dinner and a tankard of ale back to the alcove, where Kes squawked even after Maggie fed her more beef. Clearly the bird wanted cheese too. "Sorry, beautiful. Birds can't eat Dutch gouda," she lied, keeping every morsel for herself, nibbling it like a mouse to make it last longer.

When she finished eating and Bash still hadn't returned, she sought him out on deck, looking for a job she could do, but the consensus seemed to be that she'd earned her rest and wasn't needed.

"Honest, Magnus, double watch calls for double rest. If anyone's earned it, that's you," Langley said, shooing her back to her hammock, but the truth was, below deck she was about to start climbing the walls. Visions of the navy plagued her every thought, of the captain striding aboard, sword in hand, and hacking off Bash's other ear. If the navy did indeed come aboard, there was probably not a single thing she could do to save him, but she wanted to be near enough to try.

Last night on the platform hidden away in the top of the rigging had been... transformative. Blanketed only by the magnificent starry sky, Bash had filled her so fully she would never be empty again, sealing cracks she'd long forgotten were there, healing wounds she had no longer believed could be made whole. She began to tingle just recalling it. His every touch was gentle and calculated for her pleasure, tinged with barely restrained passion and hunger and need.

She flushed and shivered all at the same time. Last night had been everything her younger self once imagined, and yet, like nothing she'd ever dared to dream.

It consumed her, even now, though their lives were, if not quite in mortal peril yet, then certainly peril adjacent.

If Jeremiah were watching up from his grave, he must surely feel vindicated for all the times he blamed her frigidness on whoring with other men, using up her lust to cuckold him, like lust was an expendable resource.

She knew better now.

Bash had unlocked something in her which had been hidden away, something Jeremiah had never reached. But Jeremiah was gone, and she wasn't wicked. How could she be, when she loved Bash so very deeply?

If only she could think of some way to show him as much. If only she could be useful to him, now when he needed it most.

But that was ever the problem, wasn't it? It wasn't helpful to need to be told what to do. Ellen and Jory were so very good precisely because they didn't need to be told. They put themselves to work, carving out spaces, forging paths all on their own. Bash didn't have time to educate a silly stowaway on what needed doing. He needed her to help intuitively or stay out of his way.

It had been high on the list of Jeremiah's many complaints, too.

Maggie's nature was to daydream. She could lose herself for hours, not even noticing her own hunger or a chill from the fire burning itself out.

In Jeremiah's mind, her failure to anticipate and wash his shirts before he noticed he'd run out was purely spite on Maggie's part, to punish him for some perceived slight. If he had to remind her, it was somehow as bad as having to do the chore himself. He'd rather rail at her and wear a dirty sark than tell her he'd donned the last clean one.

Never mind she didn't particularly love him, and he knew it. If she was distant, he would accuse her of being cold and heartless, deserting her wifely duties. If she tried to summon the energy to shower him with affection, he would push her away, annoyed by her clinging suffocation.

Maggie had always found it better to be perceived as apathetic than to suffer the shame of rejection for being needy. Even now, that fear kept her below deck where she couldn't make a nuisance of herself. Because she *was* needy.

Bad enough that before last night, their interactions had all been one-sided. He'd given so much, and like a glutton Maggie had allowed herself to take and take and take, indulging in her own pleasure and never providing his in return.

Was that simply who she was—who she'd always been? Yet another character flaw she was only now seeing clearly?

It put her in mind of Ellen and all her sister had done for her growing up, all that Maggie had allowed her to do. Suddenly homesick and guilt-stricken, she busied herself writing a letter to slip inside a bottle in case the navy caught them and they should all be drowned. Or hanged. Or worse.

Addressing it to Lady Len MacKenzie of Castle Leod, Ross, she apologized for every cruel poke she'd ever inflicted as a child, and thanked Ellen for being the very best of sisters. She explained why she'd run from Orkney, her regret for any worry she'd caused. She described the wonders she'd seen, the thrill of climbing the tops and trying to count the endless stars. And then she wrote of Kes and Custard, of Langley who'd become like a little brother, of Roo's cheese, and of saving Bash's ear.

And Bash.

She confessed to her big sister that she'd fallen in love.

And then she sealed it up like a secret in an empty bottle from the galley, tight so the tide wouldn't seep in, and she crept back onto the deck and cast it out into the sea.

THROUGHOUT THE DAY AND INTO THE NIGHT, THE CREW OF *Auldfarrand's Revenge* worked tirelessly to put a great deal of distance between themselves and the naval ship. Though he didn't allow her close enough to know for certain, Bash believed her to be the *Pursuit*. She flew a red duster, unmistakable as the standard of the British Caribbean fleet, and that was enough to convince him.

The christening of HMS *Pursuit* might've been irony, unless the ship was actually named for them as they liked to joke it was. Sometimes Bash wondered if they'd rechristen her the *Victory* once *Auldfarrand's* pirates were all finally dead.

Their course would have taken them between Saint-Domingue and Santiago de Cuba, but in trying to outrun fate, Bash had tacked north. Now he intended to shoot around Nassau and skirt the Spanish coast of Florida. From there, it would be easy to hide out and bide their time in the Dry Tortugas. At least they could dine on turtle. Most importantly, the *Pursuit* should not expect such a move.

The only drawback to this plan was the added delay in sending

Maggie straight back across the ocean. Every moment they tarried brought her one step closer to the danger Bash and his companions flirted with daily. But he could only manage one crisis at a time.

If they were finally unlucky enough to be caught, Bash would claim he had kidnapped her and kept her as his concubine. But he would do everything in his power not to come to last resorts. It was like a hand of Ruff and a sailor's jig, this game he played with the navy man. He had to wager everything on the Tortugas keeping them safe until they could dance their way back to Kingsport.

Dance a waltz, then dance again...

Beyond exhausted, he was hearing his mother's favorite song on the wind, almost like a message.

Dancing was exactly what Maggie should be doing—waltzing alongside hordes of polite admirers. She should be in ballrooms filled with naval officers in pursuit of courtship, not here with the likes of him, who could offer her nothing but heartache, an empty belly, and an ocean of naval ships in pursuit of their destruction.

Too tired to risk falling asleep standing-up or climbing the taller mast which would forever remind him of his and Maggie's lovemaking, he tethered himself to the foremast, so he might continue his vigil for the return of Constantin's ship.

Bash couldn't be near her right now. To go near Maggie was to want her, and wanting her was a distraction he couldn't possibly afford. He needed to save her, not maul her. Like his mother, she deserved so much more than a grizzled pirate lover full of sweet words and empty pockets.

Hear the bells but not the sea...

That was another line of his mother's song. It came rushing back to him as the bells were rung for shift change, but Bash had nowhere else to go, so he sent Samson away when the young man tried to relieve him. Besides—he needed to be right here in case the ship turned up again, as it had briefly done in the noon hour. They had doubled the men at the oars after that. Everyone was all used up.

The scratching sound of ropes on wood alerted him to someone's approach, and soon Dutch heaved himself onto the platform and stared down at Bash, hands on his hips.

"You're no good to anyone dead, son."

"As you can see, I'm not dead."

Dutch sighed and squatted down beside him, noting the rope he'd secured himself with. "Really?" Dutch asked. "How many fingers?"

Bash blinked, counting six swimming before his eyes.

"How many shifts have you been up here?"

"Just one, I'm sure."

"Four."

Bash refused to look at his friend. "If I go to sleep and the *Pursuit* returns—"

"She'll return whether you're asleep or awake, and when she does, you'd best be in top form. You think Mad's going to figure a way out of this on his own?"

Bash laughed. They were out of food. Hadn't slept in days. Even their top form would be no match for the Royal Navy.

How many times had he played out this exact scenario as a lad? He'd line up his laundry peg sailors and let them blow the corsairs to smithereens, taking no prisoners. The navy of his youth were the good guys, and the bad guys didn't deserve to win. It was only adulthood putting him on the wrong side of things.

"What's on your mind?" Dutch asked.

Bash swallowed. "I fear for the crew."

"All the crew? Or one in particular?"

Bash turned away, his breath speeding up as he scanned the ocean.

"We've been in tough spots before, had to outsmart and

outrun the *Pursuit* more than once. You've always kept a cool head and trusted us to wake you if the situation changed."

Blast the man for being right.

"You cannot protect anyone if you're not rested."

He couldn't go to her, either, for his own sake as much as hers. He'd already broken his promise to back off and not take things further, scaled that fortress as easily as the rigging. Normally the most disciplined of men, around her he lost his self-control. He lost all sense of self entirely and became nothing but consciousness entangled in her scent.

He couldn't trust himself to be alone with her, but especially not now, when danger was courting their every move. If the *Pursuit* snuck up on them because he was below deck drowning in the swirls and eddies of her eyes, he could never forgive himself— though it likely wouldn't be a long period of loathing before he was dancing on the coals of hell.

But what would become of her? Mad would never let the ship be taken. He'd sooner send *Auldfarrand's Revenge* to the bottom of the ocean along with every soul aboard. His only chance to save Maggie was to outrun the navy long enough to see her safely ashore.

Except this time, he couldn't seem to shake Constantin.

The hunter was too wily, as though all the times they'd outwitted him before hadn't been skill or luck, but a trick to build false confidence, as though they'd only escaped because the *Pursuit* had allowed them to. He was beginning to sound like Mad. Was the chase all in Bash's own head this time? Had love turned him paranoid and delusional?

Love. Christ. How had that happened? And yet what else would you call it when another living being consumed your every thought and hope and desire? After all, the navy didn't have him worried for his own sake, but for Maggie's.

"The *Pursuit*," he said finally, looking Dutch dead in the eye.

"Others have seen it too, have they not?" The unasked question lay between them. *I'm not being driven mad by this like my sire?*

Dutch nodded slowly. "I was too hard on you before... about... Magnus."

Bash shook his head. "You were absolutely right."

He could feel Dutch's brown eyes watching him, burrowing under his skin to the very marrow of his soul.

"When you were injured... well, it's not one-sided. You know this?"

Bash tried to shrug off the implication. "Loyalty. Nothing more." It was entirely one-sided, this pull he felt towards Maggie. It had to be, else how could he possibly let her go?

"No," Dutch argued. "Not nothing. My concern was honest, but I can admit I was wrong to cast stones."

"Doesn't matter. This is no kind of life."

"Then choose another, son," Dutch said with an earnest sort of desperation Bash had never heard from him before.

Bash turned what must be a pathetic look on his friend, but something on the horizon caught his attention. "Damn."

"My wisdom has that effect on occasion," Dutch teased.

"He's caught up to us again. Constantin is determined to have the *Revenge* for dinner. How can he match our speed?"

"Perhaps God is on his side."

"If we can just make it to the islands, we'll stand a chance." Bash jumped up to shimmy down the rigging, but his tether yanked him back, cracking his tailbone against the platform.

Dutch gave him a look.

"I was testing it," he lied.

"You are testing me. If you will not sleep in your own berth, then you'll sleep in mine. Give your orders for the new course and then put yourself to bed, or I will put you there. If you continue to bury yourself in work, son, then you'll bury us all."

Bury not my body there, in earth too rich and scented air.

He blinked at Dutch, and then climbed down to relay his orders.

Instead of cutting between Nassau and Freeport, they would head north around Freeport. Then they could follow the Florida coast and turn sharply south, weaving amongst the low islands and reefs on their way to the Dry Tortugas. A shiver of dread reminded Bash that de Leon had named those islands Los Martires, The Martyrs, for a reason.

"Row through the night," he told the men. "And into the morning. Thirty minutes on, one hour off." None dared to risk his neck in protest.

Bash slept but little in Dutch's hammock, and when Langley came to wake him, it was because they'd still not managed to shake the *Pursuit*.

So he took the helm alongside the captain, and as they'd done many a time, they darted around the inlets and islands scattered along the New World coastline until at last there was no sign of their pursuer.

Mad's usual smirk was long gone as he simmered with rage at the naval captain who dared give such chase, yelling at every man who entered his sightline, ready to tear Bash limb from limb. And when at last they sailed around a reef into the protective archipelago, only to find the *Pursuit* there waiting for them, he howled, "It can only be Constantin! Now what, boy?" he demanded between clenched teeth, shoving Bash back against the mast, though Bash was his equal in height now he was grown.

There was a time, even into adulthood, when Bash would've shrunk from the captain's rage to placate him, but somewhere over the last few months he'd decided to stand his ground.

"Galleon Harbor," he said. "With any luck, they'll think we've made for Port Royal. It will buy us some time at least."

And at this point, time was all he could hope for, just enough time to smuggle Maggie off one ship and onto another.

Mad nodded curtly and stormed off the bridge, cuffing Duffy

on the side of the head when the lad got in his way and shoving Roo into the Butcher when the cook tried to offer him an ale.

"Get us out of here, boy," he roared down the deck. "Give those bastards the slip once and for all before I throw you overboard and find someone who can."

Chapter Eighteen

In the wee hours of the morning, before sunlight was even a suggestion, Maggie woke to a hand covering her mouth and soft lips against her brow. She startled awake, fighting off the shadow who loomed over her for only a second before she realized it was Bash. He had finally come to her.

"Gather everything you wish to take," he breathed into her ear. "Quick as you can."

It was then she noticed the difference in the ship's movement. No longer flying swiftly forward—they almost wobbled, pummeled by surf as they had been when she first snuck aboard a lifetime ago. Had the navy finally caught up to them and anchored them with iron chains? Was Bash going to try and slip her overboard on some sort of raft?

He handed her a bundle, the skirts and earasaid she'd worn when she fled Orkney, folded and held fast by an old laundry peg decorated with chipping paint. Then he slipped a necklace of leather string over her head.

"What's this?" she whispered.

"Nothing," he replied, kissing her cheek and then lingering like he was smelling her, like he never wanted to step away.

Kes trilled softly at them, and Maggie gave her a piece of dried beef to quiet her.

"We must hurry," Bash whispered, eyeing the bird skeptically when it flapped to Maggie's shoulder.

"Shh, shh, shh," she hushed the bird, and Bash led her out of the alcove and up to the deck.

Delicious warm air hit her face, and Maggie realized they were not moored in the middle of the ocean but in a secluded harbor near a beach lined with shadowy trees.

"Can you swim?" he whispered, hardly louder than a breath.

Maggie nodded once. She might be overselling her abilities, but her cousins had taught her to swim as a child in Loch Moy, while Ellen watched steadfastly from the shore.

Bash nodded back and put a finger to his lips, then pointed to a rope ladder folded at the port side railing.

Her hand felt safe and warm inside his calloused one before he dropped it to secure the ladder with a fancy knot, then he helped her up and over as Kes took flight. Bash watched her descend, and when she reached the cool water and slipped silently in almost up to her neck, her bundle of clothes piled on her head to stay dry, he followed her down with practiced ease.

Paddling together, the distance to the beach was much further than it looked, but Maggie couldn't suppress her elation. The water was pleasantly refreshing, the exercise after being cooped up, divine. And best of all, free of the *Revenge*, Bash could do anything—be anything—with her!

When they finally straggled out onto the shore, she collapsed, breathing heavily and shaking with silent giggles at how they staggered as though the land pitched beneath them, but Bash wasn't laughing.

"No time," he whispered urgently as he dragged her to her feet and into the safety of the scrub.

His serious voice and eyes made the weight of their escape sink in. If they were found out, dozens of pirates could descend onto this beach to take them back in a heartbeat. Would they be flogged? Sweated? Garroted? She'd no interest in finding out.

They ran in silence until a cramp forced Maggie to slow down. Walking side by side with Kes following from tree to tree, she could almost pretend their situation wasn't dire, pretend they owned this land, pretend they were Adam and Eve, the only two people in all the world.

Gradually, Bash stopped looking over his shoulder, though he still changed direction every few minutes. After two hours, the sun had long since risen, and it was clear they weren't just wandering lost. The navigator had a perfect sense of direction. He obviously had a plan.

"Where are we? And where are we going?" she finally whispered.

"Welcome to Jamaica," he said, with an air of reluctance. "When we reach Kingston, you can book passage back to England and on to Scotland."

"We, you mean."

But he looked away from her, facing forward, and a sick dread settled in her stomach. He couldn't mean to stay behind, not after everything they'd shared. She couldn't bring herself to ask.

After another hour they stopped at a stream and Maggie gulped the clean, fresh water like she'd never tasted it before. It was glorious. On her life, she would never take water for granted again.

Sitting back on her heels to catch her breath, she studied Bash. She didn't want to take a single moment with him for granted either. He was unfailingly good and devilishly handsome, especially when he was concentrating.

Now, as he looked anywhere but at her, it seemed the thing he was concentrating hardest on was avoiding eye contact or conversation, and she couldn't pretend the hard questions away any longer.

"So I'm to leave on my own and you'll do what? Go back to

pirating one step ahead of the navy, little better than a prisoner until the day you die?"

He didn't answer at first, squinting into the distance. When he finally did, he said simply, "Aye."

"Well, I don't accept that."

"You must." His voice sounded so resigned. Not angry or cruel, just tired and sad and determined.

"Was it something I did?" she asked. "I was selfish, but I can do better. I will do better."

"Selfish?" he asked, perplexed, and shook his head. "Never. But you're too comfortable with the idea of being a pirate."

Maggie laughed, sad and bitter. She didn't want to be a pirate. But she would choose it again and again to keep her freedom and stay close to her favorite pirate navigator.

" 'Tisn't a joke," he said solemnly. "This is no kind of life."

"We're free now. Both of us. We could go anywhere."

He shook his head. "Mags, I'm sorry. I only have enough saved to book one passage."

Blinking back the tears that threatened to fall, she shook her head. She didn't accept them, not any more than she accepted his words. "Then sign onto the crew in exchange for your passage. Isn't that what men do?"

"Boys, maybe—"

"Then I'll do it. I can work hard and you can buy your own fare."

"I'm a pirate, Mags. They'll see me coming and shoot me dead before I so much as open my mouth."

"Then I'll stay."

"No. You won't. You deserve better than running and hiding, starving on hard tack and rum," he said, standing up and heading off again, leaving Maggie to follow.

For a moment she considered just not following him. That would teach him, all right. If he was willing to let her go, then he might as well start right now. On her terms.

Except he paused to wait for her, leaning against a tree, and she'd rather be at his side now, fighting with the idiot, arguing some sense into him, than not be near him at all.

She'd been so stupid, allowing herself to get close to him, allowing herself to fall in love and be loved in return at last. Love was a fairytale for silly little girls whose fate fell to their fathers to give them away to the first willing man who came along.

"You're angry with me," he said, after they'd trudged in silence for another quarter hour.

"Does it matter?"

"Course."

"Why?" He didn't answer, so she asked it again. "Why? I didn't want to marry Jeremiah, but that didn't matter. I didn't want to move to Orkney, but that didn't matter, either. I wanted to have children, then I wanted to stay a widow—none of it mattered, Bash. All that ever seems to matter is what men want for me."

"I just want you to be safe," he said in a small voice.

"No," Maggie said, and she sounded loud and strong, and not like someone who was about to shatter. "No, you want to feel comfortable believing you've made me safe." Then she pushed forward into the bush without him, even though her sense of direction was more likely to send her circling back into the arms of the *Revenge*. Or right off a cliff.

"I have nothing to offer you," he called in a piteous voice that brought her up short. "Nothing but the coin to book passage back to your home, and you deserve everything."

"You are everything—"

"No. I'm the pirate by-blow of pirate scum. You deserve better. My mother deserved better. Christ, maybe *I* deserved better, but this is the only life I've known since I was nine years old. I've no skills. Not a fool would employ me. My only hope is to find my sire's fortune if it even exists. Then, I might escape and perhaps one day endeavor to deserve you."

Maggie's brain was whirring so fast she didn't know which piece of his declaration to focus on first. "Your sire—"

Bash inclined his head in affirmation, and her heart turned to molten fury for all he'd suffered at the hands of the captain, Cornelius MacLeod. A father in name, perhaps, but in name only.

"Then I shall help you find it."

"It's too dangerous. If the navy hasn't caught them yet, he'll be searching for it even now."

"I'm not afraid," she lied.

"You should be. I'm a thief and a scoundrel, raised by men who measure human lives by how hard they can row or how fast they are with a knife."

"Your mother raised you first," she argued, and his face clouded over, nearly breaking her heart.

"We have to keep going," he said in a raspy voice. "We've at least another two hours."

"It's starting to get dark," Maggie pointed out, as a cool breeze made her shiver.

Bash looked at the sky in surprise and in the distance, thunder sounded like a rumble of cannon fire. "Come," he said, putting his arm around her and tucking her under his shoulder before setting a faster pace in the direction they needed to go.

It was torture, leading Maggie towards Kingston, but it would be an even greater torture putting her on a ship in the morning. Bash kept track of the transit schedules as best he could, and if he was right, there should be a ship departing for England—so long as it hadn't been delayed or its captain hadn't set sail early to capitalize on more favorable winds.

Deep in his heart, he'd secretly hoped stopping in Tortuga

would cause them to miss the outbound vessel by a few days, allowing him to revel in Maggie's company a bit longer. When the navy beat them to Tortuga, forcing them on to Jamaica right away, he knew better than to question Providence. It was time for her to go.

But walking towards that fate, on legs that already felt like a newborn fawn's after so long at sea, made every footstep heavier, like marching to his own execution. He sometimes thought he'd sooner survive being drawn and quartered than watching her sail away, taking a piece of his heart and all the good parts of his soul with her.

Maggie hadn't spoken since they'd fought about the journey, which he hoped and feared meant she'd accepted his plan. They were probably an hour from Kingston still, both of them covered in mud from the heavy downpour, and she was beginning to tremble. When she sniffed, he asked softly, "Are you crying?"

"No," she snapped, and who was he to argue, when the heavens themselves seemed to weep for their plight.

"Then you're catching a chill," he reasoned, scanning the forest around them. "We must get out of the rain."

"Perhaps a nearby kirk will grant us sanctuary," she quipped, and he chuckled. Even when she was angry with him, she could tease. It was one of the myriad little things he loved about her.

"Come." He led her under the wide, sheltering leaves of a banana tree. "Wait here. Promise?"

"Will you bring the ship to me now, anchored on your back like the rest of the weight of the world?" she asked, catching his sleeve, and he laughed again.

"I go in search of a kirk." He grinned, delighting in her perplexed little frown. Then he took the liberty of kissing her cheek, and she didn't pull away. In fact, he felt her eyes on him as he wandered off in the direction his gut told him to go.

He was only delaying the inevitable of course, latching on to any excuse to stop time before they had to say goodbye. If a ship were leaving today, it would have already done so, and if not, it could wait until the morrow. Soon he found what he sought—a small cave, empty and dry.

Bash held his breath all the way back to the banana tree, half expecting Maggie to have plunged off into the wilderness on her own without looking back. But there she was, sitting at the base of the tree, small and vulnerable, with her knees tucked up and her head resting on the bundle of clothes he'd first met her in. She looked tired, thirsty, and achingly sad.

"Come," he said, helping her to her feet, and then sweeping her up into his arms so her head rested against his shoulder, her damp hair tickling his nose.

"I can walk," she murmured sleepily. "You needn't carry me."

"I know," he agreed, his heart beating so wildly at the nearness of her that he dared not set her down.

"A cave," she said with wonder when she spotted it.

"We can dry off, at least," he said, setting her gently on the ground inside. "I'll have to find some chert to start a fire."

When he turned to go back out into the rain, Maggie called, "Wait!"

Unfurling her bundle of clothes, she dug in the pockets, finally fishing out a piece of flint and grinning angelically. The little wonder.

Bash gathered some twigs and branches which had been mostly protected from the rain, and he took them deep into the cave to build a fire. Then he spread out Maggie's old clothes nearby to dry, and he laid his own plaid a bit closer to the entrance, cheeks burning at Maggie's little gasp when she realized he'd hidden the cloth amongst her things. He'd meant her to discover the gift only after she was long gone.

"I'm filthy," Maggie announced, breaking the awkward silence and looking down at her mud-spattered legs. "I'll get it dirty."

"Doesn't matter."

"It matters to me," she said, and then with an impish smile, she pulled her sark over her head and tossed it to him. She was completely bare from the waist up, having unbound her breasts last night to sleep.

Bash stared at them a moment, beautifully round and freckled, before she turned her back to him, stripped off her trousers and skipped out into the rain wearing nothing but her smalls.

"What are you doing?" he laughed.

"Washing. In freedom, if this is my last night to be free!"

She danced and splashed, turning her face up to the rain like a wildflower before scrubbing the mud from her legs. After a moment, Bash joined her, though his hardness would be immediately evident, since he was not wearing any smalls.

"You're the wildest woman I ever saw," he confessed, scraping the mud from his leg hair with his fingernails.

Maggie laughed again. "You've spent your whole life on a ship. You haven't had the luxury of meeting many women."

He caught her wrist, pausing her frolic. "Not one of them could have measured up to you."

Her lips parted, quirking up to the side in wonder more than laughter as the rain grew heavier until they ran hand in hand back into the cave, breathless and giggling.

"Oh no!" she exclaimed with a hand to her throat, realizing the gifted necklace had been soaked.

Bashed waved it away. "It's survived worse," he said, but she took it off and nestled it, as well as her smalls, to dry by the fire.

"Was it your mother's?"

"Aye. But I want you to have it now."

She turned back to him, suddenly shy about her nudity.

"Don't be ashamed," he whispered, gazing at her in rapture. "You're so beautiful."

She studied him, the full length of him, lit by the jumping shadows of firelight, and he swallowed. Christ but her very glance seemed to singe his leathered skin.

"You should lie down and get some rest." Useless words to fill the moment. After all, what would he do? Stand all night, a naked sentinel, prick at attention, until his breeches were dry enough to try and subdue his arousal?

Maggie took his hand and led him back to the tartan, the one which had been his grandfather's back on Lewis. They lay down together, facing each other, and she pressed her head into his chest in a way that could almost crack it open.

"Tomorrow I must sail away," she whispered.

"Aye," he agreed, his voice breaking a little. "Aye, you must."

"And you must stay to seek your fortune."

"Aye. 'Tis the only way. When I do, I shall come and find you, be you in Orkney or Inverness, or any other place in all the world. I'll find you."

"Then I shall wait," she said, kissing his throat, and he swallowed again but the lump lodged there wouldn't budge.

"No." He closed his eyes to everything he wanted and forced himself to say, "You mustn't wait. If you find a good man—a kind man who loves you and knows how to let you fly free—you must marry him for me, with no regrets, and have eleven children." He kissed her forehead.

"Eleven!" she gasped.

"Aye, and name one of them for me."

"My bravest, most favorite child," she agreed. "To remind me of my love for the sea," she added, and his heart began to splinter.

She nudged him onto his back and climbed up to straddle him, kissing him fiercely, urgently, as tears ran down her cheeks which this time neither of them could pretend was only rain, but he wiped them away under the guise of pushing back her hair all the same.

I love you, his heart screamed to hers, but he swallowed it down and kissed her harder, because if he let those words out, he knew she'd never leave. And more than likely, before the week was out, he'd swing.

"You have to go back," he whispered. "So somebody remembers me."

She swiped his hair out of his eyes as she'd done so many times while nursing his ear, studying him hard like she was trying to memorize every detail.

"Remember you? Don't you know you've become a part of me?"

He nodded, tears stinging his own eyes now, and she lifted up and eased onto him, taking him all, and gasping just as he did. She rode him slowly, deliciously, setting his scalp on fire as he drifted towards oblivion.

Maggie gasped his name over and over, not Bash, but Bastian, as though he alone could protect her from all the ills of the world. It occurred to him in the moment when she threw back her head and cried out as his seed spilled into her that perhaps if he was very lucky, more than just his memory and name would live on.

Chapter Nineteen

The sun rose bright and cheerful, as though no storm had forced them into hiding, as though Maggie's world wasn't about to be torn asunder. She woke with a stomachache that had nothing to do with hunger and everything to do with the empty, Bash-shaped hole about to be punched through her heart.

Careful not to wake him, she donned her old clothes. They no longer fit, belonging to a different girl in a whole different lifetime. Despite having bound her breasts flat for weeks, the bodice felt tight and restrictive, like one more cage from which she couldn't escape. The skirts were too loose, the sleeves of her chemise much too tight, where new muscles had formed, and she longed to wear the comfy sailor attire she'd quickly grown accustomed to.

As Bash dozed in fitful slumber, she inspected the pendant he'd given her. He'd offered no words of explanation, merely hung it around her neck as though it had always belonged there. It was a lovely oval carved from soft wood, with a marquetry flower inlaid in lighter shades. And though she'd feared the wood might swell and be ruined from the damp, it looked as perfect as it had when he'd given it to her.

Like her own folding frame, inside it held two tiny sketches. One showed a beautiful black woman with long coiled hair, the other was unmistakably baby Bash. Unlike the wood, the portrait of his mother had begun to curl from the damp. Maggie blotted it gently, but it fell out of the locket into her hand.

There was writing on the back. The faded inscription was difficult to read so she moved to the mouth of the cave for better light.

> Mahogany, cedar in a row
> Coconut palm and pimento
> Bury not my body there
> In earth too rich and scented air
> Dogwood blossoms, moonlight glow
> Fondest dreams of sweet mango

A shiver ran down Maggie's spine. It was the song Bash had awoken singing after taking the medicinal hashish, *sure as beans*, as Langley would say. He'd been humming it for weeks, struggling in vain to remember all the long-lost words. Carefully, she peeled the picture of baby Bash from the left side of the locket and turned it over in her palm.

> The king once built a town so fair
> Red hibiscus lined the square
> Dance a waltz, then dance again
> Down the hill, an empty lane
> Andrew's spire calls out to thee
> Hear the bells but do not see

"All right?" Bash asked in a groggy croak, and Maggie whirled guiltily around to find him raising up on an elbow and blinking at her through sleepy eyes.

"I'm not sure," she whispered.

"Mmm?"

She knelt beside him, opening her hands for him to see. "The pictures got wet, and I tried to dry them out, and well—she's your mother, isn't she?"

"Aye," he said, gazing fondly down at the likeness.

"Could she have been sending you a message with her song?"

"Her song?" he asked, running a hand through his sleep-tousled hair.

She wanted to run her fingers through it too, but now was not the time.

He shook his head. "It was just a song—just a nonsense rhyme."

"Or was it?" she asked, growing excited as her mind whirled with all the possibilities. "Your father loved her enough to make a baby with her. Maybe he told her where he buried the gold," she said excitedly, but Bash frowned, and reached for her hand as if afraid to impart bad news.

"I don't know if he loved her or not, but she was already gone when he buried it."

"Are you certain?" she asked, deflating.

"Mad had a woman in every port. Perhaps she was one of his particular favorites, but that's all she was. She didn't even know he was a pirate until she arrived in Lewis. My auntie tried to tell her he was no good, but she was dazzled by him. So when she realized she was with child, she took herself to the Hebrides to find him and gave birth to me on the journey. I was born at sea, and I'll die at sea," he muttered the morose afterthought to himself.

Maggie squeezed his shoulder. "The captain said he buried the gold for his son," she reminded him.

"Aye. Coming to Kingston meant coming to see her. Only she

wasn't there. Folks told him she'd taken her babe to find its father. He knew about me, and he knew where she was, but he never came looking until years after she died. Maybe in a drunken moment of paternal pride he thought to save it for me, but she couldn't have known it existed, let alone where he left it."

He seemed to realize he was clenching his fists and opened them to study the words written on the backs of the pictures, his eyes misting over.

"It's her song, isn't it?" Maggie asked. "The one you woke up singing after..." Her eyes darted to his unbandaged ear, which looked almost as good as new, though she still caught him cupping it protectively as though it pained him from time to time.

Bash brushed his dark locks down to cover the ear self-consciously and turned the portraits over again to gaze on mother and son.

"*The king once built a town so fair*," he whispered. "She used to make me sing this song over and over. 'Memorize it, Basti, and one day...'" He squinted. "One day it will lead you home."

His eyes widened and he stared at Maggie in wonder.

"Could he have buried it at her house when he went to find her?"

He shook his head, dazed by the idea.

"Your auntie, the one who told her he was no good, what happened to her?"

Bash shook his head again. "I tried to go and see her once. When I was twelve. I snuck off the ship at Port Royal but I didn't make it to Kingston before Mad caught me."

"The scars on your back?" she whispered, knowing his answer even before he nodded, lost in the distant memory.

"*Andrew's spire calls out to thee.*" He blinked twice. "There was a church spire. I could just see the top of it from Gallows Point. I remember thinking it must be the tallest thing I'd ever seen, when Mad's shadow fell across me. I'd never felt so suddenly cold as I did then."

He blinked again, a few more times, as if coming back to himself. "We have to get you to the harbor."

"What? Now?"

Bash nodded. "You've helped tremendously. I promise I'll go and look for the gold. If it's there, I'll find it. But after all the business with Willy Walsh, Mad's going to tear up this island looking for it too, and God help anyone in his way."

Maggie understood this was something Bash felt he needed to do alone. She didn't like it, but she understood.

So she didn't argue when he folded his plaid and made a gift of it to her. She didn't protest when he put out the last dying embers of their fire.

They set off for Kingston arm in arm, and she didn't even complain when he gave her the money for her passage back to Scotland, or cry when he embraced her on the outskirts of town. They held on to each other as if they were drowning, and part of her wanted to drown. She bit her lip to keep from crying.

"It's too dangerous for you. I can go on from here alone," she reasoned. "You must go and seek your fortune."

He frowned. "The port can be rough. Perhaps I should take you all the way."

She shook her head. "You mustn't be seen. Go. Now. And after, you can come back and find me."

Then she gave him the little frame with pictures of Ellen and Jory. "Find them, and you'll find me," she whispered. She clung to him, fighting off tears as she added, "I *will* wait for you, Bastian MacLeod. I saved you once, and that makes you mine. Our souls are bound, stronger together than apart. I could never love another as dearly as I love you."

With a last embrace and a kiss on the cheek, she headed off towards the port with the prickle of his eyes on her sweat-slicked neck, determined that this wouldn't be goodbye.

BASH WATCHED UNTIL MAGGIE DISAPPEARED FROM VIEW AND then he kept right on standing at the edge of the road like a lovesick fool, watching and waiting and wishing she'd run back to him, though he was the one who'd sent her away, his heart as raw as an open wound in need of scarring to protect it.

He searched the sky for answers and found only Andrew's spire standing watch like a sentinel over the town.

Inside, the church was cool and empty, and Bash chose a pew in the back corner where he could observe all who entered and escape quickly should the need arise.

Was this the same spire he'd seen from Gallows Point that day ten years ago, before Mad caught him and dragged him back to the ship to be whipped within an inch of his life? He liked to think so, anyway.

He might have broken free there and then had he not been distracted by the corpse of his old friend Calico Jack, hanging over the harbor in an iron gibbet while birds pecked out his eyes. Bash hadn't been able to stomach the taste of sorghum ever since.

There had been a wild look in Mad's eye that day. What had the old man been so afraid of? Did he imagine his lover to be some sort of witch, able to divine the location of his precious gold and share it with young Bash? Stuff and nonsense.

Mad was a paranoid son of a bitch, and though his intuition was often right, Bash's mother wasn't a witch.

So what had she been trying to tell him with her song?

After the flogging, Mad had visited Bash where he lay huddled in a heap, too broken to find solace in his hammock. Delirium had turned the visitations into grotesque nightmares, but Bash realized now they may have been real, as were the confusing questions the captain asked, repeatedly demanding Bash reveal the location of his lost bounty.

Could the directions have possibly been there, locked in Bash's brain and inscribed in his mother's locket all along?

OF COURSE, MAGGIE HAD NO INTENTION OF BOOKING PASSAGE back to Scotland and leaving Bash to struggle on his own. He'd been fighting his own side with almost no one to help him since he was just a little boy being passed from home to home, and she would never let him fight alone again.

But he was stubborn. Being more than a little hard-headed herself, she knew he wouldn't give in. He wanted to protect her, and she loved him for it. He believed he had to go on from here alone as he'd always done before, and she understood that, too. She just didn't accept it.

Maggie reckoned, though, if she could just lie low near the harbor, she might be able to wait him out. She had every faith he'd find Mad's old treasure. He would find it, and then he'd rush back for her, and she'd be ready. If he didn't make it back today, well, she had a little bit of money, perhaps enough to rent a room for one night. And if he didn't find it by the morning, then he couldn't be too angry when she turned up to help him.

Everything in Kingston harbor was new and strange, and the people seemed to think the same of her, so clearly overdressed in her earasaid and skirts, with her usually pale skin now sun-browned from her journey.

Finally locating a reputable looking ale house, she slipped inside. It was mostly empty, so she took a seat in the corner, daring the few denizens to stare.

A cautious barmaid approached her. "Bread and butter?" the girl asked.

Maggie nodded eagerly, licking her parched lips and hearing Bash's guttural, *Drink*, as though he were standing right beside her. "And tea, if you have it."

"Three pence," the girl replied, eyeing Maggie's somewhat disheveled appearance with a skeptical air.

When she withdrew her purse to pay for the meal, inside she found Bash's locket. Maggie gasped, but quickly handed over the coins, and once the girl left, she examined the necklace again, hoping he'd at least kept the pictures and the poem.

He hadn't of course, and she couldn't help stroking a finger down his likeness's little cheek where a scar would one day speak the cruelty he'd endured. Panic swelled within her.

What if he couldn't remember the words without seeing them? What if he couldn't find the gold without the locket? What if he never had any intention of trying? She had to find him, to return the pendant, pictures and all.

She flipped them over once more.

The king once built a town so fair

If this was indeed Kingston, that was a good start at least.

Red hibiscus lined the square

Maggie didn't know what a hibiscus was, but it was time she found out.

The moment her food arrived, she wrapped up the bread and shoved it in her pocket, regretfully leaving the piping hot tea untouched. Bash would be displeased with her, but she'd have to find him first.

BASH ROLLED HIS HEAD AGAINST THE CHURCH WALL BEHIND him. There was nothing here. He was no closer to figuring out the poem than he had been an hour ago. Why had he started with the church? Did any of it even mean anything?

The king once built a town so fair, obviously referred to Kingston. *Red hibiscus lined the square.* Bash and Maggie had come upon the town from the jungle outskirts instead of the port, but he seemed to recall massive hibiscus flowers around the harbor all those years before.

Dance a waltz, then dance again. Down the hill an empty lane.

Some sort of dance hall in the town center? Or directions from there? He should have asked Maggie to teach him how to waltz. She would look so lovely floating through the air in a flowing ball gown on someone else's arm.

He banged his head against the wall. Had he come this far to be stymied by social graces?

Sing the words, Basti, his mother used to say. She drilled him on it over and over. He'd thought it was a game, but she'd given him everything he needed, as they danced around the beach singing.

They danced, with him on her feet as she glided.

Bash closed his eyes, and he could see her feet beneath his babyish ones as she moved: right foot back, left foot to the left, right foot to the left, left foot forward, right foot to the right, left foot to the right.

His eyes snapped open. *Right, left, left. Left, right, right.* He slipped out a door towards the harbor and the town square.

When Bash reached the square, the church bells began to ring, and a heaviness settled on him like the bells were heralding Maggie's ship's departure.

He shook himself back to the moment.

Dance a waltz. Right, left, left.

He turned right down the first road off the square, then left at the first corner, which took him down a long and winding hill.

Andrew's spire calls out to thee. Hear the bells but do not see.

He'd misremembered the line, supposing it was about the ocean. Pausing to look back, he could still make out the spire above the trees.

At the bottom of the hill, he turned left once more, then another left, and then right, and right again. The bells still rang, but from this vantage point he could no longer see that towering spire.

THE TOWN SQUARE WAS EASY ENOUGH TO LOCATE, AND ONCE there, Maggie stood gawping at a massive red flower, its petals spread as wide as a dinner plate, its color more vibrant than an ocean sunset. There were dozens of them planted all around the square, and she was losing precious time, staring transfixed at the flowers, these hibiscus, and their ghostly, scentless beauty.

"Ya lost?" a voice at her elbow asked, and Maggie whirled around to find a young man with dark brown skin and luminous eyes staring curiously at her.

She shook her head quickly. Thirsty? Yes. Frightened? A bit. But she wasn't lost. She had a feeling she was right where she needed to be.

When the boy shrugged and wandered away, Maggie drew back into nearby shrubbery and shadows, and opened the locket once more.

Dance a waltz, then dance again
Down the hill, an empty lane

What on earth could it mean? How was this any kind of map? Unless Amoy meant for her son to follow the steps of a dance... where each turn about the floor indicated a turn down another lane or byway? Mercy, the poet was clever. Maggie was starting to understand where Bash got his sharp mind for languages and mathematics from.

If her hunch was correct, that meant the first turn off the square was to the right. She turned and her gaze was drawn to a figure with warm, golden-brown skin, disappearing around the corner. Throttling her impulse to run after him, she kept low and out of sight as she followed. He needed to do this on his own.

BEFORE BASH LAY A LANE OF TIDY HOUSES. THE PATH WAS LINED with fragrant trees.

Mahogany, cedar in a row. Coconut palm and pimento.

Gardens were dotted with coconut palms to be sure, but none held pimento trees.

He heaved a sigh, and perhaps it was wishful thinking, but he could almost taste the spicy fragrance of pimento on the breeze, growing stronger as he continued down the lane.

And then he saw it. In front of a dilapidated house where the roof had recently caved in, there stood a pimento tree, its scraggly branches raised like wide, open arms, its ripe, purplish berries hanging in clumps just begging to be picked and dried. Tears sprang to his eyes, as though with recognition. Was this old place where his mother had lived with his auntie and fallen in love with working the soil to make things grow? What had become of that wise woman who warned her little sister about Cornelius MacLeod all those years ago?

Bury not my body there, in earth too rich and scented air. Dogwood blossoms, moonlight glow, fondest dreams of sweet mango.

Slowly Bash circled the house. White dogwoods bloomed at the corner. What a difference it must have been for his mother compared to the windswept Isle of Lewis.

He'd enjoyed a happy boyhood there, but he could see why she spent so many hours attempting to transform her little patch of earth into a paradise like this one. She was a marvel in the garden, and there was something familiar about this place, like the imprint of her soul upon the soil.

In the back corner of the property, where the garden grew feral trying to catch up with the surrounding bush, he spied a mango tree.

He should have brought a shovel, but he hadn't planned on treasure hunting when he whisked Maggie off the ship. He had only his hands. And so, under the shade of the mango tree, he clawed away the damp, rich soil, shifting it easily until his blackened nails scraped against the wood of an old chest.

Working faster, he dug away the earth all around the top until there was almost enough room to pry it out.

Bash held his breath as he knelt in the dirt and worked first one side and then the other to free its handles. When it wouldn't budge, he attempted to lever it open with his knife, just to be sure it was worth the trouble. For all he knew, this might be a box of rocks. But whatever it contained was locked up tight inside.

"Good work, boy," Mad's drawl sounded, low and to Bash's right. He should've known. The captain had probably been following since the moment they slipped off the ship.

He glanced up at his sire, expecting to see a blunderbuss leveled at his heart, but it was so much worse than a blunderbuss. Mad stood about ten feet away, one arm all but choking Maggie, a knife to her throat.

Using only his eyes, Bash tried to tell her to stay calm, not to worry, everything would be all right. He'd make sure of it. Inside, though, his stomach tied itself in the tightest of knots, his mind racing with impossible ideas. All he could think to do was keep Mad talking.

"I always suspected the bitch knew where it was," Mad sneered.

"My mother? How could she have?"

"Savryna. Amoy's sister. Your aunt. She must have seen me bury it that night. But over there. She'll have moved it. I turned this place upside-down year after year, and all along, she knew."

"You could have come to Lewis any time," Bash spat. "Asked Ma about your precious gold. Why didn't you?"

"I knew there was nothing for me on Lewis."

Bash nodded. It was maybe the most truthful thing his sire had ever said. But then something else occurred to him. "If you thought I knew where it was, why didn't you keep following me ten years ago instead of dragging me back to the ship?"

Mad's lips curved into a cruel and calculating smile. "Couldn't give you an inch, could I? And risk you getting the idea I wasn't the one in command? Look how well it worked. Tamed you into a perfect little lapdog. At least 'til this one came along," he added, tightening his chokehold on Maggie, making her grunt. "Now which is it? A boy in girl's clothing or the other way around? Shall we check?" He reached into her bodice and groped her breasts, squeezing them hard enough she winced.

A fiery rage was building in Bash's stomach, but again he tried to communicate to Maggie that everything would be all right. Her eyes were locked on his, and she didn't seem angry or frightened, only sad, but in a way, he thought perhaps she understood.

"I'll take that back now," Mad said, nodding to the chest still in the ground. "You'll forgo your cut, of course, on account of the mutiny and insubordination. But I'll let you live. For now."

"A tempting offer," Bash said. "But you're not getting anything while your knife is at her throat."

"You're not in much of a position to bargain," Mad sneered.

"You want the chest, don't you? I'll trade you the girl for the gold."

From behind his back, Mad raised his other hand, aiming a blunderbuss. Check and mate. "Perhaps I didn't make myself clear, boy. Bring my gold over here and put it in the cabin boy's hands, and if you try anything funny..." he finished the sentence by turning the muzzle of his gun to point at Maggie's head.

Bash had committed a multitude of sins over the last decade, but perhaps none so egregious as the hate now coursing through him for the man who was his sire, because murder was a sin, and in his heart, he knew they couldn't both come out of this alive.

Chapter Twenty

The perfect future Maggie had envisioned crumbled before her eyes, as Bash attempted to pry the old chest from the earth to hand off to his father. She was forced to stand by, helpless, immobilized by the captain's knife, while Bash lost everything and she lost any chance of a life with him.

This was all her fault.

She hadn't wanted to spend their last hours fighting with each other over her refusal to sail away alone, but now she wished she had fought him. Anything would have been better than this. Instead, she'd gone off on her own, searching for both him and the treasure, and when she found him, sneaking silently behind, ready to emerge for the celebration when he found the spot.

Had he been less intent on solving his mother's riddle, he'd have undoubtedly noticed her following him. Had she been less intent on creeping after him unseen, she might have noticed the captain following, too.

But she didn't—not until Mad grabbed her, the cold steel of his knife pressed against her throat.

"If you so much as breathe, I will slice your neck so deep your head falls off and vermin will crawl inside the gaping hole," he had whispered, pinning one arm so far behind it made her back arch.

Now Bash was staring at them, his eyes ablaze with fury, and Maggie glared right back at him, trying desperately to convey that he shouldn't, under any circumstances, follow the captain's orders and hand over the gold. Not on her account.

He seemed to be getting the wrong message though, or else he ignored her, because he kept on digging.

There were two weapons trained on her now, the knife and a blunderbuss, and she half wondered just what Mad intended to do. If he shot the gun, wouldn't he blow his own knife hand off in the process? Was he too far gone to care?

What a terrible hash she'd made of everything, just like always, when she only ever wanted to help. Well. To help and, selfishly, to run away with Bash, she admitted. Such selfishness was about to be her downfall, and his. That was the unfair part. He didn't deserve any of this. It was just one more bad thing heaped atop his lifetime of bad things.

After several excruciating minutes, Bash extracted the heavy chest and stepped towards Maggie.

"Let her go," he tried again.

The captain laughed. "You'll have to start joining the lads for Ruff. You don't seem to understand I'm holding all the cards."

"Except one," Bash said. "One very heavy card. The only card you've ever cared about, at least so long as I've known you."

"True," Mad agreed. "But I'm holding the prettiest card. So which do you want more, boy? Wealth or beauty?"

When Bash didn't answer, his wretched father chuckled.

"That's what I thought. Now bring it here and put it in her hands."

Maggie shook her head the tiniest bit, but, sensing the movement, Mad pressed the knife tighter to her throat, and she held her breath, not even daring to swallow.

Bash did as he was told, staring into her eyes with so much

sorrow that she wanted to weep. The gold was his by rights, earned if nothing else, through toil and the lash. The one thing which could finally set him free from the cruelty he'd known all his life, and now he was being forced to sacrifice it to save her. She was grateful, but she wasn't sure she was worth it.

His hand brushed against her arm as he surrendered the chest. Like the day he found her, St. Elmo's Fire sparked between them, and Maggie almost stopped breathing. When their eyes met, his were filled with sorrow.

The gold was heavy, and she grunted under the weight, nearly forced to her knees. The captain cackled at the most unladylike sound.

"Now what?" Bash asked, stepping back only a pace or two as the captain waved him away. "You have your long-lost treasure. Let the girl go."

"Have I taught you nothing about the value of a hostage?" Mad asked with a disappointed tone.

"You've taught me nothing except how to hate."

The captain threw back his head to roar with laughter, his dagger scraping against Maggie's throat. The stinging cut brought tears to her eyes, or would have done, if her vision wasn't getting cloudy around the edges, her legs threatening to buckle.

"A worthy lesson every boy should learn."

Instinctively Maggie turned her head away from the knife and noticed a third man creeping up to join them. He wore a naval coat of blue serge.

"Cornelius MacLeod," the man said calmly. "At long last. Care to introduce me to your friends?"

Realizing he must be the captain of HMS *Pursuit*, Maggie's breathing grew shallow, and she darted her gaze to Bash, who stood frozen, weaponless and exposed.

"Constantin," Mad exclaimed, swinging Maggie and his gun around to face the officer. She staggered to her knees, dropping the chest, as the man raised his hands in supplication. "You're here just in time. I caught these two red-handed."

"Come now, Cornelius. After twenty-two years, you must call me Frederick!" the officer said jovially.

Both captains laughed like old comrades and Maggie grew faint. The warm air she had once longed for was too thick and humid. She couldn't catch a proper breath, especially not wearing her horrid bodice and stays. How had she ever stood them before?

"This woman is a pirate thief," Mad continued. "She boarded my vessel uninvited and in disguise. She stole from me. I followed her here, only to discover the two of them attempting to hide what they took."

Bile surged up Maggie's throat, sour with the taste of regret. Was this how her foolish adventure would end? Prosecuted as a criminal when all she'd ever stolen was a kiss?

"Lies," Bash said, his voice soft but strong and cold.

Constantin turned his way as though noticing him for the first time, but Mad remained focused on the navy man.

"She's no pirate," Bash explained desperately to Constantin. "Just a silly girl, forced into hiding when she snuck aboard the wrong vessel by mistake."

Tears burned her eyes, but she refused to let them fall. He would implicate himself if he didn't stop talking. She shook her head once more, ever so slightly despite the blade still at her throat.

"I'm the one responsible for all of this," Bash went on. "It was me who took his property. Believing we were lovers, he kidnapped her to get it back."

Constantin looked at each of them in turn with an inscrutable expression on his face. "Which is it, miss? A thief or a victim?" the officer asked, and Maggie opened her lips to plead with him, but her throat was too dry to make a sound.

"Please sir, you must believe me," Bash implored. "She's innocent in all of this. I should have put her on a ship straight back to Scotland as I intended, but I was a coward. I couldn't watch her sail away from me."

The last, he addressed to Maggie, and when she blinked to ease the burning in her eyes, salty tears began to trickle down her cheeks.

"I see," the officer said, though as far as Maggie was concerned, he saw nothing at all. "And you are?"

Bash stood up straighter. "Sebastian MacLeod, sir." And then, apparently resigned to his fate, he added, "Sailing master and boatswain of *Auldfarrand's Revenge*."

"Now that does interest me," Constantin said. "I've been searching for you a long time."

"For me, sir?" Bash asked.

"Indeed. You're all under arrest. Kindly drop your weapons."

"Come, now, Constantin, we've led a merry chase, you and I. Be a shame for our little game to end this way," Mad growled. "Tell you what I'll do. I'll let you have the boy and a third of the gold. You get your hanging and become a very wealthy man. Everybody wins."

"Everyone except Bash," Maggie exclaimed.

And then several things happened all at once.

Mad yanked Maggie's hair, tipping her head back to better expose her throat.

Bash lunged for his father.

A gun went off, singeing Maggie's cheek with the heat of the powder.

The captain threw her to the ground, slicing another cut along her throat.

Someone covered her body with theirs.

And then, mercifully, everything went dark.

"No!" Bash screamed as Maggie fell before his eyes.

Without a thought to the naval captain, he raced to her side, shoving Mad off her.

What had the fool been thinking, firing a pistol while Mad was using her as a shield?

She was covered in blood, slick and sticky and warm. In contrast, her skin was white and cold.

"What have you done?" he gasped up at Constantin, who merely scowled.

From both sides of the house—his mother's former home, perhaps the same structure in which he was conceived one dark night when the devil came to call—a dozen more officers converged, marching in two straight lines.

Bash was pulled away from Maggie and yanked roughly to his feet before being clapped in irons as he watched them encircle her, his beloved, his life. Then he was jostled around so he couldn't see her at all, no matter how he twisted or craned his neck. Instead, he came face to face with Mad, whose shoulder was covered in blood.

Mad sneered at him. "I always knew. From the moment I heard she was up the duff, I knew you'd be the end of me."

"Fitting," Bash spat, "since you were only ever the beginning of me."

They marched him away, tripping in his leg irons, back up the same streets and through the town center, as villagers who might once have been his mother's friends, who could just as easily have been his mother's sister, threw rotten vegetables at him until he smelled like his own death. A chill ran through him when they passed the permanent gallows before turning into a gaol ripe with the stench of piss and the bowels of hell.

He'd known in his heart it would come to this someday. There were only two ways for a life such as his to end. His grandparents had known it, too. It was why he couldn't allow himself to give his heart to Maggie, more fool him. She had it already—all of it—every beat and the skipping pauses in between.

Bash had also known better than to go looking for Mad's lost gold. Just as the search had driven the captain mad, that way could only lie destruction. But the lure of freedom had been too tempting, as was the idea his mother might be guiding him and would somehow protect him from her ghostly realm.

When faced with only two bad options, seizing a third had seemed worth the risk, but only when the risk was his alone. Never Maggie's. She was supposed to be safe.

His only consolation was that if she was dead, he would soon join her. And if she wasn't, they would go together, side by side, on the gallows come dawn.

It was a very shallow consolation. They'd surely end up in different places for the duration of eternity because she was a kind, loving, free-spirited woman who deserved every good thing, and he was pirate scum unfit to clean her boots.

In a nearby cell, Mad raised a ruckus, by turns cursing and moaning, then snoring until he started all over again.

There was no sign of his darling Maggie, no weeping or murmured prayers, none of the soft sighs she made in her sleep. Bash supposed she must be gone, and he wept for her—silently at first, until something like a sob tore from his throat when he drew a wheezing breath.

"At least we go together, eh, boy? Father and son, at last," Mad called out to him.

Bash settled himself and steadied his voice to answer coldly. "You were never my father, Cornelius MacLeod."

"Ungrateful fucking wretch," Mad muttered, but he made no further attempts at conversation and soon went back to snoring loud enough to rattle the iron bars on the door.

Finding a corner that smelled the least like human excrement, Bash curled up in a ball, rocking back and forth as he waited for morning.

When he finally dozed, he dreamt only of her. Free of blood and dressed in breeches, she appeared the way he liked her best—sun-dappled and smiling as the ocean breeze tousled her short, chestnut hair and Caribbean waves sparkled in her azure eyes. She kissed his cheek, and he grew hard with longing, but on reaching out, her hand slipped through his grasp, and she was gone—his cheeky, wild girl from the Scottish Highlands.

He only wished he'd told her in words how much he loved her. He only wished his cowardice had not prevailed.

Chapter Twenty-One

Blinding white light surrounded Maggie, awakening her to the throbbing ache behind her eyes. A menagerie of strange birds sang relentlessly joyful songs, which should have made her soar in dips and swirls like her own dear Kes, but her heart was much too heavy to fly.

When she finally wrenched her eyes open, she found herself on a cot as soft as a cloud, in a bright, cheery bungalow with windows drawn open to an ocean breeze and lapping tide. It was the kind of peace that would have been her dream two months ago. Instead, tears dampened her eyes before she could even remember why she was grieving.

Bash.

He'd been arrested by Captain Constantin, would be hanged at the Crown's convenience. Had it happened already? Was she too late to try and stop it or even say goodbye?

And why wasn't she with him? Mad had accused her of piracy as she clutched the stolen gold to her chest. But then Bash had stepped forward, taken the blame, sacrificed himself and all he'd overcome—for her.

A door opened, and a women entered, her hair wrapped up in a scarf, her eyes warm but serious, like the picture of Bash's mother.

Maggie reached for the locket at her throat and found instead a bandage and now the tears streamed down her cheeks and into her ears.

"Dry your eyes," the woman said. "Best not waste a drop of water left in you. Drink this."

The woman helped Maggie sit up against lovely plump pillows, and then handed her a cup filled with mild-looking tea, but Maggie's hand tremored, rattling the china cup against its saucer, so the woman reached out gently and guided it to Maggie's parched lips.

"Good." She nodded. "Finish that, and I'll brew some more. You've been terribly fevered. I've never seen a body so dried out as you."

"I've been worse," Maggie whispered. At least this time she could still cry.

"That's a point of pride, is it?" the woman asked, and Maggie shook her head.

"If you keep the tea down, I'll bring you some broth later."

"Thank you."

"Have a name?"

"Maggie."

"Ryna," the woman said. "Don't you fret, Maggie, I'll take good care of you until the ship's ready to sail."

"Ship?" Maggie asked. Was it a prison ship, then? Would she be indentured in Virginia like Langley's brother?

"To England," Ryna explained. "You're going home."

More tears burned her eyes, blurring the image of her kind caretaker. "I can't go back," she whispered, scrunching her face. Not while Bash's fate was unknown, not when he might be...

Ryna sat on the side of the bed and took Maggie's hand

sympathetically. "A young woman can always go home," she said fiercely. "Haven't you any family?"

Maggie nodded, blinking back tears. "A sister," she said, "and a cousin." She couldn't say why she left her parents out. Would they be as happy to see her as Ellen and Jory? Would relief outweigh their anger? Did she even want their forgiveness?

Squeezing her hand, Ryna nodded. "They'll be overjoyed to welcome you back."

And she was right, of course, this stranger. For a moment, Maggie allowed herself to imagine the soft comfort of her sister's arms, and the ache in her heart cracked wider. What she wouldn't give to have Ellen beside her right now.

Somewhere in the distance, church bells began to ring, and Maggie realized she didn't know the date or how much time had passed since the horrible scene in the fragrant, shady Eden. Could those be the bells of St. Andrew's? Her heart squeezed. She had to know whether the emptiness inside of her was real or imagined.

"Are there a great many pirates around these parts?" she finally asked.

Ryna frowned. "Some. But none will trouble you here."

"What a relief," Maggie gasped. "I suppose they're hanged fairly often?"

"Not so often as they used to be."

Maggie closed her eyes. "Have there been any today? Hangings?"

There was a pause in Ryna's voice before she said, "I don't think so. Why don't I bring you some more tea?"

Maggie nodded and relaxed against her pillow. At least maybe Bash was safe for now. Had he fought his captors? Slipped quietly away while they were busy with her and Mad?

No. He would never.

Had he gone quietly, then, after trading his life for her own? She had no idea how she might free him, but she'd cling to the hope that he was still alive for her to save.

. . .

THE NEXT DAY, RYNA BROUGHT HER A VISITOR, THE NAVAL captain who had caused so much trouble. For a moment, when his impressive figure graced the doorway in his blue uniform, tricorne hat in his hands, Maggie wondered if she was indeed under arrest for piracy after all but treated gently on account of her sex.

"Captain Constantin," she rasped, pulling the bedclothes up to cover her borrowed shift.

"Madam," he said with a curt bow. "I trust you're improving?"

"Ryna has been most attentive," she said. "Her teas are quite irresistible."

A small smile tugged at the captain's lips. "Yes. She tells me you should be fit to travel in a few more days, when we're ready to depart."

"We?" Maggie stuttered. "I'll be sailing aboard a naval ship?"

"Yes, if you've no objection. I should feel more confident in your safety if you allow me to escort you home aboard the *Pursuit*."

He was kind, but she wasn't sure she could stand it. Six weeks or more aboard the vessel responsible for... well... nothing had happened yet. Had it?

"You're troubled," he said, reading her face. "I assure you, we'll be quite unmolested. No pirates would dare—"

"Of course not. Thank you, Captain."

He bowed and turned to leave.

"Sir?" Maggie stopped him. "The men I was with?"

"I must apologize for shooting so carelessly close to where you were standing. It was only because I could see you were ill, and because I have remarkably good aim. MacLeod's shoulder was my target. Ryna assured me you suffered no more than powder burns. Still, I do sincerely beg your pardon."

"Oh," Maggie said. She hadn't remembered it was his weapon and not Mad's which had rent the silence, sending birds squawking into the air. Putting her hand to her throat she fingered the dressing where he'd cut her. "Then he's—the captain, that is, he's—?"

"Quite dead."

A sick dread crept into her stomach, and she licked her lips. "I seem to recall you placing us *all* under arrest," she said.

Constantin shrugged. "Pirates are hanged, madam. Hostages are not."

Maggie blinked rapidly, fighting the tears which threatened to overtake her.

"Then might I beseech you, sir, if it's not too late, to show mercy on the younger man—Bash? Bastian? He is all that is good, truly. He saved my life when I so recklessly stowed away in search of... adventure. He's kind and gentle though he's known a life filled with suffering. He was as much a prisoner as I, please. I beg you, and if you cannot," she went on, giving him no time to answer, because she was too afraid of what the answer might be. "If you cannot show him mercy, then please have mercy on me and allow me to hang alongside him because, you see, I love him. I love him, sir, and I cannot fathom the endless torture of living out the rest of my days without him."

Through her tears she managed to discern his sympathetic smile. "Pirates are hanged," he said again. "Hostages are not."

Then, with another curt bow, he took his leave, and Maggie collapsed into her pillows and wept. She wept until she was flushed with fever, blood pounding in her temples. Ryna quite despaired of ever getting her to stop.

She begged to be taken to the gaol to see him, but she didn't have the strength, and when at last Ryna coaxed her into sipping some tea, Maggie drifted off into another fitful sleep.

IF SUCH A THING WERE POSSIBLE, THE SUN SHONE BRIGHTER AND even more cheerfully a week later when Ryna walked Maggie to the port where she would board HMS *Pursuit* to sail away from Jamaica leaving everything behind.

She had gone out walking the day before, but the gaol was empty except for a drunk sailor sleeping off a rowdy night.

"If you're here for the hanging, it were last week, miss," a small boy informed her as she stared up at the gallows.

She'd thrown up then, right there in the street, much to the dismay of the little boy, who wrinkled his nose, stepping back in disgust.

So, she could barely look Constantin in the eye when she was escorted to his quarters.

"Are you well?" he asked with warm concern, directing her to a padded wooden chair.

Maggie nodded. Though her eyes pricked, she didn't cry. She was all dried out, as Ryna would say.

"I believe this is yours," Constantin said, sitting down at his desk and pushing an intricately carved chest forward. It was small, about a foot long and half as wide and deep. A fancy brass key protruded from an equally ornate brass lock.

"You're mistaken." Maggie shook her head. While lovely, the chest was unlike anything she'd ever seen.

"I'm certain I am not," Constantin said, turning the key and opening the chest to reveal dozens—perhaps hundreds—of shiny gold coins. Mad MacLeod's lost treasure.

She looked up at Constantin in confusion.

"The chest is new, I'll grant you," he said, with a flourish as though waving away her questions. "But the gold was in your possession when I intervened on your behalf."

"But..." Hadn't he been trying to recover this very gold for more than two decades?

"I understand, you must be concerned about the provenance of such wealth, and the belief by some that it was once stolen cargo."

"Isn't it?" Maggie breathed.

"No, madam. It cannot be. It's true the *Annabel Grace*, of which I was once the guardian, was robbed some twenty-two years ago. However, *that* gold was written off by the Crown many years hence, and reparations paid to the baron for my failure. As far as the Crown is concerned, it no longer exists. Therefore, this cannot be *that* gold. So it must be yours. Or else funds left by Bastian's auntie for his keeping."

Maggie stared at the chest of gold—more wealth than she'd ever seen in her entire life, but at what cost?

"So much coin," she whispered. "Could it have been used to buy a man's life, I wonder?"

"No, madam. Such a thing sounds an awful lot like bribery. You must never repeat it," he said, eyeing her seriously until she shook her head. "Good."

He snapped the chest closed, turned the key, and then handed it to her. "For safe keeping. Come. I'll show you to your quarters. You must be very tired."

Constantin carried the chest for her and offered Maggie his arm. As he led her through the ship, she tried hard to block out memories of her first days aboard another ship, of the way Bash's hair curled at the nape of his neck, and the slight swagger in his step. Finally, they reached a cabin with an actual door.

"Small and cramped, I'm afraid. But it has a nice view."

She nodded her thanks and opened the door to go inside.

A man turned from the window to face her, and her jaw dropped, mirroring his stunned expression.

"Bash," she breathed, bursting into tears as she flew into his arms, touching his face, his hair, his shoulders, kissing ever part of him she could reach just to convince herself he was real.

She cast a glance back at Constantin who set the chest on a ledge built into the bulkhead and, smiling to himself, quietly shut the door.

Pirates are hanged. Hostages are not.

He'd understood everything after all.

Bash spun Maggie around and they clung to each other, hugging and kissing and crying until Maggie's knees began to buckle and then he guided her to the tiny bed along one wall and lifted her onto it.

"I thought you were dead," she whispered, clenching his shirt in both fists and refusing to let go until he climbed up beside her.

"I wanted to be," he murmured into her neck. "Because I thought you must be."

"But if Mad was shot, then who was hanged?"

"A superficial wound," Bash explained. "Not enough to prevent the hangman his pound of flesh."

Maggie began to cry again, in shock as much as relief. Bash kissed her eyelids, murmuring softly, "It's all right, my love. I'm here."

They kissed slowly, hungrily. Her fingers shook as she tried to unbutton his shirt, so he took over for her, wrestling out of the garment. Maggie drew a ragged breath, once again marveling at his broad chest, sculpted from years of laboring aboard the *Revenge*, a chest she had thought never to set eyes on again. He was here. He was whole.

He helped her out of her skirts and stays, and finally his breeches were off, and she rolled onto her back to welcome him, but he continued to take his time, kissing her neck and between her breasts, teasing her nipples into hard little points.

"Please," she begged, and he grinned that roguish smile and entered her slowly, gently, sliding part way and then studying her with dark, starry eyes before capturing her lips once more and sliding forward to fill her all the way up.

Maggie gasped as lightning seemed to shoot through her and out each finger and each toe.

"Did I hurt you?" he asked.

"No," she panted, pressing up to meet him, encouraging him to do the same. "Only I'm afraid if you ever leave, I'll completely shatter."

"Never," he whispered, his breath hot against her ear as he continued to rock into her like the undulating tide, building, and building, and building until it washed over both of them completely, but instead of drowning it replenished them with the promise of new life and a future ripe with possibility.

Chapter Twenty-Two

Though Bash wouldn't have traded those first weeks of Maggie's adventure for anything, transatlantic travel as guests of a naval captain was in many ways far superior to life aboard a pirate ship, largely because they were left entirely alone in their tiny berth at the stern of the vessel. If they wished to take the air, they were allowed to do so at their leisure. If they required food, the galley chef was more accommodating than he might have been to ordinary sailors.

But when the bells rang the watch, they had only to look at each other and smile. They could stay wrapped up in bed for days, and no one seemed to notice. It was perfection. Climbing the rigging with Maggie would always hold a special place in his memory, but, though he loved to be out in the fresh sea air working under a hot sun, Bash had never been more content to remain idle. He kept an eye on their course out of habit, but no one looked to him for orders.

In fact, the only person aboard the ship who noticed them with more than idle curiosity was Constantin. Every night they were invited to dine with the captain, and most evenings they accepted. He seemed intrigued by Bash's knowledge of navigation and curious about his childhood.

He never once treated either of them as though they'd been anything more than prisoners aboard *Auldfarrand's Revenge,* but his empathy left Bash feeling unsettled. His sire's old nemesis was not at all the sea monster he'd expected, and Bash kept waiting to learn it was all some elaborate hoax, the rug pulled out from under him the moment he relaxed. Especially once he noticed the cages for homing pigeons, not unlike those aboard the *Woebegone Whale.*

At last, one night, about three weeks into their journey, Bash worked up the nerve to ask about the gold.

"Why did you keep chasing him? If you didn't care about recovering it?" he demanded. "You used Walsh to lure us into an ambush, did you not?"

Constantin took his time wiping his mouth and placing his napkin upon the table. "Once the theft was written off, I wasn't interested in Cornelius," he admitted with a shrug. "I was interested in you."

Bash stiffened, and Maggie took his hand. Was he about to learn he wasn't actually the son of a pirate, but of a temporarily disgraced naval officer? It couldn't be. He had Mad's nose and jawline, and his grandfather's before him, not the features of this fine-boned Englishman.

"You don't remember me, do you, Bastian?"

Sitting up a little straighter, he searched Constantin's face and all at once the years melted away, and his youth came rushing back—a fishing rod and basket weighed down with the day's catch, an officer who'd been asking after the pirate Captain MacLeod.

"Freddy?" Bash asked, and Constantin grinned at him. "You said you were called Freddy. You wanted to take me back to Jamaica to live with my auntie. At least that's what the adults whispered once you'd gone." A warmth flooded him along with the memory and the sudden realization that all this time, someone somewhere had cared.

"I knew you were the sort who liked to listen at windows," the captain teased, but then he turned sober. "They were afraid the lure of Jamaica was what turned your father into a pirate. They thought keeping you on Lewis would keep you far away from such a life."

Bash snorted. "Until they handed me over to him for the price of a meal."

"Mmm," Constantin agreed.

So many questions rattled around in his brain. Had the man visited more than once? Had he met Bash's mother? Maggie and Constantin continued to eat, waiting for him to process it all.

"This fish is very good," Maggie murmured. "What did you say it's called?"

"Tuna," Constantin said, holding out the dish to offer her more.

How could they go on eating like the world wasn't spinning off its axis?

"How did my mother know where the gold was buried?" Bash interrupted them.

Constantin smiled. "I've only theories on that score."

Bash glanced at Maggie with wonder, and then back to the captain.

"Amoy—your mother—and I were acquainted," he began. "Because I was besotted with your Auntie Savryna. They lived together in that little house, and I stayed with them often when I had leave. I wanted to make Ryna an officer's wife, so she could travel the world with me. But she's determined never to leave Kingston. 'Every ship needs a port to come home to,' she always says."

"Ryna?" Maggie gasped, a look of amazement dawning on her face.

Constantin nodded. "She makes very fine tea, does she not?

After Cornelius's heist, I tracked him to Kingston, and then lost him in the town, so I went to Ryna. I noticed fresh dug earth beneath a dogwood tree, but I was young and hot-headed. I didn't care about the money. The baron had more wealth than any man ought. Most of it was secure on my own ship. He wouldn't miss the stolen chest. But I wanted the pirate who embarrassed me by stealing it. He brought dishonor to my name, and then he slipped through my fingers. By the time I swallowed my pride and dug up that hole, it was empty."

"She moved it," Maggie said, smirking.

Constantin smiled some private smile. "I never asked, and she never told me. But the next time I sailed to England, she requested I deliver a letter to her sister on Lewis."

Bash sighed and Maggie squeezed his hand.

"I bore another such letter the day you and I met. We hadn't yet learned of her passing. I'm so sorry, Bastian. I wish I'd fought harder. The one and only time I ever convinced Ryna to board a ship, we sailed to Lewis so she could bring you home. But we were too late."

Bash shook his head and swallowed, smiling at the man who was sort of like an uncle to him. He owned no blame in the tragedies of Bash's life, and how could anyone even call them tragic when they were steps along the journey that led to here and now and Maggie?

"Now I have a question for you," Constantin said, turning his sharp gaze on Maggie.

"Me?" she squeaked, choking on a bite of tuna, and setting down her fork with unsteady hands. Under the table, Bash squeezed her knee as she'd done for him moments earlier.

Constantin smiled disarmingly. "What on earth compelled a young widow from Orkney to sneak aboard a pirate ship in the first place?"

"Oh." Her cheeks reddened. "Well. I didn't know it was a pirate ship, for one thing. Although, I was so eager to leave I might have snuck aboard anyway. I'd received distressing news from my father. Since my mourning period was over, he had found me a second husband and was coming to fetch me back to Inverness for the wedding."

Bash bristled, even though he already knew the story.

Constantin raised his eyebrows in shock. "I see. And I take it the arrangement was not amenable?"

"It was not."

"Do you suppose he'll insist, when he learns of your return?"

Maggie scrunched her face. "He may well try," she said, and Bash rubbed her neck and shoulder to comfort her. He'd like to see the man try. Maggie's father or not, he wouldn't allow it. "Though, I suppose it's possible this interlude may have weakened the gentleman's resolve, it will only have strengthened my father's."

"Then, if I may offer a solution?" Constantin asked.

"If your solution is impressment, my mother may object."

The captain burst out laughing.

AT SUNSET, UNDER A CLOUDLESS SKY, BASH GAZED INTO THE freckled face of his beautiful bride. He couldn't believe his luck. Finally free from the chains of his childhood and the life he'd never asked for, there were riches to start afresh with the most perfect partner at his side.

She was willful and courageous and unflagging in her willing-ness to jump in up to her elbows and help a man out. She had even saved his ear, though he liked to tease her that it looked lopsided now. He couldn't imagine a better friend or more suitable bride.

"Will you, Sebastian MacLeod, take Margaret Mary Mackintosh Budge, here present, to be your lawful wife, to live together according to God's covenant? To love her, comfort her, and honor her, cleaving only unto her?" Reverend Glaser, the chaplain of the *Pursuit* asked.

"I will," Bash replied, glancing away from Maggie for long enough to grin at Constantin, who winked.

"Very good," the enthusiastic young chaplain said. "And will you, Margaret Mary Mackintosh Budge, take Sebastian MacLeod, here present, to be your lawful husband, to live together according to God's covenant, cleaving only unto him?"

"Yes," Maggie said, gazing up with adoration gleaming in her endless blue eyes. "Most reverently and unabashedly, I will."

Bash laughed.

"Excellent," Reverend Glaser said. "Is there a ring?"

"Not as yet," Bash said, frowning and feeling a bit silly that he, a reformed pirate, didn't have one on hand for emergency betrothals, not even one made of sea glass.

"Oh," Constantin exclaimed, and they all turned to watch as the captain patted first his trouser pockets, then the breast of his jacket, from which he produced a simple gold band with flower-shaped filagree.

Bash stared at it and Constantin shrugged.

"It was my mother's."

"Thank you, sir," Bash told him, struggling to restrain his emotions.

The chaplain nodded his head towards Maggie. "With this ring, I thee wed," he said softly.

"With this ring, I thee wed," Bash repeated, his voice cracking although he was far away from the twelve-year-old boy who was flogged under a sunset much like this one.

"I believe it's customary at this point to kiss," the reverend told them, rocking back on his heels and grinning ear to ear. So they did, and all the stars in the night sky came out to bless their union.

Epilogue

Maggie stood on the beach looking out to sea. The vast, open ocean always filled her with both contentment and longing.

"Penny for your thoughts, Maggie May," Len said, taking her arm and squeezing her close.

Maggie shook her head and smiled. She couldn't put into words what she'd been thinking. That was what feelings were invented for.

"I suspect," Jory answered instead, taking Maggie's other arm, "she's contemplating the sailor who keeps doing that to her." She nodded at Maggie's belly, which was only just beginning to swell. No one else had noticed yet, except for Bash.

"Goodness," Len teased. "When do you plan on stopping? You'll soon be quite outnumbered. You know we don't need a christening as an excuse for a visit."

"Bash says he wants eleven," Maggie giggled, delighting in the way her cousin winced and her sister's eyes bugged out.

"Mercy," Jory said.

"Well," Len told her, "at least there's plenty of room for them to run wild here but still be somewhat contained."

As if to prove the point, Alex and Marjie, Ellen's two children, ran past shouting, "Run for your lives!" while little Sav and Amoy chased after them hollering like banshees.

Maggie laughed, delighted to see her banshees playing with their older cousins. Their joy was infections. "They're so funny. Maybe we won't even stop at eleven," she said, only half joking, and Jory and Len squeezed her tight.

Though he was very much loved by his mother and grandparents, Bash hadn't enjoyed the sort of closeness the Mackintosh girls had taken for granted growing up. If he wanted two dozen children to fill up his heart, she would happily carry them. She adored watching the bond her little ones shared with each other and their adoring da. "This was delivered to Leod just before we left," Len said, taking a rolled-up parchment from her pocket. "Sealed inside a green glass bottle."

She held it out for Maggie to see, and a tiny thrill ran through her when she recognized her own familiar scrawl.

"Did you read it?" she asked, but Ellen shook her head. "You should read it," Maggie told her, a little stunned the message she'd thrown into the ocean as they attempted to outmaneuver the navy had finally found its way to her sister. For a second, she wondered if Constantin himself were responsible—fishing it out of the brine and delivering it all these years later. She wouldn't put it past him.

Taking Jory's arm, she led her cousin back up the beach where the others had built a great bonfire.

"I wasn't sure I'd like it out here in the islands," Jory confided. "It's quite lovely. You've made a wonderful home."

"You should stay," Maggie told her. "We could always use a physician."

"From what I hear, you could fill the role."

Maggie warmed with pride. "I only know what you taught me. Stay and teach me more?"

"A tempting offer."

"But your Highlander longs for home."

"He does," Jory said fondly, glancing at Finn who turned their way at once, as though deeply in tune with his lady. He smiled shyly, the tips of his ears going pink.

"I never thanked you," Maggie told Jory.

"For what?"

"Showing me what marriage could be like."

Jory's smile held a moment's sadness, and she squeezed Maggie a little too tight.

"It's all right," Maggie assured her. "If one single thing had been different, I might never have run away and found Bash. Now every day's an adventure. I wouldn't have it any other way."

Her cousin peered into her face, as if making sure Maggie meant it. Then she smiled. "You used to be so fearful of freckles. But they suit this beautiful, adventurous face."

They joined the rest of the family by the bonfire and Finn, the former Shaw Wretch, embraced Maggie. "Congratulations, Magpie," he whispered, and so there were five who knew about the baby, despite the loose fitting dress and shawl she had donned instead of her usual breeches.

"This one wants a feed, I think," old Mrs. Leask said, bringing a fussy baby Freddy over, though she was clearly reluctant to part with him so he could nurse.

More likely he was cranky because the milk didn't hold him long anymore and he wanted some gruel, but Maggie was happy to let him suckle as long as he would.

"Chamomile will help the teething pain," Ryna said, joining them and putting a necklace of copper coins over Freddy's head. "Same as it helped your migraine when you hadn't had enough to drink."

"I'll give him some before I put him down," Maggie promised, kissing her adopted mother-in-law on the cheek.

They'd been shocked six months before when Bash's auntie arrived with Constantin, proclaiming that a vision had sent her to help with Freddy's birth. The labor had been worse than Maggie's first three combined, and without Jory there, she'd been so very grateful to have Ryna's steady, calming presence.

Once the baby arrived, Ryna decided to stay through the summer, vowing to return to Kingston when she'd had enough of the cold. Now autumn was encroaching, and still she and Constantin remained.

Maggie hadn't told them yet they might as well stay another six months rather than leaving and coming back again, but sometimes when she caught Ryna watching her or exchanging a look with Constantin, she supposed they had probably guessed as much.

So perhaps the count was up to seven who knew. Or eight, given the way Mrs. Leask was eyeing her. Mercy, it was hard to keep a secret among this lot.

Then again, anyone who knew Bash could probably tell just by glancing at him. Pure joy radiated off him in delicious waves. If Maggie weren't already pregnant, that might be enough to make her so.

She glanced around for him, but he wasn't there at the fire with the rest.

"He took the children up the hill to the stones, right before they came tearing back down again like a pack of demons," Ellen said, having returned from her solitary walk with Maggie's letter, eyes rimmed red and cheeks rosy. She kissed Maggie. "Thank you for writing to me."

Upon seeing his wife, Silas MacKenzie drifted over, away from the conversation he'd been sharing with Mr. Leask and Captain Constantin.

"Ladies," he said, in his staid way, hugging Len and tousling a dozing Freddy's wispy hair.

"Do you want to take him?" Maggie asked, and her brother-in-law's eyes shone with the memory of his own children's early days, so she handed the baby off once more. "That's a good boy," she cooed. "Go to Uncle Si, and I'll go find Da."

ATOP THE HILL, IN THE CIRCLE OF STANDING STONES, BASH looked down at his firstborn child. Seb was quiet and studious, so different from the others, so much more like himself—the only one of his children to have been conceived at sea.

He was lying in the middle of the stones, staring up at the endless blue sky, as blue as the little boy's Mackintosh blue eyes, a laundry peg soldier in one fist, while the old cat Custard curled lazily at his side.

"What game is this?" Bash asked him.

"As the sun moves across the stones, the shadows change," his elfin child answered. "But you have to be still and quiet to notice."

"Shall we go and see what the others are up to?"

"Mischief," the little boy replied, and Bash coughed to hide his laughter. "They're not still or quiet."

"No," Bash agreed. "Not unless they're asleep."

"Do you think the new baby will be more like me?" Seb asked, and Bash's eyes widened.

"Did Mama tell you there's a new baby?"

The little boy shook his head solemnly. So he had guessed.

Bash squatted down to his son's level and Seb sat up to listen. "Pretend you're surprised when she does tell you. Promise?"

"Promise," Seb agreed, taking Bash's hand and getting to his feet.

Bash lifted the little boy up onto his shoulders. At the ripe old age of four-and-a-half, he was still light as could be, but Bash wasn't sure how much longer he'd tolerate being carried, so he reveled in it every chance he could find.

They could see far out into the Atlantic from here, and Bash pointed. "Looks like Uncle Dutch is on his way back in. Shall we go and see what he's caught for us to eat?"

His son used his fist like a spyglass to peer out at the little fishing boat. "It's him," he exclaimed.

Bash had been grateful to return to Lewis and start his adult life over. With the help of his new fortune and some of his uncle's naval contacts, he had built a successful shipping business, though he rarely sailed himself these days. He missed the feel of the deck beneath his feet, but he was much too busy never leaving Maggie's side.

After Mad had been captured, Dutch took control of the *Revenge* and her crew. But with the gold Bash had set aside for him, he, too, soon abandoned the brigantine for a smaller vessel of his own and settled on Lewis, making an honest living as a fisherman. Langley had returned home to Hull to look after his sister, representing Bash's business interests in York with Samson and Duffy by his side.

"Hungry?" he asked.

"Ravenous," Seb replied, and this time Bash couldn't contain his roar of laughter. "Mr. Leask says it means the hungriest hungry you've ever felt, where it crawls up from your belly and grabs you around the throat until your mouth waters."

"Does he now? Well, I suppose Mr. Leask knows what he's talking about. Look, there's Mama come to find us," he said, putting Seb down so the boy could run on ahead to meet Maggie.

Rosy cheeked and windswept, she had never looked more beautiful. It was almost a shame they had so many guests out to the island for baby Freddy's christening.

When Bash caught up to his wife and son, Maggie cupped his cheek, running a thumb over his scruff and his scar.

"You need a shave," she said in a raspy murmur that shot straight to his groin. "I almost can't see your lovely scar."

"Have you the time to assist me, darlin'?" he asked.

She pursed her lips in a tiny smile, because he liked to pretend he was nervous about re-injuring his right ear.

"After dinner," she said, with a heat in her eyes that lit another fire in his belly. With so many people crammed into the house, they would have to be very quiet later making love. Twice, on account of it was Sunday.

Seb caught each of their hands and swung between them as they walked back down the hill together, and Bash smiled to realize he'd never been more content.

"Have I ever told you how glad I am you snuck aboard our ship that night?" he asked, and her eyes danced at him over Seb's head.

"Have I ever told you how glad I am you didn't throw me overboard?" she teased, and when Seb released their hands to run down and greet Dutch at the beach, Bash pulled her close, tucking her into his side where he could bury his face in her short-cropped hair.

Author's Note

I never expected to write a pirate story, but just like Maggie, her tale was desperate for attention and practically wrote itself. When I was brainstorming titles in the early days of book one, *Maggie and the Pirate's Son* popped into my head with zero context, and three years later, it wouldn't let go. As I set out to begin Maggie's story in earnest, I knew I either had to find a new title or write a pirate tale. Titles are hard, so the choice was clear, and I've never had more fun in my life.

The Golden Age of Piracy was really on its last legs by the time Maggie was old enough to set off on her adventure, with most historians placing the end between 1720 and 1730, the perfect time for a story about an unravelling captain and unsettled crew. During the late 17th and early 18th centuries, there were thousands of pirates sailing the high seas, but the Golden Age was largely sponsored by the English crown, who, after rewarding civilians for attacking Spanish vessels, was faced with a crisis of its own making.

Not strictly a British undertaking, however, other nations produced an abundance of pirates during those golden years as well, including the Dutch. To my great amusement and utter disappointment, neither country's National Maritime Museum offered a single mention of pirate history within their exhibits when I visited, focusing instead on the East India Tea Company because capitalism, I suppose. They're very proud of their tea. Still, they were fantastic museums for seeing historical navigation artifacts, old ship figureheads, and so much more—and, if you time it right, an amazing exhibit of astrophotography contest winners in London. For real pirate history in England, though, I understand you need to make your way to Cornwall.

For a pirate history in the United States, there's a wonderful museum down in St. Augustine, Florida, which proved instrumental in the writing of this book. At other museums I found tools just a little too old or a little too new, but the Pirate and Treasure Museum was the perfect combination of historical stories and authentic, period artifacts that helped me understand navigation and add lots of little details to the story. Calico Jack, for example, was a real pirate I learned about there. If you're a fan of *Black Sails*, you might remember him as Rackham, but I first found him in St. Augustine.

After half a century of piracy, the English government realized their sanction had gotten out of control, and pirate hunting became a full-time job. In 1718, leadership in the Caribbean offered a royal pardon to any pirates who gave up and left the life. Blackbeard famously accepted such a pardon, as did Calico Jack and Stede Bonnet, who both later returned to piracy.

In Jack's case, he returned to the life with one of the few known female pirates: Anne Bonny. When they were captured, Jack met his end as portrayed in young Bash's memory.

Life at sea was hard, and despite rarities like Anne Bonny and Mary Reid, pirates often had strict rules against letting women aboard. It was considered bad luck to the most superstitious captains, probably due to concerns it would cause jealousy and fighting amongst the men.

It may seem surprising that pirate ships had rules at all, and while they might have been less strict than the navies of the day, maintaining order was still essential, so most captains would have a code the men were expected to sign and abide by. Mad MacLeod's code is modeled on that of pirate Captain Bartholomew Roberts. The ships were surprisingly democratic, too, almost like the earliest worker unions, voting on men to fill key leadership roles and to choose what prizes to hunt.

When crafting these tales, I always try to borrow authentically from history. In the case of Bash's map of South America, I used the actual Spanish description of the Amazon River from a slightly older 16th century map in the Rosenwald Collection at the Library of Congress. The Spanish varies slightly from what we would use today, but shows the evolution language can take over time.

While there's no authoritative source for the idiom's origin prior to 1834, I read an article that suggested 'bull in a china shop' comes from the 16th or 17th century, when cattle being herded to market broke loose and rampaged through London. True or not, I love the idea of such a story making the news all the way up in Inverness or even Orkney, where Maggie would delight in the tale of those bulls having a grand adventure of their own.

Little is known about just how many women actually served as pirates in disguise. In such close quarters, would they be able to keep up the ruse for long? I like to think some, like Maggie, were sneaky enough to get away with it for however long they needed to, and to find allies who helped keep their secrets.

Acknowledgments

Maggie and Bash were absolutely the most fun to write. Still, as always, bringing their adventure to life was a team effort.

First and foremost, the story would not be what it is without the brilliance and generosity of Doctors Stephen R. Sullivan and Helena Taylor, plastic surgeons who performed a ground-breaking procedure to reattach a young woman's ear with the aid of leeches. When I first read about their surgery, I just knew Maggie had to try it in a historically plausible way.

Thank you, thank you, thank you for being so kind and responsive when I reached out, and for taking the time to tell me more about your work and answer every single question I could possibly think to ask. I will be forever grateful for your help, and my book is so much richer for it.

Thanks also to the St. Augustine Pirate and Treasure Museum for offering such a comprehensive curation of artifacts and educational plaques. They allowed me to root myself in the story, and I did my best to sprinkle what I learned throughout the novel like lagniappe. Special thanks especially to Matt Frick, the curator there, who settled the issue of "grog" once and for all.

To Jessie, who loved it so much you offered to read it twice and demanded a screenplay. Your friendship, unabashed belief in me, and encouragement mean the world.

To De, who is always just a text message away for everything I could possibly need. You know there won't be a single book where I don't bug you as my sounding board.

To Krista, my reader, my mentor, my inspiration.

To my beta readers, Angi, Jennifer, and Jennie who were there every step of the way and who, along with the rest of the Writerly crew, fondly dubbed the working draft as "Sweet Pirate Booty"—Mark, Christian, Megan, Sarah, Tabitha, and Trisha. I love you all so much. The internet might be a cesspool sometimes, but it brought me to you, my community. I couldn't do this without you, and I would never want to.

Thanks to my editor, Susan, without whom I would endlessly fret over complex grammar rules and punctuation, and to my chiropractor, without whose migraine relief I would not have hit my deadlines.

To my parents, who made me the hard worker that I am, and to my husband, my biggest ally, my partner in crime. Thank you for being my lodestar, and for always lugging my books around. I love you so much.

As always, a special thank you to the libraries, book stores, and book clubs who have supported me, and most of all, my readers. This would all be for nothing without you. I love my goofy cinnamon rolls, but the best cinnamon rolls are shared.

About the Author

Rose Prendeville's fascination with pirates most likely began after visiting St. Augustine as a child. Now a librarian, she lives near the water in Middle Tennessee with her husband and a garden full of bees, writing stories about found families and flawed people doing their best. The first place winner of the 30th annual Writer's Digest Awards for her debut *Last Blue Christmas* is passionate about books with happy endings and their ability to brighten a sometimes dismal world.

The fearsome pirate Rose, circa 1991.

If you enjoyed this book, please consider leaving a review at your favorite marketplace.

To stay up-to-date on this series and other news, scan the QR code and sign up for Rose's newsletter or visit: 
    roseprendeville.com

Books by Rose Prendeville

Last Blue Christmas

The Unknown Birds

Brides of Chattan

Mistress Mackintosh and the Shaw Wretch

Lady Len and the Mysterious Mac

Maggie and the Pirate's Son

Tennessee Hebrides

Grace on the Rocks

A Faire Affair